SWEET

and

GOLDEN YEARS

by John Preston

The Alex Kane Missions
Books 1 & 2

Foreword by Philip Gambone

ReQueered Tales
Los Angeles • Toronto
2022

Sweet Dreams
Golden Years

by John Preston

The Alex Kane Missions, Books 1 & 2

First American edition: 1984

This edition: ReQueered Tales, January 2022

ReQueered Tales version 1.22
Sweet Dreams: Kindle edition ASIN: B09MWNZNNW
Golden Years: Kindle edition ASIN: B09MV71HKH
Print edition ISBN-13: 978-1-951092-49-8

For more information about current and future releases, please contact us:
E-mail: *requeeredtales@gmail.com*
Facebook (Like us!): www.facebook.com/ReQueeredTales
Twitter: @ReQueered
Instagram: www.instagram.com/requeered
Web: www.ReQueeredTales.com
Blog: www.ReQueeredTales.com/blog
Mailing list (Subscribe for latest news): https://bit.ly/RQTJoin

Praise for the
Alex Kane Missions

"The Alex Kane adventure novels expand the boundaries of family constructions. Alex, his young lover Danny, and Joseph Farmdale, his late lover James's father, unite to exact justice for hate crimes directed toward gay men. A precursor of Queer Nation's activists, superhero Alex Kane does not sit idly by as terrorists and bigots extort and kill factions of the gay male community: he pulls out an Uzi. Preston's theme in these works is literature's most enduring: the conflict of good and evil – this time with homosexuals being the good guys."

— Jane D. Troxell,
Contemporary Gay American Novelists

"John Preston published six cases, collectively entitled The Mission of Alex Kane (1984–1987). They have the quality of comic books, and the dynamics between Alex and his young lover, Danny Fortelli, resemble a sexualization of the Batman-Robin myth ... The books provide pleasure on several levels. They acknowledge the harsh world in which we live, and they appeal to our need to think someone is standing up for our rights. They embody a set of values that we can emulate: [a] heady sense of individualism is firmly coupled with the need to participate in a partnership and in the community to work for the common good. A prominent message throughout the series is that the closet kills. Out people are not only happier but also become positive role models for other gays as well as ambassadors to the straight community ... Though the superheroes are unbelievably good-looking and impossibly skilled, the cases are particularly notable for portraits that are missing from much of gay literature. In a vision of the way things could be, gays and straights thus work together to make a better world."

— Drewey Wayne Gunn,
The Gay Male Sleuth in Print and Film

3

By JOHN PRESTON

THE ALEX KANE MISSION NOVELS

Sweet Dreams (1984)

Golden Years (1984)

Deadly Lies (1985)

Stolen Moments (1986)

Secret Dangers (1986)

Lethal Silence (1987)

SWEET DREAMS

and

GOLDEN YEARS

by John Preston

The Alex Kane Missions,
Books 1 & 2

Table of Contents

Foreword

I knew John Preston primarily as the editor of a trio of essays I wrote for his anthologies *Hometowns* (Dutton, 1991), *A Member of the Family* (Dutton, 1992), and *Sister and Brother* (HarperSanFrancisco, 1994), the last co-edited with Joan Nestle. John was meticulous, thorough, intelligent. He would home in on anything – a word, a sentence, a detail – that he thought inconsistent with the overall intent of the essay and suggest, quite persuasively, that I make changes. I loved working with him. He was a dream editor. But until I began preparing for an extensive interview I conducted with him, I had never read any of John's fiction.

The interview was part of a radio program I hosted in 1993 for WOMR, a small local station in Provincetown. At the time, John (who died seven months later of complications from AIDS) was the most prolific gay author of his generation. According to Michael Denneny, an editor at St. Martin's Press and gay literature maven, John may also have been the "best-known gay writer" of his generation. During that hour-long conversation, John and I talked about many things, including his early career as a fiction writer. Almost all of John's fiction fell into the categories of pornography, SM novels, and male (straight and gay) adventure novels. All told, he wrote more than thirty of these books, mostly during the 1980s.

John was the first to disavow any high literary pretensions for his fiction. His first foray into the world of erotic novels was *Mr. Benson*, which he'd begun in 1978 as a short story about an SM master for the gay male magazine *Drummer*. With the encouragement of *Drummer's* editor, he expanded that story into a novel. Published in book form by Alyson in 1983, it was John's breakthrough book and quickly achieved the status of a cult classic. Several other *Mr. Benson* novels soon followed.

In everything he wrote – fiction and nonfiction – John was, he told me, "very much aware of being in conversation with my readers." Put off by the elitism of the Violet Quill gay literati circle, he had set out to create an audience of his own. As Michael Lowenthal observes in the posthumous collection of John's essays, *Winter's Light*, "John came to rely on his gut sense of his audience, his almost primal identification with other gay men ... He knew right away that he wanted to communicate with the 'gay guy on the street.'"

And communicate John did! "All I'm doing," he told me in that Provincetown interview, "is turning myself on, fleshing out my fantasies, and having a good time with them." In the process, he turned on countless readers.

John's dream was to earn his living as a writer, but after publishing those first few gay fictions, he realized that novels with gay content, even highly charged SM content, was not going to provide financial security. It was at that point, that he turned to penning a series of straight male adventure stories inspired by the Rambo novels and television shows like the "A Team." Under the pseudonym Mike McCray, he began "whipping off these books" – his Black Beret series – at the rate of one a month.

"When I did this," he told me, "all the 'gay lit' types watching me were extremely disdainful. You know, this was a 'degradation of my skill,' this was going to be the 'ruination of my career.'" But when Sasha Alyson, the publisher of John's early gay novels, saw the sales figures for the Black Beret books, he decided John should write a gay version of the genre. And thus The Mission of Alex Kane series was born.

•   •   •

The first two volumes of The Mission of Alex Kane establish the basic parameters of the six books. Kane is a former Marine, a Vietnam vet whose lover, James Farmdale, was brutally murdered by a homophobic sergeant. Back in the States, after hitting rock bottom in San Francisco's Tenderloin, Kane is rescued by James' father, who encourages him to become a warrior for justice against those who would rob gay men of their dignity and dreams. The elder Farmdale, who is fabulously wealthy, bankrolls these crusades against evil; Kane, who is fabulously everything else, provides the cunning and the muscle. When the crimes are vast and the halls of justice slow to redress them, Kane resorts to physical retribution, executing "the ultimate judgment."

As Jane Troxell once so neatly summarized, "Preston's theme in these works is literature's most enduring: the conflict of good and evil – this time with homosexuals being the good guys." In our Provincetown interview, John told me that much of his writing was motivated by anger. He wanted to show that gay men could be "heroes, not victims."

Like all literary heroes as far back as Gilgamesh, Alex Kane is a larger-than-life fantasy. With his piercing green eyes, glistening black hair, thick moustache, and sleek muscles, he is "a perfectly torsoed specimen" of manhood. (He's also endowed with a "good-sized cock.") Capable of "unendurable amounts of exercise," he has learned to use his body in ways that other men never can. His usual sexual partners are men who have information he wants, and Kane uses his "depth of sexual ability" to extract that information from them. There is an "air of inherent command" in his very words.

In fact, Kane's superlative command of any situation,

no matter how perilous, is one of the delightful over-the-top elements in these novels. John called his books "entertainments," and watching Kane soundly trounce his enemies is, as long as you have the stomach for blood and vigilantism, part of their entertainment value. Even more entertaining is watching Kane's capitulation to the charms of Danny Fortelli, a high school senior and superb gymnast, whom Kane saves from a sex trafficking ring. Much to Kane's surprise, he and Danny become lovers. Soon they are also united in a mission to "save the dreams of gay boys everywhere."

• • •

Rereading these books has been for me, an older gay man who has lived most of his life in Boston, a trip down memory lane. The Boston depicted in these novels – a city of Irish toughs from Southie who attack gay men with switchblades, of the lurid cruising blocks around Park Square, of a predominantly gay ghetto called the South End (not to be confused with Southie) – that Boston, by and large, no longer exists. But the injustices Alex fights – child abuse, the exploitation of vulnerable elders, corrupt cops, blackmail, and the lonely self-destructiveness of gay men – that world is still very much with us. Despite the somewhat dubious methods to which Kane resorts in his crusade against the bad guys, it's hard not to take some guilty pleasure in rooting for him all the way.

By the end of the second book, Alex Kane and Danny Fortelli have begun to forge a life of dignity and meaning. They share a vision of "two men existing in a state of complete cooperation and coordination." It's here that John Preston brought together his talent as a genre writer and his lifelong commitment to healthy, fearless gay pride. Read these novels for the delicious entertainment they provide and for a reminder of how far we have come as a queer tribe.

— Philip Gambone,
Boston, September 2021

Philip Gambone is an award-winning writer of fiction and nonfiction. He has published five books, including a collection of short stories, a novel, a book of interviews with gay fiction writers, and a collection of profiles of LGBTQ Americans. Phil's most recent book, *As Far As I Can Tell: Finding My Father in World War II* (Rattling Good Yarns Press), is a memoir about tracing his father's route across Europe during the Second World War. It was named one of the Best Books of 2020 by the *Boston Globe*.

SWEET DREAMS

by John Preston

To

David and Terry

With reasonable men I will reason;
with humane men I will plead;
but to tyrants I will give no quarter,
nor waste arguments where they will certainly be lost.

— William Lloyd Garrison

I

Danny Fortelli had a secret.

It wasn't a bad secret. It was just something he knew that very, very few other people knew. Not his parents who adored him. Not his teachers who daily thought he was a gift. Not his coach who thought Danny really should be on the football team but who wasn't about to give up winning a suburban gymnastics title for the third year in a row if that's what Danny wanted. Not his friends who thought he was the nicest guy you'd ever want to meet. Not the girls in his high school who said he was the best thing since Sean and Chris combined. None of them knew.

Danny kept his secret very quiet. It wasn't that he felt badly about it or that he was upset about it. He just understood that it was something he had to keep undercover for a while longer. He had read enough to know that it would have been different a few years earlier. But not now. Not to Danny Fortelli.

It was a funny thing to keep secret. It was on the cover of *Newsweek* and *Time,* and reported on the news almost every night. It was something that everyone knew about. They just didn't know that Danny Fortelli was part of it.

But that was all right because Danny was in control of it. He'd let them know when he wanted to let them know. The idea of the timing made up a lot of his most pleasant daydreams. Whenever his mother said he'd be a wonderful teacher, Danny thought it'd be great to be a teacher when he let his secret out: he could be a hero to the students who shared it. When his father told him that he'd make a wonderful politician, what with his good looks and his inherent sense of decency, Danny thought that'd be great too: maybe he could be the first Governor of Massachusetts who told the world his secret. When one of the girls at school had tried to be coy and suggested in whispered tones that Danny should be a movie star, Danny liked that one a lot: he would daydream about the cover stories in *People* magazine that would proclaim him the greatest star with the secret ever.

But his favorite came when his coach gave him one of the big pep talks about Danny going "all the way." That meant the Olympics. The coach was exaggerating when he said that, and Danny knew it. But it wasn't a total impossibility; it had a certain truth to it. Danny was a senior. He already had a dozen college scouts looking at him. They were impressed, and had already started to talk about scholarships – and it was only September. There'd be more of them.

And maybe, just maybe, if Danny went to one of the really big schools and got really top-notch coaching he could become Olympic material, just maybe. His father had always thought so, as long as Danny was okay with his studies. And Danny was always okay with school. Danny didn't date girls and he didn't drink with the guys. He didn't waste time and – this was one of his parents' few regrets – he had given up the church a long time ago. Danny had time for school and he had time for gymnastics and maybe he could do it.

Whenever Danny had a few minutes in the afternoon to think about it, the dreams came quickly and easily. He was on the podium of the Olympics and he was being given a gold medal. After he got the medal he would tell all the world about his secret. All the people who shared the secret with him would applaud and Danny would become one of them and be happy and be able to fall in love.

His parents would be hurt, but he'd work hard to make

them understand that it was all right and they'd see the light. Especially when they saw that Danny was in love. Danny would be famous. He would be happy. And he wouldn't have to carry his secret around alone any more.

II

Sam Karpeck had dreams too. But his dreams were on the sheets of accounting paper that covered his desk. He loved those ledgers with all their black ink: the way they had so many numbers in his profit columns and so little in his costs just made him glow.

He was glowing so much he didn't even hear the man walk into his office and sit in the fake leather chair on the other side of his desk. He didn't pay any attention until the man spoke to him. "With all the gay guys you have working for you you'd think you'd have more class showing in your office. This stuff's shit."

Karpeck looked up quickly. The man was handsome enough that he might have been one of Sam's "models." Sam went through the files in his mind, reeling off the names of his latest movie releases: *Jailhouse Rape*, *Suck Boy Stud*, and his top grosser, *Jungen Meister*. The guy he was looking at had a classic clone look: sharp features, moustache, luminescent green eyes. But Sam Karpeck couldn't place him. He had a hard time remembering these fags when they had their clothes on.

"Who the fuck are you?"

"Alex Kane." The man offered his name easily; it was just an offering of fact.

"Well," Karpeck assumed the guy wanted a role in one of his movies. Too old, Sam decided in a snap judgment. He was sure that the market only wanted guys under twenty-five or so; this man was at least thirty. Sam never did understand how it was that some of his films with the older ones made money. But he didn't trust the tastes of his market; it must have been a fluke. "Well," Sam repeated, "I'm not casting right now. 'Fraid you wasted your time."

"I'm not after a job, I already have one." Alex Kane seemed to find some humor in this statement. His eyes had lit up with a smile.

"Then what do you want?"

"I want to watch your face while your business goes up in flames."

A psycho. The guy had to be a psycho. Karpeck reached under his desk and pressed the buzzer for the guards. It was a subtle move but the strange man knew what Sam was doing.

"Don't bother," he said nonchalantly.

Sam Karpeck looked at him quizzically.

"They're ... asleep." More humor showed on Alex Kane's face. "They're asleep for a long, long time. Long enough for the fire in your warehouse next door to do its job."

"The alarm!" Sam said quickly, almost as though he had just remembered another secret.

Alex Kane held up a couple feet of coated wire. He shook his head in a silent "no."

Sam Karpeck smirked. "What the hell. It's insured. Besides, I got all the masters to those films anyway." The warehouse was a shipping depot for Karpeck's many mail order and wholesale businesses. They sent out hundreds, thousands of 16mm and videotape copies of some of the most vile pornography still being made in the United States. It was a business that made so much money Sam sometimes thought he was running a mint. A goddamn mint. He wasn't about to leave the masters sitting around unprotected. They had been kept separate just in case Sam ever had to remanufacture his golden goose.

But Alex Kane didn't think it was going to work for Sam. Once again he just shook his head.

Now Sam Karpeck was getting worried. He was puzzled.

The man held up his other hand. It was a loop of exposed negative film. He let it unravel. How'd he get to the studio *and* the warehouse? Beyond all those guards? Karpeck was getting frightened; he began to sweat. He had heard about the Mob moving into porn, but he figured his outfit was too small for them. It was the biggest thing that ever had happened to Sam Karpeck, but it was chicken feed for the Mob.

"Mr. Karpeck," Alex Kane said very slowly and very deliberately, "I'm going to tell you something. You stink. You have taken laws that allow some very decent people to do some very decent things – express themselves sexually with a lot of consent and a lot of concern for what they're doing – and you've turned those laws into a license to help a lot of good kids ruin their lives. You are vermin. You are a rodent."

Each sentence had been a little louder than the other. Sam Karpeck understood that this man named Alex Kane cared too much about what he was saying. "You should have stayed in the used car business where you belonged. You should never, ever have moved into porn. You especially should never have moved into gay porn. Never, ever."

Karpeck spoke reflectively, just as his lawyer had taught him to. "The artistic expression is protected by the First Amendment, first because I produce films that are beyond the vision of a moralistic –" He never got to finish the sentence. The other man had reached across the desk and, even though Sam Karpeck weighed something over three hundred pounds, this guy had a remarkably easy time lifting him up off his chair. Alex Kane didn't seem to strain at all while he did it.

Karpeck was dragged over the desk and Kane said, "Look at your First Amendment rights." He nodded toward the window. Karpeck could see the flicker of flames reaching out of his warehouse windows next door. "Millions ... those prints are worth millions." Karpeck said the words in a whisper.

"They've already cost too many lives. Young kids, good kids, wonderful futures have all gone down drains because of your stinking films."

"No one ever forced anyone to act in my films," Karpeck protested.

"You helped them forge birth certificates, you helped them find drugs to spend the pittance you paid them. You sent them around to a bunch of assholes who cared only for their bodies for a little while and were glad to drop them on Santa Monica for the rest of their lives – however short they might have been.

"Don't misunderstand, it's not the movies, it's not the hustling. Guys want to do that, fine by me. But they should be old enough to understand what they're getting into and they should be making their own choices. They should have friends. They shouldn't be on drugs. They shouldn't be wasting their lives."

"A bunch of hustlers," Karpeck was speaking his own truth now, not the words his lawyer taught him. "They're just a bunch of scummy hustlers. You find them anywhere. You give 'em a buck and they drop their pants. What's the big deal?"

"The big deal," Alex Kane's eyes shifted, not in the intensity of their bright greenness, but in their emotion, from some ill-defined contempt into a violent hatred, "is that young guys get a right to look forward to a decent life that they choose for themselves, not what some scumbag like you manipulates them into.

"That's bad enough, Karpeck, I would have come after you just for that. Those films, those sixteen-year-old boys in your stinking films. And then there's the drugs, Karpeck, the drugs."

"Hey, I'm not involved in drugs." Karpeck was more scared now.

"Oh, not that the police would ever be able to prove. But you are, Karpeck, we know you are. You get the kids to the dealers and you take your cut. You get sixteen-year-old boys who don't have homes and you give them a taste of drugs they can afford only by selling their future. No more, Karpeck.

No more."

Sam Karpeck looked into Alex Kane's green eyes. Was that insanity that stared back at him? Was that something more than anger? He didn't know. He never would.

"You have no more films. You're not going to make any more films. What you do have is two million dollars in liquid assets. Now, when I leave I want you to walk out to the next room and see what I did when your guards tried to stop me from getting in here. I want you to look at them carefully. They're pretty good, so far as goons like that go. But they'll never be good enough to keep me from you if I come back again.

"If you want to never, ever see me again, you take your two million dollars and you give it – in cash, tomorrow – to the drug rehabilitation center down on Santa Monica. Tomorrow. And you go back to selling used cars like you used to. The next day."

Alex Kane let go of Sam Karpeck's shirt and the man fell back onto his swivel chair. Then Kane reached over and gripped the handle. With a strength no one would have expected he jerked it and sent Karpeck's three hundred pounds swirling.

When the fat man had finally been able to stop the chair he was soaking in his own sweat. What the hell was all this? The Mob? They wouldn't have destroyed the films *and* the masters.

There wasn't time to think it through. Karpeck saw that the flames were building in the warehouse next door. He had to get out before the fire spread. He had to get out fast!

He stood up and ran as quickly as his heavy bulk would allow. He got to the outer office and found all ten of his security men gathered in that one room. Their moans sounded like a chorus from hell; those that came from the ones conscious enough to make noises, that is. The strange light of the growing fire lit their bruises the way the very devil would have liked to have seen them. Karpeck stood in shocked silence.

• • •

The *Los Angeles Times* carried two separate stories the next day. Both were buried in the Metro section. The first headline announced:

GAY DRUG CENTER RECEIVES
$2 MILLION ANONYMOUS DONATION

Alex Kane smiled. He didn't bother to read the article. But the second story should contain more information, and he wanted to make sure it did. That headline read:

MILLION DOLLAR FIRE SWEEPS
VAN NUYS FILM COMPLEX

Kane read the article carefully. He didn't smile this time till he found what he was looking for. "A clerical error evidently left the building uninsured. Owner Sam Karpeck claimed a total loss." That pleased Alex Kane. It meant Joseph Farmdale had done his part in the operation ... as usual.

Kane stood up and threw the paper in the waste paper basket nearby. Then he boarded his flight to Boston.

III

Joseph Farmdale had no erotic interest in men. If you had asked any of his four wives they would have told you he had no erotic interest in women either. Sex – for any purpose other than breeding – wasn't interesting to Farmdale. Money was important, that and something he called a "sense of propriety." But not sex.

Still Farmdale, like any other human being, would have admitted that Alex Kane was a handsome man. Kane's black hair glistened as though it were wet from a shower as he stood in front of a hotel window overlooking Copley Square. The bright autumn sun that shone through the glass was reflecting off the ebony mane and the matching moustache. Kane's strong chin and well-defined cheek bones gave his face a sharp appearance.

If Farmdale took into account contemporary standards of the fashionable – something he was hardly inclined to do – he might have thought the features were perhaps too severe. The nose was somewhat too exaggerated, the chin too long. But Farmdale barely acknowledged today, let alone recent fashion.

Farmdale looked at Kane and saw something that he valued much more highly. Kane was a thoroughbred just as surely as the Arabian steeds that grazed on Farmdale's ranch in California. He was able to see Alex's classic lines clearly.

He had interrupted the man in the midst of the seemingly endless exercises with which he tortured his body. Kane was standing wearing only a pair of gym shorts. Even someone without an active sexual attraction to men could appreciate the sleek muscles that appeared to be etched into the body that stood so nearly nude in front of the window.

"You did quite the competent job in Los Angeles," Farmdale spoke with a cheery voice. "Quite the job."

Kane shrugged. He didn't turn to look at the older man. "I scared a two-bit operator. I torched some films. He was getting big enough that someone else would have done it anyway. He wasn't anything. He used guys, that was enough for us. But he wasn't really big time."

Kane was staring out the window watching the hordes of people rushing back and forth across the wide plaza that stood between his hotel, the Boston Public Library, ancient Trinity Church and a block of fashionable shops. He was wondering if there was a young guy down there that wouldn't ever have to taste the poison of heroin because of what he'd done. He hoped so; it gave him a good feeling to think so.

"What did you find out?" Kane came back to the present.

As soon as business was introduced Farmdale reacted with total, instinctive concentration. He wasn't at all put out that Kane didn't want to chat or receive compliments. Farmdale picked up his briefcase and opened it on his lap. First he took out a wrapped package of $100 bills and placed it on the table by his side. He didn't even bother to mention the money. Then he withdrew a leather-bound notebook, closed the briefcase and replaced it on the floor.

Kane knew exactly what was going on. He kept staring out the window. He already knew what the notebook looked like; they were always the same. The best Spanish leather without any markings on it. Why, he wondered, didn't the old man just use a plastic binder or – fuck it – just leave the pieces of paper? Kane didn't need all these little symbols of power or class. He didn't have class. And the power he had didn't need Spanish leather binding.

"There have been some very strange things happening here in Boston: to young boys. Not terribly young, but males in their late teens. Some of the best and the brightest quit school – not all of them even made it that far. Some died. There have been an inordinate number of suicides and over-doses.

"I've sent in the usual detectives. They've gone over everything the Boston and Massachusetts State Police have accumulated."

"Them! The worst cops in the world!" Kane's voice was adamant.

"It is unfortunate that your assessment of the abilities of the city and state police here are quite accurate. Still, there were basic facts. Enough for my men to investigate. Enough for me to know that there is a pattern."

"You're sure they were all gay?"

"Of course."

"How do you know?"

"The one thing that my men discovered that the others hadn't is that all the youngsters were members of one or another of the many gay groups in the metropolitan area. There are many dozens here. All shades of political persuasion – from Republicans to Marxists. There's also one on almost every campus. Do you know how many colleges there are in Metropolitan Boston?"

"I can guess."

"More than any other city in the country. Dozens."

"What's the pattern?"

"There's never been more than one boy from one group in any given year. The pattern is not to repeat, at least not too often. My computers have checked and cross-checked everything. There's a list here of those groups that have not been ... raided this year."

"What do you think it is?"

"If I knew, my men would have taken care of it."

"No," Kane turned from the window finally and faced Farmdale squarely, eye to eye. "If you knew *and* if the law

30

would have handled it your men would have taken care of it. I only come in when you're not sure the law's going to be effective enough."

"True," Farmdale spoke without emotion. "You know quite well what my feelings are about that."

"Yeah," Kane was sarcastic now, "when your sense of propriety can't be satisfied by the law you bring me in to balance the books the way the Farmdales have always balanced the books."

Farmdale spoke after a short silence. "If it makes you feel better to create outbursts like that I won't interfere. But remember this, you are not here for *me.* You are here for *James.* You are here because you chose to be here."

Alex Kane's body stiffened.

Farmdale went on with a flat, even tone to his voice. "We agreed years ago that these things had to be done. We agreed that they were right. We agreed that you would do them and I would provide the support to make that possible.

"You have been doing admirable, necessary work. You have been doing more for your people than any single law enforcement agency in this country. While the corrupt police officers turn their backs and the decent ones still left are bound by idiotic civil rights restrictions, you take action.

"Where stupid prejudices blind others, you can see. Where others find a group of unbearably vulnerable people, you create strength. It was your wish to do so. It was my wish to give you the means to accomplish it. You have been trained as no other man in the modern world, and you have resources behind you that the FBI would envy. If you wish, you may stop the entire project. Withdraw and you can live well and quietly for the rest of your life. I will not only not stop you, I will continue to provide you the support that James's lover deserves."

Kane's body didn't relax. His green eyes looked at Farmdale and a sudden deep sadness swept over them. He went on, his voice quieter now. "Do I have to work with anyone else?"

"Only if you want some help. My men have left without a trace, as they always do."

Kane's energy picked up a little bit. "Good," he said, "those hired hands of yours only get in the way."

"Those *hired hands*, as you term them, were some of the few decent police officers left in this country. They are also the highest paid." It seemed as though Kane's words had finally gotten to Farmdale's pride.

Kane decided to end the interview. "Leave the money and the book."

"Are you going to get someone to help you?" Farmdale asked.

"I don't know yet. Maybe not. Probably not this time. Just leave it to me. There's enough money there if I need to."

Farmdale stood and smoothed his Brooks Brothers trousers and adjusted his suit jacket. He went to where Kane stood and put a hand on the other man's shoulder. "I think this is going to be one of the worst. I don't know why. But I have that feeling."

"I didn't think feelings were up your alley."

"They're not," Farmdale agreed. "That's what makes this all the more awesome."

IV

Danny Fortelli posed only one mystery to his parents. Maria, his mother, tried to ignore it but finally there was one time too many. "Where does he go every Wednesday?"

She had asked the question to Arturo, her husband of more than twenty years. Her voice interrupted his favorite cops and robbers TV show. But Arturo, who daily told the men he worked with at the Raytheon plant that God had blessed him with the kind of family others only hoped for, wasn't about to complain. Maria was good to him and Danny was his life's delight; no one had ever seen him angry with either of them.

"Who knows? But who cares? Maria, you get a son like Danny who wants a night a week to himself, you give it. He's got all As, he's gonna get a scholarship to college for that or for gymnastics, he's the best kid they got at that school. He's eighteen. He needs a little breathing space. That's all. He's becoming a man, a man's gotta have some breathing space."

Both the Fortellis smiled to themselves. Their son was becoming a man and such a man they had! No trouble. None at all. A good boy. It made Arturo feel so good. And his words made such sense that Maria stopped worrying. Her husband was right. What with the problems her neighbors had with *their* children. But Danny, that was not a problem. That was a joy.

Danny drove the family car into Boston the same way he had nearly every Wednesday night for the past year. He knew the route via Storrow Drive along the Charles River as well as he knew the street he lived on. Not even the intricate and confusing one-way streets of Beacon Hill gave him any problem. It was going to be a great night, he knew that because he found a parking space only a block away from the church.

It amused him that the meetings were in a church. Well, in the basement. His parents had given up on getting him to go back to Mass, but he knew they'd still want it. If only they knew that he went to "church" every Wednesday.

He didn't really attend services, of course. It was just that the Gay Youth Discussion Group met in the basement. The old Episcopal church had long ago thrown open its doors to a wide variety of organizations that were excluded from other public spaces in the city. They hadn't really counted on *GYDG* being one of the first tenants, but the kindly old priest had resigned himself to an onslaught with his new policy and he stuck by his guns.

So every Wednesday night anywhere from one to three dozen young men gathered in the basement and drank cider and ate cookies. They'd try to talk about oppression and politics, but most often they just wanted a breather from the world outside. The most excitement they got going was their annual dance. It was coming up soon.

"Halloween!" yelled a flagrantly effeminate young man with dyed blond hair as he greeted Danny.

"Come on, Sy, it's still almost six weeks away."

"But Halloween, Danny. I hear what they say about Halloween in San Francisco, it's the gay day of all gay days. And here we are stuck in Beantown with little kids getting the tricks and playing with the treats! We gotta change it this year."

Danny had long ago gotten over his discomfort with the wild antics of Sy – who actually would have preferred to be called Celeste, but Danny had refused. They had even become endearing.

Danny had something else on his mind, anyway. He wondered if that blond guy, Ted, was here tonight. He hoped so. He had noticed the way Ted had looked at him last week and Danny had experienced a tingle in his groin from the intensity of it. Danny had little sexual experience, but he had already decided that if Ted wanted to play around a little bit, it'd be more than okay with Danny.

Ted was there, sitting in a corner reading a copy of *Bay Windows,* the gay newspaper. Danny hated the feeling of discomfort he got around men. He just hadn't had much experience and felt awkward and unsure of himself. He had to count on another guy making the first move. He hoped Ted would do that tonight.

But right now Sy was insisting on all Danny's attention. "We're gonna knock 'em dead. I tell you it's gonna be the greatest." Sy was a tall, skinny kid. He was about Danny's own 5'11". He tried very hard to look the part of an elegant urbanite, but his thick Somerville accent and the ravages of years of acne on his face betrayed him.

Sy rambled on about the plans. The group had finally convinced a local college to let them use a hall for the Halloween party. Some members of *GYDG* were enrolled there and the school had found itself caught in its own rules.

Sy ended his recitation of the decoration plans – which he, of course, had taken charge of – with an old cliché: "Oh Mary, it takes a fairy to make something pretty."

Danny laughed and hugged Sy. They kept the embrace for a couple beats, a little longer than other men might have. They had spent every Wednesday together for a year and the sheer build-up of that time had created a bond between them. Sy especially appreciated Danny because this was one jock that wouldn't make fun of him – and it never hurt Sy's chances for him to be seen with Danny.

He had told everyone about his "friend" who was just *too* gorgeous for words. Danny was. He had thick brown hair and at eighteen his beard was already obviously heavy even after shaving. His brown eyes danced with good will and his lips were a heavy red, so beautiful they would have been femi-nine if it weren't for the muscles that went with the rest of it.

Danny was the kind of man for whom Levis clothes were invented. Sy and his friends might have to spend hours shrinking and stretching and hoping that the off-the-racks clothing would fit correctly. Danny just grabbed whatever was on sale at the Gap and put it on. His buttocks were so firm from his constant training that they filled the jeans per-fectly. His calves were so developed that even they pressed against the cloth. His shirts – a perfect medium fit – hugged the hard, high lines of his chest and dipped in to his narrow waist.

And, as Sy never tired of pointing out, if that crotch were any bigger the seams would have torn open.

But, as is the case with so many truly handsome men, Danny didn't really know it. He had always been attractive and being considered good-looking was a given in his life. He had never had to go through a childhood period of taunting the way the Sys of the world had. He had been cooed over and fawned over from the day he was born, and he could barely recall a single zit, let alone the torture of a field of blackheads that seems the burden of American adolescents.

Because his attractiveness was a given, Danny nev-er played it. It was a such a constant that he never worried about it either. It was there. In the way of beautiful people Danny ignored most physical beauty. Like others, he would be turned on to it, but he could see beyond it. He could turn down the most handsome stud in Boston; he could also be-friend a Sy because he could see some substance there.

The group was called to order by Frank, who had become president because no one else wanted to do all the paper-work. Frank loved it, just as he loved all the chances he had to be interviewed on television and to attend all the meetings with the gay community leaders who felt it necessary to have a teenager on their panels.

They had all decided to tolerate Frank and to let him steal the limelight from them. They probably weren't even aware of the real reason. They wanted to talk to one another and to plan parties. But there was some unknown rule that said they were supposed to be politically relevant at the same time. Frank performed that task for them and let them get on with what was really important.

Danny sat on one of the beanbag chairs. Sy took the one to his right. Danny tried not to be too obvious as he waited for the blond to take his own seat. He hoped no one noticed his sigh when Ted chose the one next to him.

This was, Danny decided, going to be a very good meeting.

V

Alex Kane was sprawled over the bedspread. Night had come to Boston; the bright autumn sun had disappeared. As Kane stared out the windows of his room, the reflection of a city's lights came to play. He paid them no attention.

Farmdale did it to him every time. It had been ten years, but he couldn't see the man without memories rushing into his mind and taking it over. The old man had left more than six hours ago. It didn't matter. Kane had exercised to the point of inhuman pain. The screams of his body hadn't driven away the memories. An expensive room service dinner hadn't done it either. Nothing would.

There was nothing to do but to let the thoughts wash over him, the way they always did. As he had to every time he saw Farmdale, Kane let the whole thing play itself out. He was forced to look at his past and see it all ... the hope, the loss, the unbearable loneliness of the present.

It had begun in Vietnam. So many stories did. His own started when he was a grunt, straight out of boot camp at Le Jeune. Eighteen years old and ready to fight for America and everything he held sacred.

His company landed at Da Nang. They came charging off their amphibious troop carrier right onto the beach. Gung-ho and green, convinced they could take on Ho Chi Minh single-handedly – probably take 'em in only a week, maybe two.

Along the beach was a line of seasoned veterans, the Marines who had already seen the horror of the war that would never be won. They had scoffed at the untried jarheads. They had watched the enthusiasm with deadened eyes, barely able to remember when they, themselves, had last had faith in this god-forsaken war.

One veteran had stood out from the rest. He hadn't been as cynical as the others, not as quick to put down the new men. He was a tall, handsome blond officer, a First Lieutenant. His eyes evaluated the new troops in a way that seemed different from the rest.

Later when Kane had found his quarters and was walking around the ancient city of Da Nang, once the playground of the French colonists, now the most armored fortress in the world, he had found some old friends who had preceded him. They all went for a beer in one of the many dives that had sprung up to serve the American military men.

"Hey, guys, I saw this First Loot on the beach. Big guy, blond with a beard that was so light it looked white. Know who he was?" The image of that officer had struck Alex Kane with some power he had never experienced before. Ever. He was lucky. His friends did, indeed, know who the man was.

"Meanest son of a bitch in the Corps," Gerry Maxwell said. "Just mean."

"Didn't look it," Alex had responded.

"He is. Drives his men harder than any other officer here."

"Fairest, though," Tony Andrews admitted.

"Yeah, but," Gerry added, "fair in a way that's going to get some people killed."

"What do you mean, killed?"

Gerry looked down at his beer for a minute. "Look, Alex, you haven't been here long. You don't understand. Men here aren't just fighting an enemy, they're trying to survive. It's got so the only thing anyone cares about is getting their asses out of here in one piece. Well, the only way to do that is follow Headquarters' Command. It's real simple. 'If it's dead and Vietnamese, it's Viet Cong.' You shoot first and ask later. Kids could be Viet Cong. Young kids. And women, too. You don't trust no one here if they're gooks.

"Well, Farmdale's got all these ideals, see. He won't let his men do that. Protects the civilians like they were Americans or something. Even learned to talk their lingo. His men are going to get it bad some day."

"Yeah," Tony agreed. "But hell, you can't take away that man's courage. He's led some patrols –"

"Well, that's another thing," Gerry interrupted. "He's a hot shot. He's a real, honest-to-God hot shot. Wants to win medals and all that shit. Thinks he's going to win the war and win it with something he calls honor. Let me tell you, honor died in Vietnam about a hundred years ago. This is a game of survival."

Alex had let the man talk some more about the rigors of war in Southeast Asia. The incredible heat was already evident to him. It would always be like this, so hot you couldn't tell the temperature, it didn't matter if it was 100° or 110°, it was too hot.

Out of nowhere Alex Kane announced something to his hometown pals. "I'm going to join up with him. Get a transfer to his platoon."

"Whose?" Gerry asked incredulously.

"Farmdale's. Honor's the best word I've heard since I got here."

•   •   •

Then it began.

Farmdale was a mean son of a bitch all right. But as soon as Alex was part of the group he saw that Farmdale might be the most respected officer in the whole of Southeast Asia so far as his command was concerned. He held a special control over the men. It sometimes seemed as though his disappointment in them would have been the worst thing they could have experienced.

Alex understood that. He had never needed to make

someone respect him as he did with this guy. He volunteered continually, and for the most dangerous assignments, especially if he knew Farmdale was going to lead the troops himself. He took risks that were barely short of insane. Farmdale would often reprimand him, but with an expression of pride in Alex's courage that took away any sting to his words.

When an army is in battle promotions come fast, very fast. It's a combination of the deadly attrition rate and of the opportunities battle offers to a foot soldier have to prove himself. Kane was an exceptional soldier, an exemplary jarhead. Anyone could see it. He shot up through the ranks.

In only a matter of months he was a sergeant, proud of his stripes and anxious to continue to earn his Lieutenant's ongoing praise.

One day, after a particularly hazardous and successful patrol, Farmdale had announced they were up for R&R. Ten days out of the jungle; they could go to Bangkok. They were all wild with excitement at this break from the constant fatigue and ever-present danger of the war – but none more than Alex. Alex was euphoric because the Lieutenant had privately invited him to spend the R&R with him.

They had been flown down to Bangkok on military transport. Farmdale had arranged for himself and Kane to go separately from the rest of the men. Alex didn't understand why, but he didn't question the reason. In Bangkok he had expected they'd go to a hotel. There had been rumors about the Loot's being rich, maybe it would be a good one. But Alex was totally unprepared for what had come.

They didn't just go to "a hotel." They had the same suite in the best hotel in town that the General Staff often used to house visiting senators. When Alex saw the opulent surroundings he felt suddenly and completely inadequate. His longing for R&R with its private time with Farmdale was no longer something he was desperately looking forward to; it became a trial.

Farmdale saw the discomfort on Alex's face and laughed at him. Then he did the most amazing thing. He just walked up to Alex and kissed him on the mouth. Not just a peck, nothing that could be explained away as a joke. It was a long kiss, one where his tongue invaded Alex's mouth with its wet length and lingered there, as though Farmdale wanted to taste every drop of Alex right away.

Kane always wondered why he hadn't hit him or something. That would have been the jarhead thing to do. But he hadn't. Alex Kane, big bad Alex Kane from Portsmouth, New Hampshire, just broke into tears. The big brute of a First Loot had uncovered some need in Alex Kane that no one – not even Alex really – had ever known existed. He needed the love of a man. He had wanted the love of this man. It had been a carefully hidden need, one that only showed itself in shadows in Alex's mind, but now James Farmdale had given that need a body and a personality.

Kane had hoped he'd never have to admit it to anyone – even himself. But that kiss ripped away the covering and exposed Alex as naked and needy and lonely as any man should ever be. And that kiss meant it was going to be all right.

Farmdale led Alex into the enormous bathroom and undressed him. He put Alex into the shower and then stripped himself and joined him.

That's how it started. And once they had started they vowed they would never stop. Not until one of them died.

It wasn't too difficult to arrange everything. For one thing Farmdale was up for rotation to a desk job in Saigon. He had been planning to refuse it; now he wouldn't. It was simple for him to use his ever-present "influence" to get his new lover transferred to the capital city as well.

They had a bungalow. They spent every single spare moment together. "I'd been waiting for you," James had explained. "I'd expected you to come along sooner. But that's okay."

"What do you mean, me? Sooner?" Alex didn't understand.

"Waiting for the man to fall in love with. It didn't happen at Annapolis, and I was tired of the city games. That's why

I volunteered to come to Nam. I figured you'd be a jarhead, so ..." James would smile and drag Alex back onto the bed they so seldom left.

James tutored Alex, not so much to teach him as to wash away a lifetime of prejudice and an education that blocked real thinking. Alex was a willing student. He read everything that James gave him, he listened carefully to the explanations of the cuisine they were eating, how to do little things to produce great pleasure. And they learned to have sex.

Their rotation in Saigon lasted for six months. The war was picking up, the omens weren't good. Farmdale could have kept them out of battle, he could have gotten them back to the States. But he explained that it wouldn't be honorable. "When you have power – and my family does," he explained to Alex, "then you can't misuse it. Ever. You certainly can't misuse it to become a coward, to protect yourself. You and I are Marines. We chose to be Marines because we believed in something. It's hard to find that something in a hellhole like Vietnam, but the last thing we can do is let the rest of them define what's right and what's good. That has to be what we know it is and we have to hold on to it hard.

"Right and good aren't easy things to know. Not at all. But they're there and they're important, Alex. People back in the States are as bad as the crazies over here. It's as stupid to think you can protect right with speeches and marches on the Capitol as it is to think you can keep it alive by killing innocent women and children. The right thing for a soldier to do is to protect what's good ... however he has to do it."

So they went back, back into the rotting, stinking jungle. They went back and they marched their patrols again. "The Lieutenant and his sergeant" was what they were called. Alex Kane was proud of that.

But there was another sergeant in the platoon who hated those words. Sergeant Johnson, a big, beefy man from North Dakota, was jealous of all the things that went between the Lieutenant and "his sergeant."

One day Johnson came into the tent where James slept

and found out just why he was cut out of so many of the private conversations between Alex and James. James was on his knees, Alex's pants open, his long, thick penis hard and stabbing the air. "You faggots," Johnson growled with a sneer.

James had told Alex to forget it. Forget it ever happened – he'd have Johnson out of there within a week and the man had been warned to keep his mouth shut. It made Alex nervous to think about it, but he took James's word.

There was a sudden enemy movement. They had to go on alert and out to patrol a particularly dangerous sector. They were willing and ready – as ready as men in Vietnam ever were.

At a point a few miles from their camp they were attacked. Bullets shot through the air and whined death close to them. Alex and James were face-down in the damp, stinking Asian dirt. They fired their M-16s with deadly accuracy. The enemy dropped back. It seemed as though the fight was over. James lifted his body up slightly to check out the position. One single bullet sounded its call. James jerked up, then fell onto the ground.

Alex was mad with concern. He laid his body over his lover's to protect it from where the sniper's position was. He felt the weakness of James's breathing and screamed for a medic.

But his panic collapsed all at once. He had looked down at the body beneath him and seen where the bullet had landed, in James's back, right at the spinal column. He had been shot from behind. By an American. With zombie-like determination and utter disbelief at what he was seeing, Alex stood up. He looked back and saw that sneer on Johnson's face and he knew. *He knew.* Alex lifted his own M-16 to his shoulder and sent his own mortal round of bullets tearing through Johnson's chest. The sneer disappeared forever.

Then he went back to James. There was a hint of life, just a hint. He rolled the Lieutenant over and held James in his arms trying not to let his sobs jostle the dying man.

James Farmdale knew he was going to die. He lifted one hand to Alex's face with great, painful effort and rested it on the sergeant's cheek.

And then, First Lieutenant James Farmdale, U.S.M.C., left this world.

. . .

Kane knew that something was going on when he went before his court martial. The charge was the murder of Sergeant Edward Johnson. The defense lawyer the Marines had given him had said it was hopeless; he begged Alex to plead insanity.

"Never."

But when they went in front of the court martial, Alex didn't see faces of men who would be willing to send him before a firing squad. The judges were nervous, more frightened than he ever thought they would be. They called the lawyer up to the bench and had a whispered conference with him.

The young attorney returned to Alex's table with a shocked expression on his face. "The trial's closed; they have orders. From way up. *Way up.*"

The proceedings lasted minutes. In one of the fastest trials in the history of the United States Marine Corps, Sergeant Alex Kane was dishonorably discharged from the service. But not for murder. For some trumped-up charge that let Kane off easy. The judges walked briskly out of the room, embarrassed by something. Tough MPs stood beside Alex and each took one of his arms. He looked at them. "Follow us."

He did, right to the airport where a transport was being held for him. The guys inside figured it had to be a general at least – who else could have kept a plane that big sitting there so long? But it was only a sergeant, one with dark, black hair and a look of uncommon sadness, even for this part of the world where sadness was omnipresent.

They hadn't had time to even process his papers in Nam. But the documents were waiting for him when he landed in California. He took them and all his back pay and caught a bus to San Francisco.

Alex Kane, the lover of James Farmdale, a hero of the War in Vietnam, landed in the Tenderloin and began a battle like no other he had ever fought: a battle to drown himself and his hurt and his anger in an ocean of booze. He nearly won.

He still couldn't remember whole days, weeks of the hell he put himself through. The sleazy bars, the nameless bodies, the rancid bathhouses all blurred together in a haze of self-hating sex and self-destructive drinking.

Finally, one day, there was no more money. He woke up and there wasn't any body next to him either. The flophouse was even dirtier than most. *So this is the end of the line*, Alex had thought. He looked around the room. He had thought it would be someplace like Vietnam, or else someplace homey and comfortable like his grandparents' house in New Hampshire. He had never really thought that it would be like this. But if this was his fate, then so be it.

Suddenly the doors burst open and three strong men stormed into the room. They grabbed Alex; when he tried to resist one of them knocked him out cold with a roundhouse punch. They made no sense to him, not in the little time he was conscious of them. He did remember thinking one thing. *So this is the end of the line.*

• • •

When Alex Kane woke up the next time he thought maybe his prediction had been correct. He was still naked. He was clean though, and so was the bed he was resting on and the sheets that covered him. There was something wrong with his body. Was this what heaven felt like? This slow lethargy and all this comfort? But then he knew that the sensations were more commonplace. He had been drugged. He was just dehydrated with a chemical hangover.

He staggered out of the bed and stretched. The room was luxurious, and he could hear surf crashing on the shoreline somewhere nearby. He went to a set of doors that opened onto a patio, and beyond it, an Olympic-sized swimming pool.

There were no clothes around. But there appeared to be no people either.

A few laps were just what he needed to clear his head. He walked over to the pool and dove in. He drove his out-of-shape body as much as he could, until he could swim no more. He stopped and hung on to the edge of the pool to catch his breath.

Then he saw an old man sitting in an immaculate suit close by. The man was studying him intently, silently.

This makes no sense, *Alex told himself.* What is this?

Then an answer came to him and he laughed out loud. "Jesus Christ, man, you went to a lot of trouble for a piece of rough trade."

The old man didn't smile. He just stared and finally said, "I am James's father."

VI

The group lingered when the *GYDG* meeting broke up. They always did. There was the tentative testing of one another that followed every meeting. These teenagers weren't old enough to have grown callous in their sexual encounters. They hadn't learned all the artwork involved in sophisticated cruising. Well, a few had, like Sy. He knew lots. That was obvious to Danny.

But generally the kids were shy with one another. They didn't have their own apartments for the most part – most still lived at home, a few had dormitory rooms at various colleges, but only a few and they were most often scared of being discovered by their classmates.

So they simply mingled and a couple made dates to go to the movies together where they could hold hands in a balcony and go parking in one their father's cars afterwards. They were just learning.

Sy moved loudly through the crowd. "Come on guys, t-shirts, t-shirts! Say it loud, gay and proud!" He had a clutch of white t-shirts draped over his arm. Each one had bold lavender print spelling out: "Gay Youth."

"Great shirt." Danny said.

"Fund-raiser, handsome. We need dough for the Halloween party. I got 'em cheap and I'm selling 'em dear. Ten bucks. Buy a small size and you can flaunt your pretty muscles along with your gay pride!"

Danny hesitated. "I really like them, Sy. But I don't have anywhere to keep them. My mother ... you know."

"Closet case." Sy's words weren't angry. It was a long-standing rule that everyone in *GYDG* had the right to be as private as he chose. "Come on. Buy one anyway. I'll keep it for you in my place and you can come over and get it whenever you want to wear it."

"Deal," Danny smiled and dug the money out of his pockets. When he handed the cash to Sy he added something, "But a medium, Sy, a medium."

"Selfish," Sy responded with mock hurt. "You want to keep all that pulchritude from the rest of us poor peons." He pecked Danny on the cheek and flitted away, "Frank, you cheap asshole, I want your money where your cock is."

"He's a real screamer." Ted was standing beside Danny now. His comment had all the acid that Sy's hadn't.

"He's a nice guy," Danny defended his friend.

"Sure," Ted shrugged. He put a hand lightly on the small of Danny's back and held it there. He watched the youngster stiffen. But when Danny didn't move away it was obvious that he liked the touch.

"I'm more interested in masculine men, that's all. I like guys who act like guys, not girls." Ted's light touch moved slightly up and down Danny's back. "And when I like them I like them a whole lot."

Danny was excited. He could feel the urge inside himself. He wanted to go home with Ted. There was something strange about him, though, something Danny was unsure of. It was some sense that told him that Ted was much more experienced in ways Danny didn't understand, even more experienced than Sy.

He wondered about his uncertainty and debated letting everything slip away. Sure, he had thought about Ted a lot this past week. He admitted to himself that he wanted him. But ...

Sy came back before Danny had reached a conclusion.

"Some bunch of cheapos here. Come on, stud, let me buy you a cup of coffee down on Charles Street."

Danny was still confused. But then he felt Ted's hand move in a slow, almost imperceptible rotation; it was inviting and seductive and Danny hadn't had sex in months.

"I have a place just a few blocks from here," Ted whispered in Danny's ear.

The hand kept moving. Sy was waiting for an answer. "Not tonight," Danny said to Sy. "I think I'll do something else."

Sy's right eyebrow shot up in exaggerated fashion. "Well, don't do anything I would do, sweetheart." Then he walked away. The joke didn't hide his obvious disappointment.

VII

Alex Kane had finally broken himself away from the past – as well as he was ever able to. He had taken a shower and dressed. He was going to have to go out into the city and relearn the ins and outs of Boston. He had been here often, but not for years. A couple quick phone calls and he had the names and addresses of the gay bars and cruising spots.

It was Indian summer in Massachusetts, that special time of the year when the air was barely tinged with the promise of fall, with the lingering warmth of summer still coming over the city occasionally on nights like this. He didn't need a jacket. He pulled on his jeans and wore only a Pendleton wool shirt over his undershirt, then white socks and engineer boots of black leather for his feet.

He went down the elevator to the lobby of the hotel. He walked directly out onto Copley Square. It was only about ten o'clock; bars would be open till two. He had plenty of time. He nodded away the doorman who asked if he wanted a cab. He'd walk.

He had read Joseph Farmdale's briefing book earlier. The information had been chilling. He ran it through his mind as he walked up Boylston Street towards downtown, ignoring the chic shops and only barely glancing at the historic Public Gardens and the Common as he passed them. There was something wrong in Boston. Something very wrong and he knew he'd have to take care of it. That burden, knowing that he would have to handle it, made any pleasant sightseeing of the old dowager of a city impossible.

The local authorities hadn't even seen it. They had ignored the pattern. First, because missing teenagers were one of their lowest priorities. So many kids left home nowadays that there was seldom any hope of finding them. The cops would listen to parents report the absent kids and they'd shake their heads and say soothing words to the concerned father and mother – if the parents cared, which often they didn't. Then the cops would usually toss the report in the trash can. Runaways that age were hopeless.

The next lowest priority was teenagers who used drugs. The flood of marijuana and other more dangerous narcotics overwhelmed those cops who cared. The rest of them were on the take from the pushers; they weren't concerned about kids getting hung up on drugs, they wanted them to. It increased their take.

And a few college kids found murdered in the bushes along highways were too difficult for the police to handle. No motive, no evidence, nothing. They had written off the ones that took place in the "nice" suburbs as sex slayings and those in the slums as gang killings.

But Farmdale's relentless intelligence network and its incredible computers had picked up the pieces and made them whole. Someone was systematically moving through the gay youth of Boston and ruining their lives, sometimes indirectly, sometimes with murder. It was all there if you looked for it.

The cops never even noticed that the victims were gay. They usually weren't the kind that wore buttons or flashy clothes. They were all good kids, liked by their families for the most part, popular in school more often than not. They were all also very good-looking.

Somehow Farmdale's computers – which tracked crime patterns throughout the United States – had discovered that one link between the victims of the diverse happenings. They had known that Jimmy Saldo, a nice kid from Everett who had just entered M.I.T., was a member of a gay theater group before the heroin got to him. They knew that Mike Kenny, a star athlete at South Boston High, went to a gay Catholic mass every Sunday until his body was found alongside the Massachusetts Turnpike in Natick.

There were too many bodies, too many young men dead or dying because of drugs, to be explained. And they were all gay.

The knowledge made adrenalin surge through Alex Kane. He hated to see anything happen to gay men, but he especially hated to see anything happen to the kids. When he thought of the endless facts and figures and names and addresses that had been in Farmdale's briefing book Kane realized that he was experiencing something very rare. He knew he was going to get someone because of this. And this time he wasn't going to be bothered by it. Not one bit.

Kane walked into a suddenly blinding brightness. He had passed through a dark block of downtown Boston. His soldier's training had made him automatically alert to any danger. But he hadn't taken in any of the signs of the change in the social conditions of the neighborhood. He wasn't prepared for what he witnessed now.

He was in the Combat Zone. It was proof that Boston was something of an honest city. It had decided that it didn't want to try to get rid of all the slime that infected America's urban areas – that would have been a useless, impossible task. But Boston didn't want to have to look at that slime all the time, it just wanted it available when it felt like using it. So they zoned a section of Washington Street to contain it – and Kane was standing in the middle of the city's self-defined sewer. It was a garishly decorated row of sex shows, pornographic bookstores and an army of hookers on the street.

The women were so bold they stood directly under streetlamps as they plied their profession to the sounds of the raunchy hawkers who were competing with them to lure giggling college students, suburban "gentlemen" and military guys on leave.

Youngsters who should have been home doing their schoolwork were openly buying drugs from pushers right under the noses of cops. Filth cluttered the sidewalk. People aimlessly drunk didn't think anything of ducking into an alleyway to piss or vomit.

The sight distressed Alex Kane. He loathed what was happening to America's cities. He hated the cheap way that life was being ground away by this irresponsible, hedonistic waste. Was this what he and James had thought they were fighting for in Vietnam? Was this what they had risked their lives for? This was what heterosexual America wanted gay guys to live like? This horrid accumulation of human misery and personal famine?

Well, Alex Kane had been there before. The Tenderloin was just as bad – worse. The one thing that Kane knew was that no youngster needed to experience this. He'd do everything in his power to keep them out of it. Everything.

He walked up Washington Street, away from the Combat Zone. Soon he came to the nearly deserted canyons of the retail section of town. Tall department stores and office buildings stood silent guard over the empty streets. There were lots of indications of construction here. A city like Boston trying to rebuild itself from near destruction from the hands of urban planners was just answering the old problem with new problems.

Finally Kane came to his destination at the other end of downtown. A nondescript sign hung over the otherwise unmarked doorway. This was the place, the first of the bars he'd go to tonight in the beginning of his search for answers to the questions that Farmdale's computers had recognized. He hoped he found them soon.

VIII

Danny Fortelli had done it to himself again.

He was sad by the time they reached Ted's apartment at the top of Beacon Hill. *Will I ever learn!* he wondered. He had convinced himself that Ted was going to be something special; he had spent the whole week daydreaming about falling in love.

He had the whole thing down. They'd go to the same college and they'd get an apartment together. Maybe Ted would be an athlete too and they could train together, at least they'd share meals. And they'd be such a loving couple that when Danny took Ted home to meet his parents, Mom and Dad couldn't have objected to Danny's secret. You can't get upset about two people in love.

By the time they had walked up the steep back slope of Beacon Hill all the dreams were drained. Ted was like so many others. He wanted sex and he wanted his "freedom." Commitment was some stupid thing that straight people got. It didn't have anything to do with the handsome blond boy's life, that was for sure.

Just as they walked into the building's front door Danny had a sudden impulse to leave and go down to Charles Street to see if he could find Sy. A cup of coffee with a friend would be better than what was waiting for him here. But it would have been too much of a hassle to talk his way out of this and he didn't even know which of the many coffeehouses Sy would have gone to.

It's funny, Danny thought as he walked up the staircase behind Ted. Everyone's always talking about gay sex and getting laid and promiscuity. They made it sound like the best thing in the whole world. It only made Danny feel lonely. Every time he did this – had sex with someone who wasn't special and who probably didn't want to see him again – it just reminded him of what he hoped it would be like when he found someone different.

They walked into the studio apartment. It was clean, at least. Danny looked around and saw some haphazardly mounted centerfolds from some gay magazines on the wall. There was a neat pile of pornography in a corner. A single mattress was on the floor. *At least he makes his bed,* Danny noted.

The two of them went to the only other furniture in the small space, a table with two chairs. Danny automatically sat down. Ted stood in front of him. The blond lifted up his polo shirt and pulled it over his head. He ran a hand lewdly over his chest when it was naked. There was a surprising amount of body hair for a blond.

"I like guys to watch me undress. I like to see the look on their faces when they know I'm going to let them have it." Ted was smirking right at Danny. He dropped his hand down to his groin and cupped the growing bulge of his crotch. "And I'm going to let you have it real good, baby."

Danny hadn't taken his eyes away. Ted was good-looking; his body was almost as firm and well-muscled as the guys on Danny's track team. He still had a golden tan from the summer. His shoulders were too wide. Danny didn't have any great passion for this guy, so he could note the details easily.

He liked the looks of Ted's stomach; it was sleek with lines that ran down the side until they began to converge just over the belt line. Danny could see the growing length of Ted's cock beneath the denim. The whole thing was nice. Danny also knew that it was a natural build, it came from just everyday motions and not eating too much. It'd be gone in a few years. That belly couldn't keep its tautness without effort, the shoulders couldn't keep their stature without workouts.

When I have a lover, *Danny thought,* he's going to take better care of himself than this. This is something you get, this isn't the result of effort. *Somehow the idea of a lover in his future made Danny feel better. He didn't have to worry about Ted so much.*

"Man, I'm going to take you to the stars." Danny looked up when Ted said that and smiled. The blond thought it was a smile of appreciation; it was really just an expression of relief, because Danny had resigned himself to this. It was better than masturbation and, besides, he wanted to have had enough experience to satisfy his lover when one did come along. So let Ted talk and let him make a production of it.

Danny's relief allowed his own cock to swell, first something to make yourself feel good, *Danny told himself.* That's all he's offering and that's all you're looking for from him.

Excited by the darker boy's apparent response, Ted theatrically unzipped his jeans with a long, slow motion. There was no underwear. Danny could see the tanned skin as the triangle exposed by the denim grew. Then there was a sudden and stark line where it turned white, where a very brief bathing suit had protected the paleness. Right below that line was a tuft of pubic hair, the same blond color as the rest of Ted's.

Then, finally, the long, already hard tube of flesh appeared. "Suck it, suck my big, fat cock."

It wasn't that big and it wasn't that fat, but it was pretty, Danny thought. Nicely shaped and cleanly circumcised. With that secret smile of his he leaned his head forward and took in the silky smooth penis. It felt so good! It had been so long.

If Danny hadn't been concentrating so hard on his fantasy, wishing desperately that this beautiful penis belonged to a lover, he might have heard the slight whirring of the machine that was hidden behind the wall. But he didn't hear a thing, not even Ted's dirty talk.

IX

Alex Kane knew he had started in the wrong place. The bar was a dive. Not really horrible, but it obviously wasn't going to be one of the hot spots this night – probably no other night either. The men were either older than usual in a gay bar, or much younger. The music was loud and bounced back and forth between country and western to disco to rock and roll with a dash of New Wave. The schizophrenic sounds reflected the lack of identity that obviously kept the bar from being popular.

Alex sipped a bottle of Budweiser. He seldom drank. When he did, he drank slowly, so slowly that he'd never finish a bottle of beer before it got too warm. He'd often spend a night buying as many as ten bottles, but never actually drinking the equivalent of one.

Whenever Alex stood in a gay bar he made a point of finding the good qualities in all its patrons. He had done this ever since he had finished the training that Joseph Farmdale had provided him after his return to the United States. It had been obvious to Kane that he might be the only man in a place who was willing to make a priority out of liking it and its people, but he knew he had to do it.

Actually, it came easily right now, after what he had seen in the Combat Zone. These were just a bunch of guys out for the night, talking to old friends, open to meeting new ones.

The idea that there might be a trick, or a future lover, was clearly here, but it wasn't a driving force or a compulsion that overcame the rest of their wants and needs.

Kane kept sweeping the room with his eyes. He was going to have to talk to one of these men pretty soon to get the information he needed, and he was looking for a friendly face or one that displayed the knowledge of the city the way that some people's faces do. Instead he found himself watching a little duet over in the corner. He couldn't help the smile that came over his face.

There were two youngsters, just barely legal age – twenty in Massachusetts. They might not even have been that. Each was mimicking what he obviously thought the older gay guys thought was "in." One, dark-haired with a moustache that was only just full enough to be called adult, was leaning against the wall. He wore a leather jacket and was trying very hard to show off attitude. The cigarette in his hand, Kane noticed, was hardly ever dragged on. So seldom, in fact, that Alex thought it might just be a prop.

Beside him the other boy was moving to the music. His motions were a little too exaggerated, as though he were on a stage rather than standing by the bar.

Each youngster vehemently refused to look at the other, though Kane could see they were trying hard to catch a glimpse of one another from the corner of their eyes. They stood, not budging, ignoring the rest of the crowd and playing out some little game of their own. The dancer was lighthaired, wore glasses and was the same height – about 5'8" – as the guy with the leather jacket. The blond would swirl theatrically every once in a while and Kane was sure it was only to give himself the chance to check out the dark-haired boy.

The blond was wearing only a t-shirt. When he turned Kane was able to see the logo of a karate studio on the back. Great. Kane knew karate; he knew all the martial arts. It would give him the opportunity to go over and talk to the blond kid, and maybe he could break the ice for the two of them at the same time.

Kane turned in his warm Bud for a fresh one, then he crossed the room to where the two silent cruisers were standing.

"That shirt for real?" Alex asked.

The blond stopped his dancing and froze when Alex talked to him. The one in the leather jacket could barely suppress his sigh; he thought his trick had just been snatched away. He'd never be able to compete with a man this handsome.

"Um, yeah, I mean, I just started a little while back. I wanted to know something to take care of myself, you know? I mean, the bashers and everything. So I heard about this place and I signed up."

The explanation wasn't very enthusiastic. The blond was again trying to look at the other boy in the jacket to make sure he hadn't left.

As though he had walked into a conversation between the two of them Alex turned to the brown-haired boy and said matter-of-factly, "They a problem here in Boston?"

If the kid in the leather jacket was surprised that Kane had addressed him this time he didn't show it. "They were, down in the Fenway, over on the Esplanade, you know, where people go in the parks."

"Yes, but even around the bars, on the little side streets there have been some muggings, especially in the South End," the blond grabbed his excuse and was talking to the other boy.

"I heard that, too." The brown-haired one wasn't going to let this chance pass either. "I'm Kurt," he stuck out his hand to the blond.

"Roger," the other one smiled. There were a few minutes there when Alex Kane didn't know if they would ever stop staring directly into one another's eyes, or if either would ever give up his grip on the other's hand.

"What's anyone doing about this?" Alex was honestly sorry to interrupt the moment.

"Oh," Kurt shook his head as though waking from a dream. "Well, the Association's doing a lot, they're organizing protests about police protection and that."

"Yeah, do you know Erin Frost?" Roger asked Kurt.

"Well, sure, I mean, I know who he is," Kurt replied.

"Have you ever been to Association meetings?" Roger was interested.

"Nah, I live way out in Boxford and it's hard for me to get in town. I don't have my own car," Kurt explained.

"I could maybe pick you up."

"Where do you live?"

"Only in Weymouth," Roger said.

"But that's on the South Shore. It'd take you nearly an hour to drive up to Boxford and ..."

"No problem," Roger insisted. "I love to drive. Do you want to go to the next meeting? It's tomorrow night."

"Great!"

"Hey, just a minute," Alex tried to stop the conversation before the two decided to rent an apartment together. "Who's this Frost person?"

"Erin Frost," Kurt was brought back to the present again. "He's the head of the Association, it's the big gay group."

"That, and he's involved in nearly every other gay thing in town," Roger added.

"Any one that's worthwhile," Kurt agreed.

"Do you know where I can find him?" Kane asked.

"At the meeting tomorrow, the one we were just talking about," Roger suggested.

"Well, but everyone knows Erin's into leather. If you wanted to you could probably go to the Stiffbeam and he'd be there. He hangs out there," Kurt added.

"Thanks. That's the one out by the Fenway?" Alex wanted to make sure.

"Yeah," Kurt said. But his eyes were back on Roger whose hands had quietly and unobtrusively found both of Kurt's hips. They were oblivious to Alex, that was clear.

"Can I buy you guys a drink for the information?" Alex offered.

"No, no, that's okay," Roger said. This time the two boys

didn't even look at Kane. "I got a lot of driving to do tonight. I don't think I should have any more."

"Nah, you shouldn't." Kurt said.

When Kane got to the bar door he looked back over to the corner where he had left the two of them. They were in a deep embrace, kissing with quiet passion. Alex silently wished them the best and left.

• • •

Alex Kane took a cab across town. He paid the driver and stood outside the Stiffbeam. The bar was in the shadows of Fenway Park, home of the Boston Red Sox. Strange place for it, far from the hustle and bustle of downtown.

Alex went to the door and entered. He expected that he'd have to barter his body for some of this information; he'd done it often before. He just hoped it'd be something he'd enjoy for a change. Too often it was boring, or involved sticky, often false emotions. Alex Kane liked men, he lusted after men. But he wasn't open to any big affair and he wasn't looking for a lover.

Not like those kids at the other place were. God, they'd be a cute couple. Young love, innocent, trusting young love. Something Alex Kane had long ago decided he'd never experience again.

His work was in the sewers of gay life, in the wards of its most victimized inhabitants. His cause was their protection. His life was devoted to making sure that kids like Kurt and Roger could have just that experience he had just witnessed. They would never have to know the humiliation of cameras owned by a pig like Sam Karpeck. That was what it was all about.

It was a consuming obsession with Kane. Once he had seen his own lover killed and had been brought out of his own near self-destruction with the aid of James's father, Kane had decided no other gay man should suffer that way. That had been the pact that Joseph Farmdale and Alex Kane had made. That he, the soldier Alex Kane, would go out into this world and fight to protect the sweet dreams of gay America wherever they were threatened.

He could do it because he had none of his own. His quest for others' peace was his satisfaction. Sex was a tool, except for those very, very occasional moments when another man as individualistic and as self-reliant as Alex Kane came along and made it clear that that one night was all that was expected, or all that would be offered.

As he went into the Stiffbeam Alex Kane thought about all that. And he thought about Kurt and Roger. He imagined the tastes of the bodies, young and firm, clean and healthy, full of the promise and hope of life. He thought of them and he realized that he would never know the way they touched one another. His sex was utilitarian. Or it was athletic. It no longer carried with it the indefinite but exquisite possibilities of whatever it was that someone called love.

He had had it once. It had been taken from him. He never again expected to know the touch of a man who loved him.

A primeval sadness descended on Alex Kane. One he had experienced too, too often.

The door to the bar slammed behind him.

X

Alex Kane went to the bar and ordered a beer. When the bar-tender delivered the usual Budweiser, Alex stopped him. "Is there a guy named Erin Frost here?"

The bartender, obviously used to being asked for information, nodded towards the crowd. One man stood out in particular. That must be the one. Kane walked over to him.

He was enormous. Well over 6'3" and he must have weighed close to 200 pounds. But Alex could sense that it wasn't fat. There was strength behind that bulk. The man's hair was slicked back in a pseudo-punk style, heavy with grease. His eyes were hidden behind reflecting aviator sunglasses. He wore only a strapped t-shirt over his not-too-tight button-fly jeans. He had on heavy work boots. The man moved slowly to the music that came over the loudspeaker as he surveyed the crowd with the cool ease of a veteran of the bar scene.

Kane spoke to him, "I hear you're the biggest gay politician in town."

The big man didn't answer. He didn't stop moving. He didn't even look at Alex but kept staring straight ahead.

"Are you the big shot in Boston?" Kane asked.

The man's eyes didn't meet Kane's. But his voice finally spoke. "I didn't hear anything about you, but if you think I'm going to talk about politics in the middle of a bar this late at night when I'm this horny, you're an asshole."

Kane liked him immediately. The voice was good, deep and well-practiced. You could sense the man was used to speaking, probably from all the activities he was supposed to be involved with.

Alex followed the big man's gaze over the room. There was a crowd; it was heavily dominated by men dressed in leather, sometimes just jackets, often in chaps and hats as well. The boys had been right. If this was Frost's bar, he was into it.

There weren't any outstanding numbers, though. Besides, if the man was still here it meant that he had already had the ones that were attractive. He would have scored by now if he had wanted to. Kane realized that this was one of those times he would enjoy his information-gathering.

He checked out the body more carefully. Frost was incredibly hairy, you could tell from the growth that covered his shoulders and back where it was exposed by the scant shirt. And from the thick, long beard and hairy arms.

"I got what you want," Kane told him. "I got it better than any one else here. So why don't you just talk to me a little, make me happy. Then we'll go someplace else and make you happy."

The giant looked at Alex Kane now. The expression on his face didn't alter. "You should find out what I want before you go making such big promises, boy."

Alex hadn't been called "boy" in years. At least not by anyone who was left standing a single minute after the words had been uttered. But this man was using the word as a sexual challenge. Kane felt an uncommon charge go through him. This man knew what he was up to. Maybe it was going to be a *very* interesting night.

Kane didn't speak; he let Frost's words stand and simply smiled back at them. He stood stock-straight. It was his own challenge back to the Frost. The giant understood and let the slightest smile crack on his face.

"What do you want to know?" the Bostonian finally asked.

"Whether you know anything strange going on in the city. If you know about anything peculiar happening to gay kids."

"Why are you asking me?"

"Because the best authorities I've found said you were the straightest shooter here. They told me if you were involved, they followed. Theirs was the highest recommendation I could have gotten." While the words might have sounded a little overblown and misleading, Kane thought of Kurt and Roger and realized he sincerely meant every one of his statements.

Erin waited a bit before answering. "Are you some kind of cop? A fed? A narc?"

"No," Alex assured him.

"Then what do you want to know all this shit for? You're not from here. I'd know you if you were. So what's the deal?"

"I just want to get some answers, some understanding so I can ask some other people the right questions. Come on, I'm going to pay you back for it. Tell me about Boston." Kane didn't change his own challenging attitude, but he did move closer, close enough that his hips straddled Frost's right leg ever so slightly, just enough for Frost to feel the mound of Kane's crotch.

The big man smiled just a little more. "You think you're convincing, don't you?"

"Aren't I?"

"Yeah, you are." Frost brought down a hand onto Alex Kane's ass. The palm was big enough that it nearly cupped the whole of Alex's left cheek. He pulled the man in and gave him a wet, masculine kiss. Alex Kane let Frost think that his tongue was able to pry open Alex's lips.

When the man was done with the embrace and had relaxed his hold on Kane's buttocks, he had a strange expression on his face. "How did you do that?"

"Do what?"

"Make me feel that way. I just kissed you, that's all, and you did something."

"You learn," Alex Kane said easily.

As though he had to retest an unexpectedly good dish, Erin Frost brought their mouths back together again. He tried to be his usual rational self as everything was happening, to be able to study this phenomenon while it was taking place. But a unique wave of warmth went through him, just as it had the first time. It enveloped his groin and tingled at his anus. Alex Kane hadn't moved, hadn't touched him; his arms still hung by his side. But a powerful eroticism came from him. He was weird, Frost thought.

But it was a good kind of weird and Erin Frost wasn't about to let it slip away.

"How about going back to my place first? We'll talk later."

Alex Kane shrugged; he was all for seeing this through. Everything told him that this guy was trustworthy, and there was nothing he could sense to suggest otherwise.

They left the Stiffbeam. Frost had a pick-up truck parked close by. He unlocked his own door, then lifted the lock on the passenger side from inside for Kane to get in. They drove in silence through the Fenway and into the South End. Frost parked the truck on the street in front of one of the rows of Victorian mansions that had been turned into apartment buildings and rooming houses. The debris of construction was all around them.

They got out of the truck. While Frost was locking up Alex Kane looked at the evidence of the rebuilding. This wasn't like what he had seen in downtown Boston, where faddish architecture was creating inhuman congestion and unrelenting ugliness in the heart of a once-proud city. Downtown Boston was being built up with nondescript buildings that were indistinguishable from those in Pittsburgh, Los Angeles, Podunk. What Kane saw here was the reclamation of the unique soul of a city.

These buildings were being rebuilt, saved from demolition and misuse, they were being saved by the hard work and commitment of gay men. While moralists indulged in ridiculous speculations about the effect of homosexuality and gay liberation on the society, here was the proof that gay men were often the only people who had the guts and the determination to commit themselves and their little money and their labor to saving the cities from turning into empty shells.

Find a rebuilt neighborhood in an urban center and you've found a gay ghetto in the making. Kane knew that. Someday the rest of the country could rid itself of its prejudice and see the reality of just what gay life meant to America. Someday.

Frost took his arm and broke Kane's thought. The two men walked up the large, once-grand stairs to one of the red-brick buildings Kane had been admiring. The multiple locks of urban dwelling had to be undone. Finally the door opened and they walked in. Then Frost had to relatch all the protective devices that kept the crud of the city outside.

They went into the first-floor apartment. Alex knew that the furniture and the fixtures were authentic. There had been a lot of artistic work done here, and it had a real sense of masculinity about it. This wasn't a decorator's image, this was a man's home.

They kept their silence as Frost led the way into a bedroom in the back. He turned and faced Kane, then took off his glasses for the first time. His eyes were clear and intense. He was smiling. He kicked off his heavy boots and let them fall onto the floor with a thump. The shirt came next, and quickly. He stood there with his remarkably hirsute body open to Alex's appreciative inspection.

Then Frost undid his belt. He didn't just unbuckle it, he unsheathed it from the pants loops and left it resting on the mattress. It was clear the belt was going to have another purpose this night. Erin Frost undid the first button on his jeans and then stopped. His smile broadened. "Let's see if what you're paying is worth what I got to give."

Alex Kane unbuttoned his own wool shirt and pulled it off, then his undershirt after it. He kicked off his boots and reached down to take off the white socks. He didn't play any games about his pants, they were removed quickly. He stood for the slightest hesitation wearing only his white cotton briefs. Then he took the elastic band, bent over and slid out of them as well.

Erin whistled very slightly. The body in front of him was a dream come true. Alex Kane was certainly a big man, but there wasn't a bit of extra flesh on him, not one ounce that wasn't prime, in hard condition. Erin usually liked men as hairy as himself, but this one time he was happy to see a nearly totally smooth body. This way he could trace every one of the exquisite lines in Kane's torso. The only hair on it were slight tufts at Kane's underarms and a dark, lush growth that topped Kane's good-sized cock and two low-slung testicles.

"Man, this is going to be fine, just fine." Erin picked up the belt and doubled the length of the leather. "I want my payment in full. I want it right now."

Kane looked at the man and felt that sexual response that he enjoyed so much, as seldom as he experienced it. He could sense his own cock filling with blood. The surface of his bare ass felt cool with anticipation.

He smiled at the bigger man. "That's what you want?"

Erin Frost nodded. "Your ass, after it's nice and warm."

Kane could have taken Frost any time he wanted to. The Boston gay leader didn't know that the same power of sexuality he had experienced with Kane back at he bar was matched with an awesome accumulation of fighting skill. *Some things you just learn.* That's what Kane usually said. What he didn't often explain was that he had learned to use his body in ways that other men never could.

But tonight he was going to just use it, just enjoy it. So this guy thought he'd get off on using a belt on Kane's ass? All right. Kane would get what he wanted, information, he'd also get the special sexual experience between two adult men that he craved.

The smile had never left Alex's face. He answered Frost's statement by going to the bed and standing at the foot of the mattress. He fell forward, his arms extended in front of him and spread his legs. His offering was going to be complete.

Frost moved close to the open man's figure. He leaned

over and ran a hand across the firm, ivory white buttocks. "You look just like a statue," he whispered, "just like a fucking statue."

• • •

The next morning the two men sat in Frost's kitchen and drank coffee together. Frost was studying Kane's face. He still couldn't get over the way things happened last night. Alex Kane's perception of Frost had been right, he was a veteran of the bar scene. He had had great sex in his life. But never anything like that.

"How do I get you back again?" Frost asked the strange man whose face resembled a Greek statue more than anything else.

Kane smiled, "I think it'll probably happen."

"So, I got to keep accumulating information just to get you into bed, is that it?" The words weren't bitter.

"Doesn't hurt." Kane's voice showed he was simply playing along with Frost. "But I think barter has its limitations. I just ... don't get involved with people. I have my reasons. So long as it's just a case of having a good time, well, fine. But I don't get involved."

Frost nodded. People had all kinds of reasons for all kinds of decisions and there were lots of them he had learned long ago not to question.

"But I do want that information," Kane said.

"Ask away," Frost spread his arms and sat back on the chair waiting for Alex to go on.

"See, there are some things happening that you probably don't know about. Kids are having too hard a time in Boston, gay kids."

"They've always had too hard a time," Frost spoke with a sudden passion.

"But there's something worse, even worse than usual. Have you noticed it?"

Frost's face frowned. "Yeah. It's impossible to put my finger on, but, yeah. It's like this: when you've been around as long as I have you start to be able to make predictions. You meet people in the bars, at meetings, at parties. The ones that have just come out. Well, you learn to read their future in a way, there are just some signs. There are men who are going to make it and there are men who won't, usually ones that are going to self-destruct in any event.

"I meet *lots* of people. I learned to know just which ones would have lovers and nice homes in two months, which ones are going to be politically active and which ones are going to spend night after night in the bars.

"But I've lost my ability to predict lately, in the last year. I never dared to mention this to anyone 'cause it seems so crazy and it's certainly not scientific, but it bothers me. Now you come and tell me there *is* something wrong and it bothers me more."

"Keep on talking," Kane coaxed.

"I've been meeting guys – the real good-looking ones. Often they've been the young ones who I just *knew* were going to join organizations or become vocal or active in some way. I would have bet money on it. They had an enthusiasm about them, it was just infectious. High energy, clear minds, good presence, born leaders.

"But they'd never come through. Next time I'd see them they'd be hustling Park Square or they'd be drunk out of their minds in a bar. They'd avoid me totally, as though they were ashamed for me to see them. Some of them I never did see again. They'd disappear."

"Now that's stuff that happens all the time in the gay world, we both know that. But it was happening to the ones I never would have expected it to. That's all I can do, tell you I know something's happening and it's bad and it's happening to the wrong people."

"But you don't know who's doing it?"

"Not a solitary clue. Not one."

XI

Danny Fortelli spent at least an hour working out in the gymnasium every day after school. At least an hour ... and that was on top of the hour he spent there every morning before classes started.

He was walking out of the locker room when he stopped in his tracks. There was Ted. A bunch of quick emotions went through Danny. He was a little scared to have the guy here, in his own high school where no one knew his secret. He was sort of happy to see someone he knew was gay here at the same time. He was even flattered that Ted had gone to the trouble. But, in the end, most of all, he wished he hadn't. He didn't really ever want to see this guy again.

"Hi," Danny went up to last night's partner and held out his hand.

Ted took it and smiled. "You sure got a lot of lookers here, a lot. Do you score much?"

"No," Danny admitted, "never here. I just never even tried. It's like I'm a different person in school than I am at the meetings."

Ted nodded. "You going home?"

"Yes."

"Come on, I'll give you a lift. I got something to show you."

Danny nearly made an excuse to get out of having to have to spend time with the other gay guy, but Ted had just turned

and begun to walk away, obviously expecting Danny to follow. The young gymnast just sighed and decided to follow the
path of least resistance.

The two of them walked out of the school building and
over to the nearby parking lot. Ted used a key to unlock the
door of an expensive sports car; Danny recognized it as a
Porsche and let out a low whistle.

"Like it?" Ted asked.

"Sure do," Danny opened the passenger door and got in
after Ted had reached across from the driver's side and unlocked it for him.

The car started and Ted poured on the power, revving
up the engine in an adolescent display that contradicted the
quiet elegance of the German vehicle and repulsed Danny. He
hated show-offs.

Ted backed up too quickly, then changed gears and laid
a patch of rubber on the parking lot surface. *Only assholes do
that*, Danny thought, and only with beat-up cars. Not with
something like this.

Ted seemed to know the general direction of Danny's
house. Danny Fortelli wondered about that vaguely, but his
sense of fear over the guy's driving was too pressing to let
him really think it through.

Ted did know exactly where they were going. He parked
the car just a little way away from the driveway on the street
and lit a cigarette. Danny opened the window to let the smoke
drift out.

"You could have a car just like this, if you wanted to."

Danny laughed, "I doubt it. We don't have much money, what we have is being saved for college next year. I don't
think my father's about to buy me a Porsche."

"No, *you* can earn it. It's easy. You're good-looking, you're
hot, there are men who like that, a lot."

Danny was uncomfortable with this conversation. He instinctively knew where Ted was going and he didn't want to
have any part in it. "I do fine. I'll wait until I graduate and get
a good job before I worry about fancy cars."

"Oh, come on, Danny, get real. There's money out there waiting for you, you can get it. Why not? Huh?"

"Nothing doing," Danny's voice was severe, he obviously intended to end the conversation. His hand went to the door handle.

"Wait!" Ted said. Danny looked at him. "I think you will do it, Danny. I know you'll do it. See, I found out some stuff about you. You're really the big man on campus here in school, aren't you? And your parents think your shit smells like roses, huh? All the kids just think that Danny Fortelli's the world's nicest guy. What are they going to say when they find out you're a cocksucker?"

"You're going to tell them?" Danny's voice was full of contempt. "Are you threatening to tell them?"

"Oh, not just tell them, Danny. Not just tell them. I got a better way to handle it. You know, when you tell someone that someone else is gay there's all kinds of ways they can respond to it. They can get mad at you for saying the words, or they can handle it pretty easy since they only have to think of it as an idea, do you know what I mean? But if you show them, now that's a different story."

Without any further explanation Ted reached under his seat and brought out a large manila envelope. He handed it to Danny.

Danny's intuition told him not to open the envelope. But he had to, he knew that Ted had him cornered. He undid the metal clasps and reached inside. He brought out a couple dozen 8x10 inch photographs. They were of him. At least he was the only person whose face was identifiable. There was another body there, represented in a large erect penis. In most of the photographs that penis was in Danny's mouth.

Some of the shots were extreme close-ups. The process of enlargement had created a fuzzy image, but not one that could hide the smile on Danny's face. It was clear he was enjoying what was happening. He flashed back on his dreams, the fantasies he had had while the sex was going on. That was what the smile was about. But no one would ever know that.

They'd just think he was having a good time.

Danny couldn't remember the last time he had been guilty about sex, about being gay. Years ago, back when he had first discovered this secret about himself, he had felt bad about it. And right now he was disgusted by it again. It was amazing how these photographs could take something he had grown to believe was beautiful and make it seems so utterly loathsome. Danny was repulsed by the image he was studying right now. It made him feel dirty. It convinced him that he was dirty .

"Now, how's Mama Fortelli going to like these pictures, Danny? Think she'll hang them up over the mantel for all her neighbors to see?"

There was a moment's silence. Then Danny admitted defeat. "What do you want me to do?"

• • •

Ted had picked Danny up in his Porsche the next Friday. Danny sat silently as the other youngster sped into Boston. He refused to answer the cute comments or indulge in pleasantries with Ted. He hated the other boy – he hated him almost as much as he hated himself.

They parked the car in the garage of an elegant apartment house in the Back Bay section of town. Just across the park – the Common – was Beacon Hill and the church where the *GYDG* met on Wednesdays. It was only a few blocks, and an entire lifestyle away, Danny realized. He'd never go back there again.

Ted led Danny to the building's elevators. He ostentatiously turned a key in a keyhole and punched the button marked PH. He was obviously pleased to be able to get into the penthouse of such a place. Danny didn't respond.

When the elevator stopped and the doors opened, they walked right into the foyer of the apartment. This place took up the whole floor; there was no outside hallway. As soon as they had walked through the entryway they came into an enormous living room. The floor was covered with a thick wall-to-wall white shag carpet. The furniture was an ensemble of various sectionals that fit together to weave a snakelike line through the center of the room. There was only one man there, sitting on one of the segments of the couch sipping a drink.

"Ted," he greeted the two boys, "you brought a new friend for us."

Danny studied the man intently. He immediately realized something. There were really people in this world that anyone could – *should* – distrust and possibly even hate, because just the way they looked sent out such intense and strong signals that you knew there was no way they could be decent. This was one of them.

Ted introduced the man as Mr. Morrisey. He was a big man, with a good-sized paunch on him. He stood about Danny's 5'10" height but weighed at least fifty pounds more. At least.

His clothes had that unusual but unmistakable mixture of being clearly expensive, very expensive, and in the worst possible taste. There was something wrong about almost everything in Mr. Morrisey, especially his eyes.

They were beady. It was the only word for them. Lips of fat rose around his eyes and nearly covered them. The little cylinders that were showing were dominated by dark, hard-looking irises. They glistened, just as though they were marbles.

The smile on Morrisey's face was as fake as any Danny had ever seen. It meant nothing. There was no warmth to it. It was a feeble attempt to hide the way he was judging Danny's appearance. The evaluating glance was as overt as the hand that gripped Danny's upper arm, supposedly a comradely gesture – this pig was just feeling the goods to see if they were adequate. Danny knew just what was going on.

"Have a seat, boys, have a seat." The two sat in a part of the couch that nearly faced the big man. A waiter who Morrisey called Bruno appeared. He looked foolish in his black tie outfit; his bulk and his bumpkin gestures made it plain that he was there more for his muscle than for his ability to gracefully serve the drinks he offered Ted and Danny.

Danny almost never drank. But for this ordeal he decided it wasn't a bad idea to mimic Ted's request for a gin and tonic. The big buffoon played at being butler while Morrisey's little chatty monologue continued.

"Yes, yes, you're going to fit right in here, Danny. I can see that right now. It's a friendly operation, or at least it can be, should be if you boys just cooperate a little bit. Aren't we friendly, Ted?"

"Of course, sir." The way the quick-talking blond immediately responded with such a brown-nosed attitude let Danny know just how scared Ted must be of this man.

"Yes, of course. Now, Danny, let me explain our operation to you. It's quite simple and straightforward. We use this little apartment," Morrisey's tone made it obvious he meant it as a joke, he was impressed with his penthouse, "to entertain some very important people. At one time, before the relaxation in social mores that's taken place recently, those people were almost always straight.

"But now no one has to hide from the obvious implications of being, shall we say, inclined towards the other side. We, being good businessmen, have expanded our operation to meet all our clients' needs.

"We have so far limited this part of our operation to Friday nights. Though that will soon change, very soon. But for now, we can only offer you employment on Fridays."

"*Offer* me?" Danny said sarcastically.

The eyes lost their fake facade of joviality. "Yes, Danny, offer you. I strongly, strongly suggest that that become the way you perceive things here. You'll find this not unpleasant in the end, after you're used to it. And you'll certainly find this very, very lucrative. Ted can tell you that."

The blond didn't say a word, but seemed a little embarrassed. He hung his head silently. For the first time Danny wondered if someone had taken Ted's picture some time in the past.

"If you fight it, if you hold on to some silly idea that you are doing something ... wrong, you'll only make things difficult for yourself. It's a question of attitude, Danny. Attitude. We want our clients to be happy. You'll make more money if they are. They often tip quite well, you know.

"Now, if you need some help with some attitude adjustment, Ted will be able to offer it to you. At our cost." The man sipped his drink. The smile was coming back to his face. "You're certainly welcome to use any of our stock from the bar, within reason. We don't want drunks falling around here.

"You talk to Ted about these details. I'll tell you more about some more immediate issues. The men and women who come here are very busy, very influential people.

"They have to be more discreet than the man on the street because of that. They have to be more worried about what the press might make of a slight expression of very basic and human needs, unfortunately.

"We give them the protection of this apartment. We allow them a slight space to let loose their inhibitions. They can do it here in the comforts of utter luxury, as you can see. But the luxury might be a little misleading, Danny. Our customers come here knowing that there's nothing forbidden, nothing that isn't allowed.

"We give them the permission to act out their fantasies. And you are here for just that purpose. There is nothing, Danny," the eyes hardened again, "*nothing* that you should refuse to provide for a customer." The smile was forced back on the man's face. "We do get a little wild, sometimes, don't we, Ted?"

"Yes, sir." Ted blushed from some secret memory.

"But, then, these are busy men we're dealing with. Men with pressured jobs and the need to blow off steam. I'm sure you'll understand, Danny, as things progress. Now, Ted," Morrisey stood up, "why don't you show Danny around and help him get acquainted with ... things."

The pair stood and Ted led Danny from the room and down the corridor that bisected the apartment. Morrisey dropped the friendly host routine as soon as their backs were turned. When they had disappeared he snapped his fingers and held up his empty glass. Bruno came to take the container and carried it to the bar where he refilled it with bourbon.

He spoke to his employer while he worked. "Not a bad one. Looks good."

Morrisey was obviously thinking of Danny himself. "He's a little too spunky. And too hairy. I don't understand why the fags go for that type."

The servant brought over the filled glass. "They do though."

"Yeah. I know. I mean, I could understand if those pansies wanted to poke some hairless butt that could belong to a woman, I guess. But it's weird that they want a dago with hair on his chest so often."

The other man shrugged.

"How's the operation going?"

The servant didn't want to answer the question, but a glance from Morrisey told him he couldn't withhold the information. "Not till next week."

"What!" Morrisey's face flushed with anger.

"Boss, they can't get the guys in. They don't dare use local talent, it'd be too easy to trace it. They gotta bring 'em in from someplace else. You're asking for a lot, you know. It's going to take a lot of muscle."

"I'm asking for a simple order to be filled. That's all. I have this thing all ready to go. It's going to be the gold mine of the century if I can only get the cooperation I need."

"I know, boss, I know," Bruno said nervously. "And you're going to get it. But not till next weekend. I got them coming in from Chicago. They'll never be traced. When you're done you're going to have the only game in town."

Morrisey seemed a little placated. "What a scam. How come no one ever tried it before? For Chrissake, they're all out there, unorganized, unprotected, hated by the cops and the 'good citizens' and they're raking in a fortune. A fucking fortune! It's just sitting there waiting for someone to pull it together."

"And you're the man to do it."

"Yeah," Morrisey's first authentic smile of the night showed on his face. It was a greedy smile, one that made his eyes appear even more beady than before. "By the time we're done the only place to buy a piece of boy ass in this town's going to be right here, right in Morrisey's."

The man toasted a nonexistent companion and started to dream about his riches after next weekend.

•　•　•

A couple doors away, inside the penthouse apartment, Danny was facing Ted. He had a look of scorn on his face. "How could you do something like this? To other gay guys?"

Ted looked away. His bravado had disappeared after their encounter with Morrisey. "It's a job, Danny. You'll find out. It's just a job. Besides," he suddenly remembered a part of his act he had forgotten, "I'm not gay."

"Could have fooled me," Danny scowled.

"Well, I guess I did then," Ted was trying to regain the upper hand. "I'm bisexual. I just do that to get guys like you."

"Sure," Danny scoffed.

But Ted was on a roll now. "And I did get you, Danny. I got you good. You're here."

Danny's attempt at resistance deflated.

Ted smiled acknowledgment. "Now, let me tell you how to do this. Get out of your clothes."

Danny averted his face while he undressed, leaving his jeans and shirt and underwear on the double bed that dominated the room. He did notice how small the space was, little more than a cubicle. He would have expected something more grand given the scale of the apartment. If he had had more experience he would have realized that the apartment was cut up into as many tiny areas as could be fit into it. Space was money here. It was one thing to give the image of opulence in the living area; there was no need to waste money making space back here. This area was strictly functional.

When he was naked Danny looked up and caught Ted's admiring glance. That little bit of rebellion returned. "Thought you weren't gay?" Danny teased.

Ted didn't have to play any more. He was in charge again, the only position that made him feel comfortable. "Let's see," he said haughtily, "what image is right for you."

The blond boy went to the only closet in the small room, and opened it. Inside was a wardrobe of various slight costumes. Athletic gear, leather, rubber … a catalog of fetishes was there.

Ted smirked at Danny. The blond boy wanted to indulge his need to humiliate the handsome Italian even further. There was a leather collar there with a length of chain attached to it; it'd go nicely with nothing more than a black jockstrap. But Ted's hint of common sense came through. That was too much too soon. Besides, just for business' sake, the kid's athletic look was a natural.

He pulled out a pair of shiny gym shorts and handed them to Danny. "Put these on."

Danny examined them. "They're too small."

"That's the whole point." Then Ted brought out a matching athletic shirt, a pair of over-the-calf white socks and a pair of running shoes. "The perfect jock."

Danny was silent as he put on the outfit. It was much too tight around his crotch, it forced his cock and balls into a tight bunch off to one side. He caught a glimpse of himself in the big mirror and felt more naked than if he had been undressed. The shirt was skin-tight as well. The gleaming fabrics clung to him and their shiny surface actually accentuated his body.

"Here are the rules. We put on a couple of shows. No big thing, but the men like to watch a lot. So someone might suggest it, and you do it, there's a little platform, covered with carpet – did you notice?"

Danny shook his head, yes.

"That's where it happens. You're new. If someone asks you to do it, find me or one of the other guys and ask to get fucked. That way you won't have to worry about getting it up this time. You'll get used to it in a while and then it won't be a problem.

"Someone asks to take you into a room, you say yes, then go and get one of the goons in tuxedos to make the arrangements. They'll collect the money. You get $100 for being here and $50 for every trick you turn.

"I better warn you about one thing."

Danny looked up sharply; after all this dullingly mechanical description what could there possibly be that deserved special warning?

"There'll be a lot of women. Mr. Morrisey's not set up for a strictly gay scene yet. So a lot of these guys ... well, they're closet cases. They have to make believe it's just a joke, you know? So they hang on the prossies and make believe it's just a kink they're going through."

"I'm just a kink to them?" Danny asked incredulously.

"Yeah," Ted's voice admitted that even he knew it made things harder, "but that's going to change." His face brightened. "Believe you me, that's going to change. Mr. Morrisey's going to have nothing but guys here pretty soon. This is going to be the biggest and best gay whorehouse in the country."

"How's he going to do that?" Danny asked.

"Oh, a man like Mr. Morrisey, he has his ways, Danny." Ted seemed the slightest bit friendly now. As much as Danny distrusted and disliked him, he caught the change in Ted's voice. "It's hard the first time. I know. Look, you want something?"

"I don't do drugs," Danny said adamantly.

Ted seemed to ignore him. He reached in his own jeans pocket and brought out a small vial. He opened the container and took out a large white pill. "Here," he held it out, "you're going to need something, believe me. It's just a 'lude. Nothing heavy, it'll just make things hazy and easier to take. If you do want something ... heavier, let me know. Like he said, Morrisey's got lots of things to help your attitude. Drugs are probably the easiest of them all."

• • •

The next morning Danny's mother went in to wake him when he still hadn't gotten up at noontime.

"What's the matter? Are you sick?" Maria Fortelli was concerned.

"I'm fine, Ma," Danny said into his pillow, unwilling to turn over and speak to her.

"But Danny, it's after twelve o'clock. Your father's waiting to watch football with you. You never sleep this late. Where were you last night? What time did you get home?" Maria was instantly sorry she had pressed so many questions on the half-awake boy. But she hadn't ever seen such behavior from him before.

"Ma, *I'm all right!*" Danny's voice rose to a yell. Maria stepped back as though she had been physically struck. Her son, her Danny, had never spoken to her like that before, never in his entire life. Confused and hurt, she fled the room and left Danny alone.

The boy got up and showered. He dressed in casual clothes and walked into the living room where his father was cheering at the television set. "Hey, Danny, BC's ahead. The Eagles are finally going to beat Penn State!"

The man's excitement was immediately crushed. "Who cares," scoffed his son. "Boston College is rinky-dink. A bunch of rejects from Notre Dame." Then Danny walked out of the house and went down the street.

Arturo and Maria Fortelli were each so upset that it took them most of the afternoon to be able to speak to one another about the changes that had come over Danny so quickly and savagely. They agreed on one thing though: the boy had to be ill, there was no other excuse for this bizarre behavior.

Whatever its cause, the behavior didn't change. It got worse. On Monday a new witness was added to the events. Danny's coach sat behind his desk and listened incredulously to a snide Danny Fortelli announcing that he was quitting the gymnastic team. He gave the coach no good excuse.

"It's boring, that's all. It takes too much time. I don't want to do it any more," was all the kid would say. Then he stood up and left the room.

On Wednesday Arturo automatically handed Danny the keys to the family car for his weekly trip into the city. "Not tonight, Dad. I'm just going to stay in my room."

"But you spend every Wednesday night out," Arturo protested.

"Yeah, well some things just change." Danny left the older Fortelli more concerned than ever. He followed Danny into his bedroom and put a hand on his son's shoulder. "Talk to me, Danny. Something's wrong. You gotta tell me about it."

"Nothing's wrong, Dad. I'm just growing up and my ideas of what I want to do are changing." The stony voice invited no further conversation. Arturo, more than anything else, respected Danny's privacy. If the boy needed to be alone with his thoughts, then let him. But, Jesus, what the hell was going on?

• • •

Danny couldn't tell any of the people who were so obviously upset. He felt guilty and sorry that he was causing them so much pain and confusion, but as far as he was concerned, the only alternative was worse. Much, much worse.

Danny couldn't deal with his parents or the gymnastic team because he thought he was unworthy of any of them. If they knew what he had done …

He lay on his bed and looked vacantly at the ceiling. What he had done … The Quaalude had made everything dull while it was going on, but it hadn't blotted out the memory. Danny had left the house on Commonwealth Avenue with $250 – a lot of money, Danny thought bitterly.

He had earned every penny of it.

The young men had gone to the party that night dressed only in ridiculously tight gym suits. They weren't allowed to wear anything underneath the outfits. "Let the customers sample the goods," Ted had explained.

Anonymous hands had constantly crept up and felt Danny's buttocks and fondled his penis. Men with heavy smells of bourbon reeking on their breath had kissed him, laughingly. Whenever Danny seemed to be pulling away or rejecting one of the men, one of the tuxedo-clad waiters had come up and put a hand on his shoulder, and the smile couldn't hide the warning they were conveying.

Danny had figured the whole thing out right away. The men weren't gay, or at least they never were going to admit it. They came to the penthouse and paid their money to be entertained by the stunningly beautiful women who plied their trade there. The boys were a sideshow, a freak addition to the usual. They were a little kink to go with the good time.

The first "good time" was had by some suburban idiot who had bet one of the women that a gay guy could give a better blow job than any female. Danny and the female prostitute had to go up to one of the rooms and compete with one another to win the bet.

Another man wanted a more involved three-way. He got it. The third – this wasn't until late in the night when the whole crowd of them were drunk or high – was more honest, at least while the chemicals were working on him. He wanted Danny all to himself.

The memory of the incidents was burned into Danny's consciousness. But the most humiliating, the one thing he'd never get over, he'd never forget, was the "show." Ted had taken him up on the small carpeted stage in one corner of the living room. They had just finished watching two of the women act out some straight man's fantasy of what lesbian sex was like, with grossly exaggerated movements and loud, artificial dialogue.

Now it was time to watch the fags. The 'lude had made the whole thing go so slowly in Danny's mind; he was almost able to separate himself from it. He watched Ted grease his erection with detachment. He observed the erect penis as it was aimed at Danny's own ass. Then he felt a fullness.

But any possible physical enjoyment had been cut by the jeers of the audience, the obscene yells and the lewd comments echoed within Danny's head.

Two hundred and fifty dollars.

Big deal. But a deal big enough that Danny thought he'd never recover. Ever. He couldn't tell his parents or the coach why he was acting the way he was. Never. He couldn't explain that he felt too filthy to have his mother or father touch him. Or that the whole basic enjoyment of gymnastics was gone, probably forever.

Danny had loved gymnastics because he had loved his body and was entranced by how much he could do with it, how much he could push it and train it. He felt beautiful when he was doing his routine. But now the body that had given him so much quiet pride was just a vehicle for the filthy wet dreams of a bunch of straights and closet cases, a thing to be joked about by hookers and gangsters.

He never wanted to use his body again. Ever. He wished he could talk to someone about it. Anyone – but who would ever understand the nightmares Danny Fortelli was having?

XII

Sy could have understood Danny's anguish. He was actually thinking of Danny the same night that the Fortelli boy was making his second Friday appearance at the house on Commonwealth Avenue. Sy could have talked to Danny because Sy was doing almost the same thing.

Danny and the rest of the Gay Youth Discussion Group thought that Sy paid the rent on his studio apartment in the Back Bay with his salary from a part-time clerk's job and money that he got from his parents. That was a laugh! Sy hadn't gotten a penny from his parents since the last time he was in their house, when he was thirteen years old.

His father had gotten drunk and started beating him again. It had happened so often that Sy hadn't really even reacted to it. How could he, why should he? Things never changed in that depressing triple-decker in Somerville. But Sy's father had been drunker than usual, madder than usual, and he had beaten Sy worse than usual. The boy had passed out from the blinding pain of the flailing belt as he was struck again and again.

He had awakened in a hospital, his body wracked with internal injuries. He had nearly died. He had faced his mother that day with a maturity that no thirteen-year-old should ever have to have. He had promised her that he wouldn't contradict the fabricated story she and his father had given the hospital, that he had fallen down a flight of stairs. But he had also promised her that he would never live in that house again. If she or his father ever interfered with him and his life he would tell the authorities just what was up.

They had made their infamous pact. He forbade her to even visit him in his hospital room again. After she left him Sy never saw his parents again, except for once, when he had spied them on a subway car in downtown. He had gotten off a stop early to make sure he didn't have to speak to them.

Sy needed a means to live, and boys under the legal age had few options. Sy had found one that many others like him had discovered. Park Square.

There's a neighborhood like in it any major city, and many small ones as well. This one happened to be nicer than the vast majority. It wasn't the honky-tonk of the Combat Zone or as dangerous as parts of the South End. Park Square was a nearly elegant section of town just off Boylston Street. It was dominated by a large first-class hotel.

On its sidewalks stood an army of listless youngsters, who leaned against the buildings or walked aimlessly up and down the blocks. They were waiting for the traveling salesmen or the horny suburbanites who would pay them a little money for their services.

Sy had started in Park Square the night after he had gotten out of the hospital. It had been easy, much easier than he had thought it would be. The men liked him. They were seldom mean, and you quickly learned which ones might be and how to avoid them. In a week he had met the other boys who lined Arlington Street and had found a place to crash.

Sy wanted more, all the boys wanted more. This was a stopping-off place for them, a limbo where their bodies gave them the time to grow up that their parents should have provided for them. Many of the kids were in school; some were paying their own tuition from the money they earned. Others were looking for a lover, either one they'd find from the ranks of johns – so many of them as lonely as the boys themselves – or from the numbers of other hustlers they could meet there.

Certainly the hustlers took care of one another. The grapevine of rumor and information was one of the most complex and efficient in the city. They all always knew when a police bust was coming, when a particular john had turned mean and just what he looked like, where there was dope to be bought, where there was an extra bed for someone who hadn't a home yet.

Sy had learned to trust that grapevine and that's the reason the news his friend Solly gave him was so strange, "What do you mean, trouble?" Sy had demanded. "What kind of trouble?"

Solly was from an upper-middle-class household in Newton. He wasn't the only boy on Arlington Street who didn't need to hustle for the money but who did it for the sense of excitement and because this was the only way he had to fulfill his precocious sexual needs. At seventeen Solly was too young to go to the bars and he was too experienced to ever be satisfied with the *GYDG* meetings that Sy was always trying to get him to go to.

But he was level-headed, more so than a lot of the others, and that made his information all the more valuable. "I haven't ever seen anything like it. But the word's out. Get off the streets. And they closed the Captain's." He was referring to a nearby bar that winked at IDs and was famous as a meeting place for the hustlers and their johns.

"They closed it?"

"Yup. Tight as a drum. And the word's out that we should get off the street," Solly was repeating now.

"But no one can do that! The police wouldn't dare do that any more. That kind of shit's over with."

"I'm just telling you what's coming down, man."

Sy looked up Arlington Street and saw that there were already nearly fifty young men on the sidewalks. There didn't seem to be anything very pressing or different going on. He was ready to dismiss Solly, no matter how good his information usually was.

But then a line of Lincoln Continentals – three of them

– pulled up and stopped in the middle of the block. The automobiles were a safe distance from where Sy and Solly stood talking, but they were right in the middle of the line of hustlers. Quickly a group of adult men jumped out of the cars. With a speedy and vicious violence the men took out baseball bats and lengths of chain. They made their way to the center of the hustlers and began to swing their weapons.

The screams of the boys rose above the sounds of the city traffic. Not one car stopped. Scared by the violence, or else willing to assume it as part of urban life, the drivers kept on their way. They paid no attention to the blood that was being spilled on the concrete sidewalks as the chains and bats made fearful contact with young, unarmed flesh.

The men knew what they were doing. They were obviously well-trained heavies, and they acted like commandos would in war. They made a quick attack, and they dealt their most vicious blows. In minutes, maybe it was just seconds, they were in their cars again and the big limos were lost in the city traffic.

Sy and Solly hadn't even had time to react. They were momentarily frozen by the sight of the extraordinary violence. As used as they were to the hard realities of the city and its streets, they had never seen anything like this, and they never saw anything like its aftermath.

At least twenty boys were hurt badly enough to be hospitalized. All of Arlington Street seemed to fill up with ambulances within five minutes of the attack. The boys' bodies were sprawled out, blood spilling on the sidewalk, their cries and moans competing with the sirens for people's attention. Sy and Solly had finally mobilized and had moved quickly through the casualties. With disbelieving eyes they saw the gore, the horrible sight of wounded bodies.

"I told you so," Solly had whispered.

Sy studied the friends who so recently had been standing around and joking with him. His face was set with anger. "I don't believe it."

"What are we going to do? You want to talk to the cops

with me?"

"Fuck the cops," Sy said. "I'm calling the Association. Right now."

•   •   •

The next day Sy was sitting in Alex Kane's hotel room. Erin Frost was there as well; it was Frost who had brought Sy to meet this strange man.

Sy stared at Alex Kane. He thought that maybe he had seen Kane somewhere else before, a common enough occurrence for anyone who spent as much time in meetings and on the streets as Sy did. But then he realized why he had that impression. Sy had been taking classes at the university part-time, and he had taken one on Art Appreciation. This guy looked just like the ancient Greek statues they had studied, the nude males that Sy had committed to memory.

"What do the police say?" Kane was asking Frost a question that brought Sy back to the moment.

"There's nothing to go on. The cars' plates were tracked. They were rented out of state – in Rhode Island. They'll check, but it's a foregone conclusion that they would have used fake IDs. It might mean that they're from out of state themselves – the goons I mean. But it doesn't make any sense." The gay leader was puzzled.

"What do you mean?" Kane asked.

"Look, the guys on Park Square are all freelance. Everyone knows that. There aren't any pimps the way there are with the female prostitutes in the Zone. These are kids, some straight, looking for money to buy their dope; some gay, looking for a good time more than anything else, most of them runaways or kids kicked out of their homes by their parents and needing a way to make a living.

"But there's no reason for any Mob guys to be after them like this. None."

"Could it be vigilantes?" Kane wondered.

"Maybe, but they usually only try for as much publicity

as possible, I mean the Moral Majority types. They don't go in for frontal violence in any case. And whatever else happened, this was violence."

"How bad are the kids hurt?" Kane's body was tense as he asked the question. He wanted to know; he didn't want to know. There are some things in this world that just made him too angry, too angry for him to contain himself. He picked up an ashtray just to have something to do with his hands.

"There were twenty-one that were taken to the hospitals. It's a miracle none of them died. One's blinded for life. He got a link of chain right across his face. Another's going to never walk again; they got his spinal cord. Two guys are going to have to have their kidneys removed."

Alex Kane let out an eerie shriek that electrified Sy and Frost both. Without any warning he let the heavy object fly through the air. They watched it bounce hard against the wall where it left a definite imprint in the plaster. They looked at one another, but said nothing.

Kane seemed to never have noticed the break in his composure. "There must be someone who knows what's going on. *Someone.* "

"It's an obvious – and effective – message to tell the kids to get off the streets. But from whom? We just don't know," Frost said, "And we don't know why."

Kane looked over at Sy and could tell from the boy's open-mouthed expression that he had frightened him. "I'm sorry," he apologized.

"It's okay, at least it is so long as you're on my side," Sy said. And after last night, he was glad someone was on his side.

"It must have something to do with the others," Kane was speaking aloud, but not necessarily to the two men sitting in his hotel room. "This has to be part of a big scheme. But who's doing it? For what reason?"

"What others?" Sy asked.

Kane looked at him quickly. Of course, there was no reason for the kid to know what he was talking out. He quickly went through an explanation, of the changes in kids' person-alities, their disappearances, their use of drugs, and some-times their death.

A cold chill went through Sy. "That sounds like Danny."

Kane spoke sharply. "Who's Danny?"

Sy blushed and looked down at the floor. "This guy I know, he used to be in the Gay Youth Discussion Group with me." Kane was even more alert; that was one of the organiza-tions on Farmdale's list of potential target groups.

"Tell me more," Alex demanded.

"Well," Sy was obviously embarrassed, "he's been coming to meetings for over a year, or he had been. We were really good friends, I thought so. At least on Wednesdays when we'd see each other. It's ... I don't know, I feel foolish about it. I sort of figured that that group, and especially Danny, they were like my start of a different life. I had a real job, and even if it's only part-time, it's not bad and they might hire me full-time.

"So, I never told them about the Square. I didn't want them to know I hustled. I'd only see them, and Danny, on Wednesdays. I guess I was playacting growing up, becoming respectable. Here I am a whore and I was there planning Hal-loween parties."

"There's nothing wrong with that," Frost said. "You have no reason to feel guilty."

"I don't," Sy said, "not really about hustling. I mean, you gotta earn a living, right? And I know my way around, I'm good at it and I don't get into trouble. But, it made me dis-honest. With Danny. I would have given anything to have had a real friend like that. But I kept him cooped up on Wednes-days and I never went to his house when he invited me. I nev-er invited him to stay over with me. I just kept him at arm's length."

"So?" Alex asked.

"So, he's disappeared," Sy said. "He hasn't been to the last two meetings. I called his house and his mother said he wasn't home, three times in a row. It seemed pretty obvious to me he was hiding, ducking calls. So, I lost a friend."

"Were you in love with him?" Kane asked with a gentle voice.

"You know, I was. At first. I had a crush on him that wouldn't stop. But, no. I get all the sex I want, easy, out there on the street. I get all the ones that fall in love and want to marry you and I've even fallen myself for some of them. But I figured Danny was more important as a friend than another trick. Does that make any sense?" Sy looked up at the two older men.

"It makes all the sense in the world," Frost answered for both of them.

"Well," Sy continued, "it does, except for one thing. Danny Fortelli's gotta be the most handsome kid I ever met. Ever. What a one for me to pick as a friend instead of a trick! And now it's too late. Danny hadn't missed a single Wednesday night meeting in over a year. He hasn't been to the last two. I doubt I'll ever see him again.

"There's something else too."

"Go on," Alex encouraged him.

"Well, I know this other guy that goes to the same school as Danny. It's one of those places where they don't know each other's gay and I just never told them. I figured they'd both freak out. But the other day this guy told me some stuff about Danny, not knowing I knew. Seems he's been really fucking up. The guy was amazed. Here was the star of the senior class and he was stoned out of his mind every day and skipping classes, the works. It just didn't make any sense."

It did to Alex Kane. He clenched his fist. He had his big break.

XIII

Danny Fortelli sat in his chair in English class. *Big deal,* he thought. He used to care about this class. He had liked his teacher, an old lady named Mrs. Petersen who'd been here for ages. She could have retired years ago if she'd wanted to.

Her excitement about her subject usually fired the imaginations of her students, and Danny had been one of those who used to be the most enthusiastic. She used to gloat over the boy, so glad that one of the star athletes held such academic promise.

Now she was just staring at him in disbelief. For the last two weeks the Fortelli boy just hadn't been his old self. He was rude, the kind of rude that she expected from one of the dumb jocks who tried to hide their ignorance behind a wall of cynicism.

Mrs. Petersen stood in front of the class and glared at Danny. She tried to remember that so very recently he had been her favorite. She would have to talk to the guidance counselor about him; she made a decision to do it that very afternoon. For now she'd ignore him. It was just a phase he was going through, she was sure of it. No good boy went bad this way, so quickly and completely.

She went on with her lessons and let Danny's latest rude comment go unnoticed.

Danny was glad. He was so stoned he doubted he could

have kept up any more conversation of any kind with the old lady. He had never used to do dope. But Ted had given him some last Friday to go with the Quaalude and it had felt good. Sort of. It made him feel things less, and that meant good these days.

The second Friday night in the penthouse apartment had been more of the same. Danny had dreaded the visit, but he had gone. The hurt looks his mother and father had given him lately only intensified his need to keep on going and doing whatever it was that Morrisey and his "friends" wanted. If the way he acted now could hurt them this much, how much worse would it be if they ever saw the photographs?

So, standing around in his gym outfit, Danny had gone along with the plan again. He had picked up some things, little things that helped some. He hated them. He hated seeing that he had it in him to use them. But he had.

The humiliation of the first time had come because Danny had been scared and had just stood around. He was a walking target for whoever wanted to have some fun. It had left him open to the most abusive and least understanding of the tricks.

But as the second Friday night began, Danny saw that some of the other boys there handled things differently. There was Frank, a real good-looking guy. He was so good-looking with his blond hair and blue eyes and bright teeth that Danny had thought he had belonged in Malibu instead of Boston. Frank hadn't gotten any of the freaks the first night they were both in the penthouse. He seemed more at ease than Danny. And Frank hadn't had to put on one of the little "shows" that the creeps liked.

In the beginning of the night Danny had taken Frank aside and talked to him. He found out that the handsome boy was a student at Boston University. The blond hair and the blue eyes didn't belong in Malibu; they were from Australia. He was there because of the same kind of pictures that had trapped Danny. He didn't like it any more than Danny did, but he knew what it would mean if the Immigration Service saw the photos; he'd lose his student visa so fast he'd have to swim back to Melbourne.

"But how do you handle it?" Danny asked.

And Frank explained: don't wait for the aggressive ones to come after you. Go after one of the meek ones, no matter how nerdy they looked. They were the ones most likely to welcome your attentions. They took the longest time. That was Morrisey's problem, not Frank's. They paid the most and they left the biggest tips. If they wanted Frank to stay for more than an hour, it was up to Morrisey to see that they paid double.

In the rooms in the back the nerds found their moments of pleasure and their fantasies in the form of Frank's body. They weren't ever one of the dangerous jerks who wanted rough stuff.

Danny took the lesson seriously and learned it well. He had found a doctor from Cambridge in the furthest corner of the room. Physically, he was the worst looking man there. But he was the loneliest as well. He was delighted with Danny. He didn't mind that Danny had to take a few breaks and smoke more dope, not so long as he could touch the exquisite body of the young gymnast.

Then there had been a visiting businessman from Cleveland who was terrified that he'd meet someone he knew in a place "like this." He was relieved to have Danny take him into a back room.

Danny had pulled in $350 that night and he hadn't had to put up with the crap in the front room. It had only taken him minutes to pull in each of his tricks. Morrisey was delighted, and even congratulated Danny.

I sure am a quick learner, *Danny thought as the meaningless words came out of Mrs. Petersen's mouth.* A real quick learner. I must have had it in me all the time. Sure thing, I'm a sure thing. A natural born whore. *Danny had to laugh at that phrase.* A natural born whore.

Mrs. Petersen shot a glance at Danny's laughter. But she returned to her lessons. She had long ago learned to ignore troublemakers, and apparently that was what the Fortelli boy was becoming.

It amazed Danny that he could actually do it. First two weeks and he was able to do it. Big deal, you take off the little pants and you wave your cock at them and they go crazy and it's over. What was the big deal? What a twerp he had been to think that it was something he had to worry about. What a twerp. What a fool to be so concerned about life. *His dreams!* College and coaches; gymnastics and the Olympics. *His dreams!*

Time to wake up to life, friend, *he told himself.* And life is full of cock and cash.

Danny was so full of the killer weed Ted had sold him that he barely noticed the bell had rung. Class was over. It didn't dawn on him till he was in the hallway that it was the last class of the day. He was finished with the stupid school. He could go and smoke another joint now.

He wandered in his slow way through the building and into the parking lot. A couple guys were in a corner and Danny went over to them. "Want some?" he asked, holding out the already rolled marijuana.

"Hey, Fortelli! Sure. But be cool. Don't let them see." The boy who spoke was Tom Larsden. Danny was looking at him while he lit the dope; Larsden was watching the joint with anticipation. Danny remembered when he thought that this kid was an idiot, a loser on a road to nowhere. They had gone to grade school together and used to play Little League until Larsden decided it was too childish and silly. Larsden was right, Danny thought. *Too bad it took me so long to realize it.*

The group stood and the other three quickly went through the tightly-rolled smoke. "Fortelli, I used to think you were such an ass-licker. I was wrong. You're a good guy." Larsden was saying that to thank him for the free marijuana.

"No problem. See you guys later." Danny walked away with a little strut to his step. The effects of the new dope had brought his euphoria back to the fore. He felt fine, just fine.

His step was light and easy and he thought he might be

floating through the air. Enough dope and he'd get through it all. No matter how badly he fucked up school, they'd have to graduate him. He could pass easy enough. Then? Danny sighed. He didn't know. Morrisey kept talking about more hours; big things were supposed to be happening.

He'd only been doing it for two weeks, but he was learning the ropes. He knew it. He was learning the ropes so quickly that it seemed that maybe this was what he should be doing. What the hell? So long as Morrisey had those pictures and Danny's parents were alive, there wasn't much choice.

Danny was walking down the street towards his house when some guy got out of a car and stood in front of him on the sidewalk. "Danny?"

Danny tried to clear his head and pay attention to the stranger. He was frightened that it was someone from Morrisey. "Danny Fortelli?" the man repeated, but it wasn't a question; he knew who Danny was.

Danny looked at him. Jesus, was he handsome. The man was just wearing slacks and loafers and a shell jacket over his sports shirt. His moustache and thick hair were jet-black. His eyes were *weird.* They were a bright green. It was the one thing about him that just electrified Danny. Those weird green eyes. He was so stoned that he didn't realize he was barely paying attention to what the man was saying to him.

"Come with me," the man opened the door to his car.

"Ah, come on, it's just Monday. I can't do more now. I just can't. Can't you wait till Friday?" By now Danny had somehow convinced himself that the man was from Morrisey – that had been his suspicion and now he was sure the guy wanted him to go back to the penthouse.

"Get in, Danny." It was really an order, not a request. Hell, Danny might as well get in.

• • •

They drove through the suburban streets and out onto an expressway. Alex Kane kept looking over at Fortelli. This was one they would have picked, he knew it. The kid was very good looking and his muscles showed through the clothes he was wearing. He was – he should have been – as innocent and happy as Kurt and Roger, the pair that Kane had met in the bar that first night in Boston.

He should have been.

There was something about the aggressive slouch that Danny was in that contradicted that idea. His hands were unnecessarily shoved into his pants pockets. He stared straight ahead. He clearly didn't want any small talk.

So this was the kind of kid they were getting hold of! The thought went through Kane's mind with force. *This was who they were corrupting.* Alex Kane's opinions of gay men didn't change just because they were effeminate or masculine according to the rest of the society's standards. But he couldn't help notice that this young man was probably the last boy in that high school that any teacher or counselor would ever expect to be gay.

Danny Fortelli had the natural grace of a born athlete, and he had the walk and stance of one too. He was the kind of kid who didn't realize that he might be intimidating, but he easily could have been, both socially and physically. He had grown up with a clear sense of himself and he must have been aware of the potential power of his body. His naturally assertive self could easily have been mistaken for pride.

If it hadn't been for that smile, the cleft in his chin made the boy look slightly vulnerable – and sexy at the same time. Right now he looked to Alex as though his eyes were dead, but they probably had sparkled once, and when they had Alex bet those lips, so full and so red, must have looked wonderful.

Alex Kane tried to take his mind away from Danny's appearance. He was a guy in trouble and it was Alex's job to help him, to remove the pressure, to excise the pain that came from somewhere else. What was he doing thinking about the young man in that way?

They drove all the way into Boston in silence. The journey only confirmed Danny's suspicions. The route to Kane's hotel was the same as that to Morrisey's right up till one of the last turns. Until that turn had been made, Danny was convinced he was being taken to the penthouse.

But then Kane did veer off the expected boulevard and had turned into a hotel parking lot. The dope was wearing off a bit. A little fear crept into Danny's mind and the unexpected events perked up his awareness. He finally asked, "What are we doing here?" when the car had stopped.

"We're going up to my room to talk."

"Oh, sure," Danny sneered. *'Talk.'* Well, the guy knew who he was and where he was from, so Danny might as well go along with it. He had to be from Morrisey. Maybe the fat man with the beady eyes was sending him out to make a few extra bucks. Ted hadn't lied – at this rate, Danny could buy his own car soon.

Danny passively followed Alex Kane into the hotel proper and into the waiting elevator. Kane punched the correct button and the two of them stood silently until they reached Kane's floor.

Then they went to the room. Kane unlocked it and stood aside to let Danny go in first. The youngster didn't hesitate. He entered and walked over to one of the two double beds. He sprawled out on his back. *Let him come and do what he wants*, Danny thought. He pushed away an image of his parents. *It's for you. It's for you.*

But Alex Kane wasn't moving towards Danny He went to one of the overstuffed chairs and sat down, "Want a cigarette? Something to drink?"

"No." Danny didn't even lift his head.

Alex Kane reached over and picked up the Spanish leather notebook that had been air-couriered to him that morning from Joseph Farmdale's house in California. It had everything in it. Alex Kane had to prove it to the boy.

He started to read, "You were born Daniel Joseph Fortelli at Newton-Wellesley Hospital on –" Danny did sit up at those words. He listened intently as the man kept on talking. He knew *everything* about Danny and his family. The boy was terrified.

Alex Kane looked up and saw it written all over him. "I have ways to find these things out. Computers store lots of information, there are always people who can be talked into giving more." He didn't like frightening Danny this way. It must be amazing to be eighteen and to have your first experience with the power of information.

"What the hell do you want?" Danny was as much confused as anything else. Was this man from Morrisey? Was Morrisey upping the ante and expecting even more from him?

"I want to know what's happened to you in the last two, three weeks of your life, Danny. It's fallen apart as fast as you could possibly destroy it. You never used to take drugs; you've been reported stoned in school five times. You never drank; the police in Brookline say you were in a bar with a false ID last week. You used to be a part of the gay youth group; you disappeared for the last two meetings. You were a star on the gymnastics team; you quit.

"Sounds like some pretty big things have been happening to you, big, bad ones. I want to know what they are."

"Fuck you." Danny was full of spite. The guy was not from Morrisey's. He would have known the whole thing if he had been. The last thing the kid was going to do was tell him anything.

Danny stood and went for the door. The man jumped and took his arm. *"Let go!"* Danny took a punch at him. The man avoided it easily. Then Danny felt the man's hands on his neck and he felt some pressure. And then he felt nothing.

• • •

When Danny woke up he was back on the bed. His wrists and ankles were tied with belts. He tested them. They wouldn't budge.

The strange man was still there. He was wearing only his gym shorts, doing pushups on the floor. His muscles were incredibly well developed, Danny could see that, but they weren't gross the way some guys' were. Just big and powerful looking.

"Let me loose," Danny said in a quiet voice.

The man stopped his motions and jumped to his feet. He didn't seem to show any sign of being winded or tired at all. "No. We'll talk first. I don't like chasing people down hotel halls."

"What is this, some kind of kink?"

The man grinned, "No, not really."

"Why don't I feel lousy?" The question suddenly occurred to Danny. "You knocked me out and I don't feel bad."

"I didn't knock you out, I just put you to sleep," the man said with that grin on his face.

"Yeah? Can you show me how to do that?" Danny was talking as though once again he were the imaginative and inquisitive student.

"Maybe, later. It's just something you learn." The man went and pulled a t-shirt over his chest.

"Willing to talk to me yet?" he asked Danny.

Danny re-tested his bonds and realized it was hopeless. "Sure," he sighed. "What do you want?"

"I want some answers to my questions."

The boy let his head fall down against the mattress. "I really don't want to talk about it."

"Too bad, Danny. You're going to." There was no room for argument in the way the man said it.

Danny didn't know where to start. He began to put the words together and his face broke into a sob. The tears he had been holding in for the last three weeks burst forth. His chest heaved with his personal pain.

The man came over and sat on the mattress beside him. He put a warm hand on Danny's back and rubbed it a little. Danny only cried more, as though the touch was more than he could bear; the idea of a caring touch was something he had given up on.

The man's hands moved and the belts came off Danny's ankles and wrists. The man wrapped his arms around Danny and lifted him a little and held him against his own chest. Danny just hoped he wasn't going to want sex. *Please, don't let him want to have sex, God, please!* The idea of the words actually coming out of Danny's mouth, the idea that he might have to describe the actions, the filth, the degradation ...

Danny cried and cried. The man just held him, tightly enough that Danny knew he was protected, loosely enough that he didn't feel any other motive from the man but to hold him and let him cry.

Alex Kane was doing it all very consciously. Not to manipulate the boy, but to keep the boy from feeling the tensions and anger that ripped through Alex's own body. What was an eighteen-year-old doing with this pain! Whoever had caused it was going to pay.

•   •   •

When Danny had calmed down enough Alex had let him lie back and relax. He had called for some coffee and when it arrived the two of them sat at the little room service table and they talked.

Danny told Alex everything. Here was someone he could talk to, had to talk to, and he could get it off his chest and not have to hold it inside himself.

When the whole story was out, Kane asked a few questions, not challenging Danny's account, but asking for some clarification. Danny answered them all with his head bowed.

"Why don't you call your parents, Danny. Tell them you won't be home tonight. Say you're at a friend's."

Danny took a deep breath. "They won't ask where I am, not any more."

He mechanically dialed his home number and told his mother not to expect him. A hurt Maria Fortelli didn't ask for details. She was tired of fighting with Danny.

"How do we find Ted?" Kane asked when the call was done.

"Ted? His apartment, I guess."

"Let's go."

• • •

Danny was feeling scared. "Look, they've still got those photographs."

The man who had finally told him that his name was Alex Kane assured him. "Don't worry. No one's going to use them against you. No one's ever going to use them again."

Alex Kane rang the bell. He had told Danny what to do when someone answered the intercom to the Beacon Hill apartment. The mechanical squawk came quickly, "Yeah?"

"Ted," Danny yelled into the little voice box, "It's Danny. I got to talk to you."

There was a hesitation. "Okay, come on up."

The door buzzer sounded and Danny pushed it open. Danny walked ahead of Alex Kane, up the stairs. Ted was waiting on the third floor landing wearing only a pair of jeans. He looked at the pair with a puzzled expression. "Hey, Danny, what's this all about?"

Danny didn't answer. Alex Kane did. He shoved his hand in the blond's chest and pushed him backwards through the apartment door.

Danny followed and closed the door behind them. "This is a friend of mine, Ted, Alex Kane. He's got some talking to do to you."

Ted looked at the tall, muscular man with an expression of immediate distrust. "I don't want to talk to him."

"Too bad," Kane said to him, "you're going to."

Danny was standing to block the doorway. He was watching carefully. He wasn't going to let Ted get out that way. The blond boy looked around in a panic for a means of escape.

"Don't try," Kane said harshly, as though he knew what was going through his mind. "You're staying. We're talking."

Kane kicked a chair away from Ted's small eating table, then he sat in the one facing it. Ted reluctantly sat down also.

"Who are you? Who's Morrisey? How'd he get you? Tell

me quick, clean and honest and we'll be friends. Play any games with me, you won't like the ones I know how to play with you."

There was an air of inherent command to Kane's words. It wasn't the fake bravado that Morrisey used, that was for sure. Ted could tell right away that he was in a jam and the only one who could get him out was this guy.

"Look, I'm small fry –"

"Not so small you can't use a net to drag in some other people," Kane said. "Talk, you have to convince me that you're not really just a bad guy for getting Danny involved. I want you to talk and I'd rather not hurt you. But you *will* talk."

Again, the sense of command and the man's obvious willingness to carry through with his threats struck Ted hard. He started to fidget a bit. "Can you ... can you make me some promises?"

"Like what?"

"Like, I won't go to jail?"

"Why are you worried about that?"

"Because that's where I came from."

Alex Kane sat back and listened to Ted's story.

He had been in a minimal security adolescent facility in the Midwest. The place had been brutal. The kids, especially those like Ted who were known to be gay, had been raped repeatedly, not just by other inmates, but also by the guards. Any slight infraction of the rules had brought swift corporal punishment. There was no way to prove it; the guards had had special private instruction on how to do things that hurt like hell but never left a mark.

Kane knew about such places. There seemed to be no end to the pain and suffering that people were willing to inflict on men they knew were gay.

"I'm just telling you this so you'll understand." Ted couldn't look Kane in the eye. "You have to understand why I wouldn't go back."

"You escaped?"

The boy nodded his head, yes.

"And Morrisey found you?"

"Yes, one of his men did. I had been there with him, he was one of the older guys."

"When did they find you? Where?"

"About two years ago. In Park Square."

The starting place again.

"When did you begin recruiting others?"

Ted hesitated only a little before going on. "Almost at once. He wanted a bunch of boys, but he didn't want them from the streets. He wanted *clean* ones he could train. He also wanted them better looking than on the streets. So he started sending me to meetings, he thought that was the best place to find them, colleges and stuff."

"Do you know what happened to them?"

This time Ted didn't answer. Not until Alex Kane brought back his hand and delivered a sharp slap right across the blond's face. "Do you know what happened to them?"

Tears watered in Ted's eyes. "Yes, I mean I know they ended up in the apartment on Fridays. And some went away, on trips."

"Trips? Where?"

"Anywhere," Ted was talking quickly now, now that he really did know the man's anger could manifest itself in quick and harsh punishment. "I took some. You know, some john wants you to go to Florida with him, or New York, that kind of thing."

"But what about the ones that never came back?" Alex asked. "Tell me about them."

Ted was trapped, he looked it, he felt it. He didn't dare say any more, but the man began to move his hand again and he wasn't about to take that punishment any more. "They just left. I never had anything to do with that. I promise you. They just left."

"The drugs. Where did they get the drugs?" Kane's green eyes had taken on a brightness that made them seem to glow.

"I had dope; I had 'ludes. The other stuff they could get from Morrisey, as much as they wanted. He told them it was good for their attitude. Sure was," Ted snorted. "It sure was, they couldn't go through with things, you know? The weak ones. The ones that couldn't handle it all with just some dope or a 'lude or a little booze. The ones that thought they'd crack up, they'd go to Morrisey and they'd beg him to let them stop. They would have done anything else."

"He loved them. They were the easy ones. Guys like Danny made the Friday night parties, him and that Australian from the university were big hits. Morrisey wanted stars like them for the parties. But the other kids were the bread and butter.

"They'd do anything for Morrisey by the time he was done. They had to. They weren't street kids like me, they didn't know where to score. Morrisey would tell them to take a little something for their attitude and they would and then he'd have them hooked."

"Heroin." Kane knew it was.

Ted nodded his head, yes. "Those were the ones who'd come by and beg to turn a trick for some smack. They were pitiful." Ted's face was sad for the first time, at least the first time he was mourning someone besides himself.

"Do you know how many died?"

Ted's head jerked up. "I never knew one did. I tell you, mister, they'd be guys up there and then some of them wouldn't show up again. That would be that. You learn not to ask a lot of questions in a place like Morrisey's."

Kane burnt inside. His anger fed on itself and he was afraid it would burst out into the room and consume the two young men. "What's the deal with the Park Square rumble?"

Ted answered slowly, "I only heard hints, I just overheard some conversation. Morrisey, he doesn't like competition. He hates seeing those kids out on the street and hustling without pimps. His business wasn't as big as he thought it should be, either. He wanted to scare the kids off the street. That's all."

"There's a blind boy at Massachusetts Eye and Ear Infirmary," Kane spat out the words. "There's another guy over at Beth Israel who's never going to walk again. Is that *all?*"

"I didn't do it!" Ted was sitting up straight in his chair now. The man's voice was crazy with anger. "I had nothing to do with it!"

Then Alex Kane reared back and slapped Ted again. He did it so hard the boy flew off his wooden chair onto the floor with a dull thud. He covered his face instinctively.

"No, you didn't do it, but you did nothing to stop it. You didn't raise a hand to help those guys out. You gave no warning –"

"*I did!*" Ted yelled in his own defense. "I did, too."

Alex Kane and Danny looked down at Ted's form on the floor, waiting. Ted went on, "I got a friend, sort of a boyfriend," he seemed embarrassed to admit to that. "Solly's his name. I told him. I didn't tell him how I knew, but I told him to get off the street and to stay off. I couldn't have told him everything –" panic swept over Ted as he realized his predicament, "– they would've sent me back to jail. But I did tell him and I did tell him to spread the word."

Alex Kane remembered Sy's story about the night when the men attacked the young hustlers. There had been a Solly who had been trying to convince Sy and some others that there was going to be trouble.

"When are they coming back?" Alex demanded. "When are they coming back to Park Square again?"

Ted didn't dare lie. "I heard them talking last night. There's a group of them coming back tonight. They're from Albany. They come from different places each time. They're from out of town so they can't get fixed by the cops. That's the set-up."

Alex Kane looked down at Ted's figure. He didn't trust the guy. He didn't trust anyone who had that much hanging over his head.

Alex turned to Danny. "Can you keep him here? Make sure he doesn't leave or make a phone call?"

Danny was still staring at Ted. "Sure. No problem. I can handle this piece of shit."

XIV

Alex Kane stood on the corner of Arlington and Boylston Streets.

After the first time the toughs had come to Park Square and had dared to leave gay boys with permanent injuries, the Boston Police had made a big show of cleaning up the area and patrolling it. They had press conferences and got front page coverage in the *Globe* and the *Herald* and lead story coverage on all the television stations. As soon as the ink on the newspapers was dry and the sound had been turned off on the last nightly news installment, the police had disappeared.

The hustlers' ranks were thinner now, and too many of them were scared. *And too many hurt,* Alex Kane said to himself. But these young men had little choice. They had nowhere to turn for housing, for food, for anything. These were the walking wounded of families that should never have had children, or of a society that systematically rejected whole segments of its people. They had only one commodity: their bodies.

At the risk of danger, they came back. They had no options.

Kane had chosen his vantage point carefully. The way the streets ran in Boston this is where any attacking vehicles would have to turn; any other route was ruled out because of the complicated system of one-way directions in the city.

Kane stood there in his slacks and his light jacket. The autumn air was chilled tonight, but he didn't notice; he didn't care. If Ted had been right then there was going to be another assault on these guys. Whoever did it was going to be very, very sorry.

Kane had to wait for three hours. It was nearly one in the morning before the line of automobiles made its turn off Boylston. They were moving slowly. There was an obviousness about them; they were clearly rented. They were all late-model cars, all the same style, just slightly different color combinations. There were four of them this time. More manpower for fewer bodies.

That was all right. Because this time there was Alex Kane.

The cars pulled up to the sidewalk. They weren't even going to change their ways of doing things. The first car's door opened and one large man started to get out of the driver's seat. He had a smile on his face. He was going to beat some fag's head and get paid for it.

He didn't count on this fag though. He saw the jet black hair and he saw the green eyes and then he watched with amazement as the door he had just opened slammed shut, with his left hand between it and the car chassis.

The man getting out of the back seat did see it. It awed him. He even heard the bone crunch and heard his driver's voice scream. It was a mistake, a bad one. He was watching all that so intently that he didn't even notice that the man with the thick black moustache had taken the chain link out of his hand and was wrapping it around his head. He never did hear the sound of his own skull crunching.

It had happened so quickly that the men in the second, third and fourth cars hadn't even taken notice until it was too late.

It was too late because Sy and some friends of his had rushed across Boylston Street dodging the oncoming traffic. They had long spike-like staffs in their hands and they accomplished the task that Kane had given them with gusto and speed. Sy and Solly and a couple of others took the sharp instruments and methodically went from tire to tire, slashing the rubber open with wide wounds that sent the air into the night and made sure these men weren't going to get away with the ease of an automotive flight.

The men hadn't noticed. They hadn't noticed because by then Alex Kane had begun moving up their ranks. The two who had been loaded in the second car were the first to meet him. One had a baseball bat. He would have used it on Kane but he never saw the man coming. He just felt him when a well-trained palm slammed into his neck and snapped it cleanly – so cleanly the man had no consciousness when his face bounced off the concrete sidewalk.

His partner did swing the baseball bat he had in his hands. He swung it hard. But somehow the guy was able to duck, the one with the black hair and the green eyes miraculously avoided contact with the wooden weapon. The force of the swing was so great, the man had been so sure he would contact, that he couldn't help but follow through. He lost his balance and stumbled. Alex Kane helped him along, right into the brick wall of the building on the other side of the sidewalk.

Frank Tecci couldn't believe it. What the fuck was this? It was supposed to be an easy score, go scare some kids. But there was Sal running into the wall and slamming into it so hard that Frank thought he must have broken every bone in his body. The length of chain link was in Frank's hands, dangling uselessly. That was too bad – because he was the next one that Alex Kane turned to, with those gleaming green eyes that made Frank think this guy was crazy.

Alex Kane walked over to Frank very slowly. Frank thought about the metal in his hands and thought maybe he should use it. But he was wrong; Alex Kane wasn't walking very slowly. He was moving very quickly – Frank's perceptions were off because of all the noise and confusion around him. There were off even more when Alex Kane delivered a thumping punch right in Frank's jaw.

But Frank's buddy, Terry, thought he had a chance to take

the guy. He saw him hit Frank and he figured the guy would have hurt his fist, at least, with a punch like that. And besides, he had to have all his attention focused on Frank to deliver that kind of knockout.

Terry moved up to the man and expected he'd be able to land his baseball bat right on his back. Terry fully expected to hear the loud crack of the man's spine. He was very surprised to discover that the man had somehow moved. The baseball bat crashed through the front window of the car Frank and Terry had been driving; it shattered the glass and sent splinters flying through the front seat. Alex Kane sent Terry flying in afterwards.

Kane turned. The last three men were just staring in disbelief at what they had seen. They knew only one thing, they weren't going to make the mistake the others had made. They were not going to go up against that man. They turned on their heels and ran.

Kane went after them. The light was in all their favor when they crossed Boylston Street. Somehow – they never would believe this – he caught up with them as soon as they were in the Public Garden. The grass was closely kept and the whole thing was like in a picture book. But they didn't like the picture Alex Kane was putting them in right now.

Kane just tripped the first man he came to. It seemed such a nonchalant thing to do, it must have been an accident that when he came flying down through the air he landed head first in a trash container.

The second one Kane just sort of bumped into. Just a little nudge, really. How did it happen that the nudge sent him directly into a concrete park bench and then, head first, onto the park's concrete walk on the other side?

The last man thought he might have gotten away. He was running over the bridge that spanned the small pond in the middle of the Public Gardens. The city was just on the other side, he could run ...

But he couldn't run. Alex Kane was in his way. The black-haired man didn't seem to move when this last gangster hit him square in the chest with the full force of his running body. Alex Kane seemed to lift him up easily, too easily. And why wasn't he even breathing hard?

Then the man was flying through the air like the rest of them. He had an easier time, though. He landed in the pond and who cared if it was stinky and polluted. It was water and he was conscious. He fought his way up to a standing position in the waist-high water, his feet caught in the slime at the bottom. He shook the rubble of the city debris from his hair and looked up at the bridge where that strange man stood.

"Don't come back," Alex Kane said to him.

"Oh, no, sir," the last gangster said. And he meant it.

XV

Mr. Sean Morrisey was sitting on one of the sectional couches in his penthouse apartment sipping fine cognac. Yes, indeed, very fine cognac. At least it was the most expensive he had been able to discover in that gourmet shop. He supposed that made it fine. Actually, he just cared that it was a good, stiff belt of brandy.

You have to have class in this business, though. He knew that. He never had discovered what that really meant to a lot of these people, *class*. But they responded to it when you had this stuff and when they knew your clothes came from one of the stores that advertised in *Esquire*. Fuck 'em. If it made them feel better about their money and how they spent it on Sean Morrisey's goods, they could have class.

He was looking out the window. The view really was superb. The Charles River was nearly a half mile wide at this point. The lights of the university city of Cambridge were on the opposite bank. You didn't have to have class to know that their reflection on the calm river waters looked good, it looked very good.

Sean Morrisey had always wanted to live in an apartment like this one. He had dreamed of it for years. It – and the money it represented – had been his obsession since he had been a teenager. He had vowed that he'd have it, he'd have it all. He had vowed that he'd pay any price and do anything necessary to get here. The really big boys had blocked most of his possible routes. The territories for the most lucrative drugs and the big gambling games had been divided up and carefully guarded. He was only given a pittance, a tiny little bit of stuff to push. It had been enough to start.

If nothing else Sean Morrisey was smart. He knew that he was smarter than the guys who were littler than he was; and probably smarter than a lot of the big ones. So he had looked at the small fry underneath him and had seen their lack of vision, their lack of imagination.

Now, take the drugs that Morrisey had been given to sell. Sure, you could move out onto the street with them and make a nice profit. But who was using them? Sean had looked around and he had seen a lot of pimps using them, that's who. Those pimps had begun to look like middlemen to Morrisey – and he had read in *Business Week* that any good distributor gets rid of middlemen.

So Morrisey had begun to take on the girls himself. He could not only get the extra profit from the drugs, he could pick up a little money for some protection and some referrals and everyone seemed much happier.

But *Forbes* had told him that the only good business was an expanding business. So Morrisey had looked for possible ways to increase his base of operations. That was when the gays had come to his attention. They had been on the cover of *Newsweek.* Again!

There were all those independent operators out there. Hell, even Morrisey knew where they were, littering Park Square. They had no pimps, they had no bosses, they had no order to them.

That was what made Sean Morrisey so happy tonight: he was bringing order to the gay world. By the time a few more of these rumbles took place, Morrisey figured, he'd not only have scared the hustlers off the streets, he would have scared the johns right into his arms.

He'd keep this place just for himself. He thought of a couple of the women he'd take off the active roster and keep right here, just for Sean Morrisey and a couple of friends. He was all lined up to buy this whole building, the whole thing, and he'd have a floor for the working girls and a floor for the working boys.

That made Morrisey giggle.

It would be easy as eating cake. Keep the streets unsafe and the fags would have to come to him looking for sex. Make the hustlers frightened of being outdoors, maybe convince them that a few hits of smack wouldn't be such a bad thing, just for discipline, mind you – and you'd have all the sleazy queer bodies you could sell.

It was a dream come true. Sean Morrisey was going to make a fortune this way. He thought idly of moving on. Maybe he could pull the same thing in New York. Washington. He was going to be one of the big boys. One of the very big boys.

He thought.

• • •

Alex Kane thought differently. He had found the building and had made his way up to the penthouse. Some gorilla in a tuxedo thought he'd keep Alex Kane waiting for a while. But it was only a little while. He had gone to sleep for a long, long time.

Kane walked into the main living room where Sean Morrisey was daydreaming about his future plans. He knew he had found the man he wanted. Danny's description had been perfect.

"You're a pig." Kane said it in a normal speaking voice.

Morrisey sat up and stared at the intruder. "Who the hell are you? Bruno, Bruno!"

"Don't bother." Kane didn't explain, but Morrisey knew that he was hearing the truth. Morrisey was trying to figure out what was going on while he watched the new man go and sit on a couch.

The man seemed tired, weary. "Some day," Alex Kane began, "you people are going to learn that it just doesn't pay to fuck around with those guys. I mean, I know they must look very vulnerable to you, all their crazy politics and the way some of them dress. It must look very, very easy.

"But it's not." The weariness hadn't left Kane's voice. But he was looking right in Morrisey's eyes now. "I'm going to make it very, very hard. Me and my friends, you see, we're making it very, very hard for pigs like you."

"There's no need to talk that way." Morrisey was honestly insulted to be called a pig.

"It's what you are. You know, I fought in Vietnam. Whatever you think of that, let me tell you one thing. When you're in war you understand that at some moment, in some ways, there is such a thing as utter, total evil. Evil that has no justification, evil that has no right to exist.

"You'd think with all this civilization we have that we'd find out what evil is and we'd erase it. But no, we're so worried about good that we don't look at evil, even when it's staring us right in the face. Well, most of us don't, our courts don't, most of us don't.

"I do.

"I see it. I see it in people who take young men and purposely addict them to heroin so they'll be easier to handle. I see it in men who destroy the lives of the best and brightest gay men for the sake of quick profit. I see it in men who dare to kill in cold blood, just 'cause someone has become difficult.

"Now, when I see it, I think society should do something about it. I think society should act to make sure it's stopped. Sometimes it does. Sometimes it acts quickly, the judicial system functions and that's great. The way it should be.

"But then there are the times when the evil is so great, the bad being done is so enormous, that you can't wait for society to act, a man himself has to act, for the sake of society.

"Now," Alex Kane had stood up and was moving around the room with a hand on his chin, as though he were a college professor trying to make a point to a philosophy class, "I think there are two times a man has to act. One is when the judicial system falls apart, when there's some loophole or some lack of law that lets a clear criminal sneak through the web of justice. It's not always clear-cut, though. I mean, do you know how complicated questions of legal procedure can be?" Morrisey shook his head, no. *Boy, this guy has class, just listen to him.*

"Trust me, they can be very complicated. But there are other times when it's clear, when the crimes are so vast, so many, so horrible, then there's no way to avoid the necessary judgment. Do you understand me?"

"Sort of."

"Good, because I want you to understand why you're going to die."

Sean Morrisey let the words sink in. The man had moved over to him and had taken the snifter of cognac out of Morrisey's hands. He had lifted Sean up onto his feet. He was moving him to the wide picture window with the beautiful view of the Charles.

How did this happen? Morrisey wondered. He was still wondering when his bulky body had broken through the glass and was falling, slowly it seemed, to the waiting arms of Storrow Drive, fifteen stories beneath him.

XVI

Alex Kane was waiting outside the high school when Danny came out after classes. This time Danny didn't hesitate about coming over to the car.

"Hi," he said.

"Come for a ride?" Alex asked.

"Sure."

They drove in silence for a while. Danny was the one who began to speak. "You know, everyone says you did the wrong thing."

"Who knows what I did?" Kane asked with a smile.

"They all guess about Morrisey. And Sy and Solly saw you at Park Square."

"Now," Kane asked softly, "what was so horrible about that?"

"A bunch of the guys think you should have done it non-violently."

"And you?" Kane asked.

Danny didn't smile. "I don't care how you did it."

They drove for a while longer. Kane spoke next, "How are you doing?"

"Not too bad. Got my grades back up. My parents are happier."

"Sports?"

"No sports," Danny said with finality.

Alex drove further along a side road. They were moving away from the center of town, the foliage was splendid, the maples a rainbow of bright colors and the air was crisp with fall.

"Why no sports?" Kane picked up the conversation again. Danny would only shrug.

They went for a while longer until they came to a small roadside stand. Kane pulled into the parking lot. This time of year there weren't many people out looking for ice cream cones. But the day was sunny enough that they ordered one each and stayed outdoors, deciding not to go into the warm interior.

"What's with you, Danny? It's over. We got the pictures back, negatives and all. It's over. You can go back to your life the way it was."

"No," Danny said.

"Why not?"

Danny had finished his cone. He walked over to the nearby trash bin and threw away his paper napkin, When he returned he lifted himself up onto the hood of the car where Alex Kane was already sitting. He began to speak, "Do you remember what you said about evil? What you told me about Morrisey?"

"Of course."

"Well, I saw it. I saw evil. It was inside me. It was in those pictures. It was a part of me. I looked dirty and ugly and I acted like a slut, I was a slut."

The words stung Alex Kane. "You don't really believe that. You did what you had to do, Danny. That's all. We all do things –"

"Not like that. Not as quickly as I did. I gave in when I was at Morrisey's those times I kept on being amazed. It was so easy, Alex. It was easy. I just took another pill or a toke of dope and I did it.

"I used to think that sex and love were wonderful. I used to dream about it and think it'd be just wonderful. I'd just wait until it came along and then the answers would all fall into place. I'd trick maybe once every six months. I think I had sex with all of six men in my *life* before I went to Morrisey's. But there was Ted and there were the pictures, and there was the money and there were the johns. I did it all."

Danny hadn't appeared to have lost his composure, except for the tears running down his cheeks. "Sex isn't love. Not for me. I read all the magazines, I knew that people said that. But I didn't believe it until now. Not ever. I figured, hell, I could make it different. I'd read the magazines and the newspapers and I'd read about all the places in New York and all the diseases and I'd think, I don't have to worry about that. I'm different. Well, I am. I'm worse."

Alex Kane tried to draw Danny into his arms, hoping the same comfort he had given the young man the afternoon he had needed to cry would be sufficient this time, hoping he could convince him he was wrong. It wasn't. Danny fought his way free from Alex's embrace. "Leave me alone!"

Danny jumped down and went around to the side of the car and got in. He waited for Alex Kane to take the driver's wheel.

This wasn't what Alex Kane had expected, it wasn't what he wanted. This was a kind of situation he wasn't used to. He felt stupid, foolish and inadequate; he felt just like ... the first time James Farmdale had taken him into his arms.

"Danny, can you get away this weekend?"

"Alex, you don't have to play social worker any more. I'll get by."

"I asked you a question." There was a sharpness in Kane's tone.

"Yes," Danny admitted, "I can get away. I told you, I'm caught up in school and I don't have anything else that I have to do."

"Will you come away with me?"

"Where?"

"Provincetown."

"Provincetown? Why there?"

"Don't you like it?"

"I've never been."

"Good," Kane said.

"Why?" Danny responded.

"Because I want to be the first one to take you there."

Danny looked at Alex Kane. "Are you saying what I think you're saying?"

Alex just smiled.

"Holy shit."

XVII

They were in a guesthouse that stood right on Commercial Street. It was smaller than most, a little more elegant. It was a Victorian style building with bright yellow paint underneath a mansard roof.

They had driven out on Friday night. It was a long quiet drive. For the whole two and a half hour trip they had barely spoken a word to one another. Danny was fighting his belief that Alex was doing this as some sort of therapy, and he had told the man that's just what he thought was going on.

"I'm telling you, Alex, don't do it for that reason. It'd be worse than anything else you could possibly do to me."

"It's not therapy, Danny. I promise you."

Alex hadn't said much more, words never came easily in times like this for him. There hadn't *been* times like this for him, at least not since James.

He had tried to understand what was happening to him. He had attempted to analyze everything. Maybe he just was lonely; that would have made sense. But Alex's loneliness had been there for years and he had gotten through it before. What would change that now?

Was he getting too old? At thirty-two? Hardly. He didn't buy that. But he was too old for Danny, at least he thought so. He would have wished that Danny had found another guy his own age. Then Alex could have wandered off, back to his accustomed aloneness. He probably would have left in any event if it hadn't been for Danny's speech in the parking lot, that plaintive cry that Kane could never have left Danny with.

But, now, what was going to happen?

He had explained his life to Danny. As much as the kid could handle, as much as he needed to know. There couldn't be anything long-term, that was for certain. He had his mission, his purpose in life, and he had to fulfill it.

But he did care. And, more, he cared physically. He couldn't possibly let Danny stay behind with those images of self-hatred.

The car had been left in a parking lot a block or so from the guest house. They had carried their small bags over and had picked up the key to their room.

Now they stood uneasily in front of one another. The room had a fireplace. More out of a nervous need to do something rather than any conscious intent to be romantic, Alex lit the kindling and the log that had already been laid out in the fireplace.

The fire caught immediately. The sounds cracked in the air and the aroma of burning wood filled the room. Alex held his hands out in front of the flames.

Danny sat down and watched him for a moment. "I thought you'd be better at this."

"What do you mean better?" Alex snapped. Danny had hit him right in his insecurities of this moment.

"Well, seduction and stuff."

Alex didn't answer for a while. Then he turned and walked over to Danny. "I'll show you just how good I am."

They went to bed. Alex ripped down the covers and left only the cool white sheets on the mattress. He took Danny and moved his body onto the surface. Then he brought his own body down on top of Danny's. He began to move the way he knew he could. His hands moving softly here, roughly there, quickly in that direction, slowly, lingeringly in another.

Danny responded. The young man lifted up his waist and hefted Alex up as well. His lithe athletic body jerked with spasms of excitement and pleasure.

Their mouths found each other. The kisses were wet and greedy. More driven by Danny's lack of practice than anything else, they were sloppy with saliva and hunger.

Hands moved, clothes came off, skin felt air, cocks got hard. They bucked, not competing for position, but anxious for contact.

All of Alex Kane's careful repertory seemed forgotten. His careful practice of careful sexuality had no place here. He didn't want to overwhelm Danny with technique now, that wasn't what this was for.

But he wanted the young man's body. He wanted it desperately and their thrashing wasn't going to give him the access he wanted. He pulled back, gently motioning Danny to relax. With his mouth he started at Danny's neck, tasting, finally, the smooth skin he had stared at for so long. His tongue led the way down over Danny's chest, through the already thick hair where it uncovered the tender, small nipples. He teased them for awhile, then went on. Over the hard muscles of Danny's stomach and to the cleft of Danny's navel.

He ignored the moans the boy sent out. He let his mouth move further, till it rested in the pubic hair that crowned the bottom of Danny's belly.

He refused to indulge himself or Danny's need with a quick acceptance of the rigid cock that was waiting for him. Instead he took in the delicious aromas of the sweat and hair and tasted the saltiness of Danny's testicles.

When he did take the erection into his mouth, he did it slowly, moving with minute precision down the shaft and leaving Danny's moans louder and more needful than ever.

Danny tried to sit up. Alex used an arm to push him back; he wasn't done. He wouldn't be done for a long time. A very long time.

• • •

The next morning Alex woke up to the sound of the shower.

He smiled at the memory of last night, the images brought to clear light with the help of the aromas that lingered in the sheets.

The water stopped. Danny was wiping himself dry. Alex made no movement or sound that would have alerted him. He watched through his half-open eyes as Danny quietly returned to the bedroom and opened his bags. He watched him put on his clean, white jockey shorts. Alex thought for that one moment, *Is there anything quite so handsome as a man in underwear?*

He was imagining the smell of the clean cotton, the feel of Danny's body underneath it. "Come here," he said out loud.

"Good morning." Danny smiled after he got over the unexpected shock of Alex's voice. He moved to the bed and climbed under the covers, then wrapped himself in Alex's arms and rested his head against Alex's chest. The touch of him and the cotton briefs was as good as Alex had imagined.

"Danny, still feel dirty?"

The young man's head moved against Alex's chest. No.

Alex's hands moved easily over the smooth skin of Danny's back, down underneath the elastic band of the jockey shorts and finally rested on one of the well-muscled buttocks.

"Still feel bad?"

The head shook, no, again.

"Still feel horny?"

This time the head changed its motion. Danny brought it up to face Alex and kissed him on the lips. "Yeah."

• • •

They were forced out of bed at noon. Each of them was too hungry to deny the need for food. They dressed and were ready to walk out the front door to find a place to eat when one of the two men who owned the house called out, "Mr. Kane, these came for you." He was holding out an enormous bouquet of flowers.

Alex was puzzled. They hadn't told anyone where they

were. And flowers?

He thanked the man and took the already potted arrangement into their room. There was a card.

"An admirable job, quite competent. And quite a decent choice for your future. I approve."

How the hell did Farmdale find out where they were?

GOLDEN YEARS

by John Preston

"When I was younger I often wondered
what happened to all the old homosexuals.
Where do they go?
You never see them around after a certain age
—they seem to disappear."
—Louis Persinger, age 61,
in *The Daily News*, April 16, 1982

Golden Years is dedicated to Senior Action in a Gay Environment (SAGE), one of the most admirable organizations in our community.

SAGE stands on the principle that no gay person should ever have to grow old alone. Its work in providing support, services and companionship for older gay men and lesbians is dependent upon private contributions.

You can help by mailing a donation to:

SAGE, 208 West 13th Street
New York, New York 10011

I

Joe Talbot stood in the entryway to his apartment building and fumbled with his keys. He finally found the right one and used it to open his mailbox. There wasn't much there; just the usual junk mail. But when you last till you're Joe's age, seventy-two, there aren't that many people left who know you well enough to write.

He slammed the box shut, then turned and opened the big front door to the tenement. He let it close behind him and then began to make his way up the stairs. He remembered when he used to be able to run up those flights without taking so much as a single deep breath. Of course, in those days Harry would have been waiting for him and Joe would have been able to climb a mountain without stopping if he had known Harry was on top of it. But Harry'd been gone for a long time ... a lot of years. And now Joe had to linger at almost every landing and rest for a bit before he reached his fifth floor flat.

He could have taken a place on a lower floor; there had been some openings. But it just didn't seem right to leave #5AR, the place he and Harry had spent so very many years together. So long as he could make it up the stairs at all, he had vowed, he'd keep the old place.

As Joe made his way he could sense one of the many things that had changed in the neighborhood over time. When he and Harry had first moved to the East Village it had been mostly inhabited by a collection of first and second generation immigrants. Jews, Italians and others had crowded into the small apartments, using them as way-stations in their drive up the social scale of their new homeland.

The strong odors of their food weren't there any more. Of course, there wasn't the sickeningly sweet smells of the drugs either. That had filled the hallways during the sixties when the flower children had moved in after most of the ethnic families had fled Manhattan for their promised lands in the suburbs.

Instead there was the one constant that had survived all the changes the neighborhood had undergone: the rich aromas of Ukranian cooking. Joe could catch a strong whiff of Mrs. Porytko's kielbasa on the third floor, just the way it had been the very first day he had moved into this building.

Joe never figured out why the Ukranians stayed when everyone else had left. But they had, and their bright colored native crafts and clothing still decorated many of the shops, their beautiful church music still filled the streets on Sunday and on their religious holidays. It was so confusing the way they seemed to use their own peculiar calendar, and Joe just never did know when they'd be celebrating Easter. But they were here, an anchor in the shifting population of the city.

It was the other smells that surprised Joe. He and Harry had never expected that the next group of urban wanderers to settle in the East Village would be the gays. But, Jesus Christ, they had moved in with a vengeance. They had a big disco down the street and who knows how many bars of theirs lined Second Avenue and St. Mark's Place nowadays? And they just packed themselves into the old tenement, turning it into a showplace, almost.

Every time one of them took over one of the apartments Joe knew that it meant the place would get new plaster, new paint – but why was it always that same grey? – and they'd start cooking their own food, food whose smell consumed the hallway more and more. Rich Northern Italian sauces and super-spicy Chinese food, both of which raised havoc with

Joe's tender digestive tract. Those, or else the suspicious health food stuff that some of them ate.

Not that Joe ever complained when one of them invited him to dinner. Hell, no! He was always pleased when the knock came on the door and there would be one of the cute young men wondering if Joe wouldn't like to join them for something to eat. Those youngsters probably thought he wasn't capable of fixing his own meal. Well, he was. It was a matter of pride for him.

But he did like their company. Especially that nice one, Sam Manetti. Jesus, didn't he cook up some great pasta! Joe often had to pay for a dish of it with a whole day's worth of indigestion, but he wasn't about to turn it down. It wasn't just that good food, it was the good company. Sam was always so polite and so interested in Joe's silly stories about the old days – or at least he pretended to be. Joe sighed to himself when he thought of the bland canned food that was in the bag he was hauling up the stairs. He certainly would rather have an invite from Sam tonight than have to eat this stuff.

But it worried him too that maybe he was intruding on the young men. After all, what use did they have for the company of a fossil like Joe? They should be out playing and dancing and doing all the things they liked; they shouldn't have to be taking care of an old man like Joe. They were always saying they didn't mind running errands when Joe didn't feel all that well. And they didn't do a very good job hiding their real intent when they'd come and knock on the door if one of them hadn't seen Joe for a couple days. They'd make some excuse, but he knew they were just waiting for him to fall and break a hip or do some other foolish thing that old people did. Hell, there wasn't any reason for a bunch of youngsters just in their twenties having to have to take care of an old man who wasn't even a relative.

Joe finally got to his door. He used the keys to undo the three different locks that kept the world out of his small space. He'd already been broken into three times in the last two years. He'd forced the Ukranian superintendent to add a new set of locks. All he needed was to have a burglar break in and mug him one night while he was asleep. That'd really get the kids riled up.

By the time Joe had opened the door, locked it behind him and dropped his bag on the kitchen table he was exhausted. He collapsed onto one of the wooden chairs and caught his breath. He was getting old, too old for this neighborhood and too old for those steps. He'd have to face it someday. Damn. It made him mad!

He looked up at the single picture of Harry that he kept on the wall of this room – one that did triple duty as kitchen, dining room and living room. "Harry, we never thought it'd end like this," he said to the photograph. "Old and alone and gay. 'Course," he chuckled, "we never expected we'd have thirty years with each other, either."

Oh, listen to yourself, *he scowled silently.* Talking to pictures of dead men!

But the anger wasn't real and it went away. He sighed. *I wish you were still here, Harry.*

Growing old was so *lonely.*

II

Frank Matson wasn't lonely. He was the pastor of the fastest growing congregation in the South. Even if he hadn't had
hundreds – thousands! – of church members to keep him
company, he had all their dollars. Lots and lots of dollars.

He was sitting at his desk and counting that night's collection. What a piece of cake. Who would have thought that
those fools would have given him – Frank Matson – so much
money just for some good old-fashioned revival meeting sermons? That and the kind of filth they loved.

Why did all those other preachers worry about the Scrip-
ture and theology and that shit when the congregations didn't
care? They didn't give a damn. They wanted to be shocked.
Shocked about the sin and corruption that they knew – they
hoped – was going on all around them. That was Matson's
secret. All he had to do was read the *National Enquirer* every day and he had a ready-made sermon to use. Drugs in
Washington! Sex in the state capital! Incest in high places!
And if those ever failed, there were always the fags. Frank
had merely to mention the homosexual conspiracy to corrupt
youth, and the collection plates would overflow.

Those idiots in the pews wouldn't be caught dead with
a sex magazine or a scandal sheet in their sanctified homes.

They counted on old Frank Matson to provide them with
the dirt and to have it all wrapped up in the clean and holy

words of religion and they could get their hard-ons and their wet pussies – those fools were probably having orgasms while Frank was preaching, the way he had learned to carry on – and they'd all pay him for the excitement. Just look at how much tonight, it might be a record for a Wednesday service. Just payment for goods delivered, Frank thought.

In his own way, Frank's visitor must have agreed. Frank didn't notice him until the man leaning against the doorway delivered his own judgment of Frank's real purpose in life: "You pimp."

The man said the words with almost no discernible emotion. Frank looked up. "Who are you?" he asked, puzzled how the man had gotten past all the guards that protected the church from atheists and communists and who knows who else.

"Alex Kane."

Frank studied the man. He was sure he had never seen him before. He would have noticed those green eyes, so close to luminescence even in the bright lights of the office. Frank felt a certain discomfort. The man was strangely attractive, actually sexual. It made Frank fidget to have to acknowledge that.

"What do you want?" Frank tried to be stern, as though he were still in his pulpit.

Alex Kane stood straight up and walked over to Matson's desk. "I want to convert you."

Shit, Frank thought, *one of those freaks that's going to try to one-up me on Jesus.* "Brother," he smiled, "I have already pledged my life to the Savior! I am called by Him, Himself!"

"I don't think we're talking about the same conversion." Alex Kane had taken a seat in a chair right across from Frank. "I do want to save you from a life of hypocrisy, that's true. I also want to save you from continuing to be a murderer."

"What the hell are you talking about?" Frank sat up in his chair. "I've never laid hands on anyone in my life, never in anger."

"But you have killed people. We discovered that you're

personally responsible for dozens of deaths, ever since you got your crackpot television program on half the cable networks in the country. Those stupid sermons of yours are directly responsible for many too many suicides. They've got to stop. So I'm going to convert you."

Alex Kane seemed to smile, even though his message was serious and his passionate conviction was obvious. He meant what he was saying. Frank Matson just couldn't figure out what that was.

Preachers get lots of crackpots. There are plenty of religious fanatics out there who somehow get through to all the big shots like himself. "Wait a minute!" Frank suddenly realized something. "How *did* you get by the guards? I have a detail of armed men out there doing nothing but protecting my person."

If Frank was puzzled, Alex Kane was amused. "Well, we'll just say they're asleep – for a long, long time. They weren't very good, you know. The Klan may talk a good line, but they sure don't know how to fight. They were probably a bunch of draft dodgers. You would have been better off getting some Vietnam Veterans. At least they know what fighting is all about. Like me, I was in 'Nam, that's where I started all this."

Whatever amusement had been motivating the man with the green eyes was suddenly erased; instead there was a sudden and great sorrow, one so deep that Frank actually wished – if only for a moment – that he was a real preacher. Even Frank would have wanted to heal that pain. Frank didn't know that it was something that many other people had seen and been forced to react to.

Kane seemed to shake his head to toss off the thoughts and to bring himself back to this situation. He spoke to Frank again, with even more passion than before. "You're going to stop those broadcasts. Now. You're going to cancel your program and you're going to disband your parish, at least the way it is."

This guy's whacko, Frank was sure now. "I'm not going to change a goddamn thing."

Kane was amused again. "Yes you are. You are because we've found out some things about you – *Jack*."

Frank went white. No one knew about that. It had all been taken care of years ago. He had changed his name and his identity. That's when he had gotten into the Jesus racket. "I don't know what you're talking about," Frank lied.

"Jack, Jack," Alex Kane was shaking his head in mock displeasure. "You shouldn't say you're a preacher in one breath and then lie in the next. Really you shouldn't. You are Jack Franklin. You were born in Manitowoc, Wisconsin. But you spent most of your life in Cleveland. We know all about it."

Fear seemed to be pressing against the minister's chest with a physical reality. "Those fuckers promised –"

"We know, we know," Alex Kane said softly. "If you'd turn evidence for the state and testify against The Family, the feds promised you a new identity, a new life. Their plastic surgeons were real good. I never would have known you from your pictures."

"You're not from them?"

"Nope. We found you all by ourselves. The federal agents didn't compromise you. It's all in the computers. We just ran all these programs and we finally found out who you were – before. It was strange, for a pastor of a big, televised church like this to have such a shabby history. The details didn't fit. We decided you were hiding something. We found it, and it was a whopper. It's big enough that we're sure you're going to see a lot of things our way from now on."

The minister's color hadn't returned. The fear was gripping him even harder. Alex Kane didn't need to give the rest of the explanation; the thoughts had already flooded through his listener's mind.

But the strange man seemed to need to make everything clear, as though he were justifying himself, as though he wanted the minister to understand just what was going on:

"The Family's never forgotten what Jack Franklin did to them. When they find out that he's still alive, that he's earning a good living here in Birmingham, Alabama, they're going to do something." The smile came back full force. "I bet it'll be gruesome, too.

"They don't know what happened to Jack Franklin. We do. The FBI needed a squealer. They found you. In return for a lot of bucks and a fake history – probably all the way down to a birth certificate and a social security number – you'd turn in your life and take a new one.

"They probably figured that a pimp – that's what you were, Jack, a filthy pimp for young girls – wasn't a big enough score. They'd let you go to get the old man. Stupid, they're so stupid. First they think they can overlook the kind of slime you were. You were the kind of asshole who'd take lonely teen-age girls and put them on the street, help them get some dope to forget what they had to do to turn their money over to you. You were the kind of pimp that even the big guys think is dirt."

"Hey, now listen," the minister stammered, trying to start a defense.

"Don't even bother," Kane waved away the protests, "we did plenty of research on you. The FBI decided that the kind of exploitation of children you got involved with wasn't worth prosecuting if – by overlooking it – they could get a bigger fish. They were stupid to think that a loathsome thing like you wouldn't find another way to earn money on the backs and minds of youngsters."

Those green eyes had heated up to an intensity that made the man look insane; he was a fanatic, Frank knew it. The man also knew too much about Frank and his past. No one was supposed to know about that.

"You can't prosecute me." Frank was getting his backbone up again. "You can't lay a finger on me. I have an official pardon ..."

The man's hand waved through the air again. "Oh, I know about the pardon. Sealed in a federal courthouse. Yeah, I know all about it. Fucking FBI thinks it can play god and decide which crimes need to be brought to justice most. That's a great flaw in our system, Jack. A great flaw."

"Don't call me Jack!"

Kane smiled wide again, the turn of his lips alleviated that impression of insanity a bit. But the sharp focus on the matters at hand didn't waver at all. Not at all. "You are Jack. Don't worry, there's no one left in the building to hear. I told you: they're all asleep. You see, if you play my game from now on, you won't have to worry about things, *Jack.*

"Now, you're right, the system fucked up and let you get away scot-free. We tried to get you on taxes, we thought you probably had been playing games with all that money you collected. But you were too smart for that, weren't you? Oh, it'd be embarrassing if your congregation knew just how much money you got in salary and expenses, but you could talk your way out of that.

"And you can't go on trial, 'cause of that agreement with the FBI.

"But, *Jack,* what do you think the Family's going to say when they find out where you are? What do you think they're going to do?"

"You can't tell them, you just can't." The little color had disappeared again. The minister was even more pale than before. "You can't turn those goons loose on me. They'll ..."

"They'll kill you, *Jack.*" Alex Kane smiled. "They'll kill you nice and slow and they'll do it with great pleasure. Now, the FBI thinks you're a hero. But they're not going to help you any more. You know that. They probably told you the deal. You work for them and they give you a new identity. But once it's established, you're on your own. They don't want too many people to know about this little program they have going. It doesn't look good for them when they've got to admit that they helped a pimp get off scot-free. So, they've washed their hands of you."

"What do you want me to do?" the minister slumped back against his big office chair. He obviously knew he was defeated. He wasn't about to find out what The Family would do against the small clique of men who were supposed to protect him. They hadn't even kept this one single man out of his office.

Alex Kane seemed to relax a bit too. He was obviously pleased with the little chat they were having. "First, you're going to stop killing people."

"I've never killed anyone!" This was perhaps the only thing the man knew he had never done. His defense was vehement.

"Those sermons of yours do the job. The guilt you lay on gay guys, the way you carry on about them and the way you make their parents hate and despise them. That stops. You've driven too many of them to suicide, you've convinced too many others that they're on the side of righteousness if they attack innocent gays on the street. That's over with. From now on, the only time you mention homosexuality on television is when you talk about David and Jonathan. I want to hear Psalms about those two, long love stories from your pulpit." Now the man's intensity was being re-directed. He certainly was some kind of fanatic. His eyes seemed to glaze over, as though he had gone far away, driven by the mere mention of love stories.

"You do all that, Jack, and you and me will be fine. You will be fine. You start liking black people some more, too. There aren't enough on your program. I think it's time you had a woman as an associate pastor, that'd be a good idea."

"I can't do those things," the preacher complained. "The church'd fall apart. The pledges would go, the money from the syndication of my program ..."

"You know," Alex Kane interrupted, "I hate to admit it, but I think you'll actually make just as much money getting on the right side of issues as you do where you are. Me, I'd rather just off you for all the harm you've done. But it's more poetic this way – to threaten you with The Family and to make you become one of the real good guys – not just testifying, but acting on some good things."

Alex Kane stood up. "Trust me, *Jack*, I know people who are in The Family. One phone call from me or one of my friends and you're a dead man. That, or you can become the new leader of a movement in religion. The one holding up the flame of social justice." Alex Kane chuckled over that one. "No more sermons on fags, no more telling women to stay in the kitchen. None of that. But more blacks and Hispanics, more money for really poor people. All that kind of thing.

"Oh," Kane stopped himself, he had been turning to leave the office. "If you doubt my sincerity, if you think you can find some new way to hide, remember that I found you this time. I'll find you again. If you think you can get more Klansmen to fight for you, go look in your dumpster in the alleyway and see what happened to those you had. You have no place to go. That is, no place to go but to get a new religion. You look at those fools, then you'll know I converted you."

With one last smile, Alex Kane left the office.

• • •

The next day the New *Orleans Star-Ledger* and half the other newspapers in the country had banner headlines:

Evangelist Hears New Social Gospel

The world of popular religion was shaken to its polyester roots. Frank Matson was going to turn it on its head. His first move was the most shocking. Matson had announced his intention to marry homosexual couples.

"That the law doesn't recognize such God-fearing marriages is its own business. The Lord knows when true vows are made by true Christians."

III

Joe Talbot fought it. He insisted that he keep himself alert to the world around him. Every morning he began his day with the *CBS Morning News,* all two hours of it. He was amused that Bill Kurtis and Diane Sawyer were probably the most important on-going relationship in his life. He turned on his television every morning and the sounds of their reports filled the small apartment while he went about his routine.

Sometimes they could be so amusing. Joe always paid close attention to even the smallest bit of gay news on the program. He cheered the little victories the young guys were winning and he mourned their defeats. But he loved the foolishness of some of the straights the most. He howled over the ridiculous Bible thumper down in Alabama who was trying to convince people he loved homosexuals now. Who'd ever believe one of those idiots anyway?

A quick shower and shave was first. Then he'd make a pot of tea and drink a cup while his soft-boiled egg cooked. The television would still be going while he ate that tasteless breakfast and sipped his obligatory glass of orange juice. By the time the program was done, the meal would be eaten and the dishes would be washed.

Then Joe would go for his "constitutional" – the long walk he took every morning. Sometimes he thought he did it just to prove to himself that he could. He'd walk up and down Second Avenue and wave at the people whose faces he had come to recognize. He'd go up to St. Mark's and get the *Daily News* and a new magazine if there was one to catch his attention on the stand. He made sure he read all the gay ones as soon as they came out. He'd take the purchases and go on up the Avenue to his favorite coffee shop – the one where there were so many young guys working as waiters. They didn't mind if an old coot like him sat and read *Mandate* or the *Advocate,* they seemed to enjoy the sight of a man his age still being interested in the stories – and the pictures.

Joe used to walk further. Only a couple of years ago he would have gone all the way across town to the West Village and observe all the men there, the ones who seemed to march endlessly up and down Christopher Street. But it was too far a journey now. He was grateful he could do what he did these days.

He made sure that he took a big trip at least once a week. Usually he went to the museums. He had never had time to do that while Harry was alive; Harry wasn't the type who would like museums anyhow. They were pretty much home-bodies in those days. Harry'd come home from his job in the ship-yard and Joe would return from his shift at the printing plant and they'd be dog tired. Well, not so much they couldn't have their own fun, but they didn't often feel like much outside the apartment.

But Joe went to museums now. There was no good reason for him to let his brain atrophy just because the bones were getting a little stiff and the breath a little short.

He usually went to the movies at least once a week as well, but he limited himself to those that were showing in the neighborhood. The jostling crowds in Times Square and on the Upper East Side had become too much for him to take.

The best part was the theater. It used to be – as it is with so many New Yorkers – that Joe only went to plays on very special occasions, maybe once or twice a year on holidays to see a big musical number. But now it seemed that every one of the young gays that lived in Joe's building was in some little theater production or another. They acted or stage-managed or something, and they always made sure that Joe had a pass to see their opening nights.

Of course, Joe could barely understand a tenth of the things that happened on the stage at those productions. But he loved going and seeing the kids.

The best one – by far – was Sam's. Just think! A twenty-five year old who earns his living as a temporary typist and a play he wrote got produced. It was the one that Joe had understood most clearly, just a nice story about a couple growing together. Sam had worked into the play some little things from Joe's own history with Harry – the East Village apartment and the way that Harry acted, the things Joe had told Sam.

That made Joe relax even more with Sam. He was always so concerned that he was wasting the youngsters' time. But if Sam was learning something from Joe's stories, maybe he wasn't being such a self-indulgent old man after all.

Sam and the others were the peaks in Joe's life. But they came so seldom and he really didn't like to ask for more of them. And the constant repetition of the *CBS Morning News,* the same walk up Second Avenue every day, the same cup of tea in the same coffee shop, the same movie theater, the same ...

Damn it was *boring* to grow old.

• • •

The last thing that Joe Talbot was going to do was to let things get him down. He would never be one of those fools that could only think in terms of self-pity. That was not Joe Talbot's way with the world. It never had been and it never would be.

Whenever he discovered himself sinking into that trap he'd infuse his life with a surge of energy. He would add an extra trip to the museum or buy a new book or do something to get himself out of that rut.

This one day he had forced himself to do just that. He had

taken the Lexington Avenue subway uptown to see the new exhibit at the Metropolitan. It had been tiring, but Joe was pleased with himself. It had been a great exhibit – all kinds of stuff from Spain. Those guys sure could paint, Joe had been thinking about it on the ride home. He had never gone to college, and even his high school education had been aimed at giving him vocational training, not cultural stuff. Maybe he should take one of those adult education programs, one that could explain to him just who those Spanish artists were and why they did things the way they did.

Joe was still thinking about that idea while he wrestled with his mailbox key. It was awkward since he had stopped at the little local store and bought a few things for the kitchen. He was so preoccupied with the lock and balancing his grocery bag and his plans for an education that he didn't hear the outer door open. He wasn't prepared for the loud and cheerful greeting, "Joe! How are you!"

Joe was startled. He jumped just a bit and the bag fell to the linoleum tile floor. "Oh, hell!" Joe muttered. The loud sound of shattering glass had announced the breaking bottle of orange juice.

"Joe, I'm sorry." Sam Manetti knelt down and tried to retrieve the packages that had fallen away from the broken bag. The sopping orange juice had soaked most of them. Sam quickly moved to place them on the counter over the mailboxes. "Look, I'll replace everything. You just go upstairs and sit down. I'll take care of those and go back to the store ..."

"Sam, I've told you before I'm not a baby. For Chrissake, I can get over a broken bottle of orange juice and if I have to I can still walk half a block to replace it. Now, you just go on your business." Joe's voice was sharp and angry.

Sam looked up with a pained expression of guilt. "Hey, I'm sorry."

Joe's coolness melted at the look from the young man. "Oh, come on, let's do this together. I can take these things upstairs." He gathered up the butter and bread and the few other loose items that Sam had picked up off the floor. "I guess you're going to have to clean this up, though," Joe gestured toward the spilt juice.

"And replace it," Sam insisted.

"You don't have to replace anything."

"Yes I do," Sam said in mock rebellion. "It's a question of honor. And you know how we Italian men are about our honor." Sam struck his own chest with a playful fist.

"I know nothing of the kind. Italian men aren't high on *my* list of honorable."

"Oh," Sam perked up. "You never told me about you and any Italian men."

Joe blushed. "Well, you don't know everything. There are some secrets left."

"Joe, you've been holding out on me. A new story? Come on, you going to tell me? What was it, a passionate affair with a Genoan sailor? A night of lost lust with a Roman diplomat?"

"Sam, you stop that."

"Joe, I know it! I know it was a Sicilian. They're supposed to have the biggest cocks of all. Tell me, Joe, come on, tell me!"

"You just let me take this stuff and my mail upstairs and you finish what you have to do. Then we'll see."

"Over a pot of tea?" Sam was being coy now.

"Oh, yes, damn it, over a pot of tea." But Joe's attempt to sound annoyed was obviously inauthentic. He was delighted that the boy would be spending time with him. He needed a bit of a perk today.

• • •

When Sam came up the stairs and into Joe's apartment he was carrying a replacement bottle of orange juice. He hadn't bothered to knock and he found the older man sitting at his kitchen table carefully reading something that had apparently come in the mail.

"Hi, Sam," Joe said, but didn't lift his eyes from the paper in his hands.

"Hi, Joe." Sam placed the juice in the small fridge and then took a chair opposite Joe's. "What you got there?"

Joe folded the paper carefully and put it in his pants pocket. "A thing that's advertising something I might be interested in."

This secrecy wasn't like Joe. Sam pressed. "What is it?"

Joe knew he was cornered. He made one more try. "Want that tea now?"

"I want the tea, I also want to know what the letter's about."

Joe was resigned as he stood and went to fill the kettle. "It's from a place in Arizona called Son Valley. I thought it was a typographic error at first, but it's just a cute name. Seems someone finally got their act together and has started an old folks' home for gay men." Joe put the kettle on the stove and stood there, hoping Sam wouldn't pry much more. It wasn't a very promising hope, of course. The younger man jumped into the subject:

"Who runs it? Who's sponsoring it? How much does it cost? How could you afford it?"

"Now, wait a minute," Joe said crossly. "All I did was read a flyer. I don't know anything about it. It's just a place where some old folks live who happen to be gay and who want to spend their last years with their own kind. It's not the worst idea in the world, you know. I'm intrigued," Joe frowned, "I admit that I'm intrigued. But I'll have to find out more about it."

"Joe, you don't need to go to an old people's house. We'll take care of you. We're your community. Right here in this building there are at least twenty gay men who can be organized ..."

"I don't want to be organized!" Joe's sharpness was real. "I just want some comfort and some peace and some people like me – gay and my own age. I ... I don't want to always have to come after you kids and get things done."

"But we want to help, Joe. And besides, you have so much here, you've lived here so long and you have your memory trunk."

Joe smiled at that. He involuntarily looked over at the big steamer trunk in the corner. Inside it were all the mementos and all the photographs, every letter he'd ever received. He'd always been a collector, more like a pack rat, Harry used to say. He had even saved the book of matches from the very first time he and Harry had stayed in a hotel together, in Atlantic City. Jesus, that was a long time ago.

Joe had started the collection as a young man. He had decided that he wasn't going to forget all the good times. Just in case he grew old, as he actually had, he wanted to have the memories to draw on to keep himself company. Whenever things got bad, Joe had only to open the trunk and look at the photo albums or reread the letters Harry had sent him during the war, and the blues just went away.

That was how Joe told Sam all his stories. The two of them would paw through all those newspaper clippings and the silly souvenirs and they'd prime the pump of Joe's remembrances or else let him illustrate some particularly funny tale.

But that folder had been so appealing. To have some of his own people his own age to talk to and to spend time with, to be able to break the rut of the daily schedule and the grinding pressure of his loneliness ...

The teapot began to whistle and Joe's attention was brought back to his small kitchen. And to Sam. "Oh, it's just something I'll look into, Sam, that's all. Just an idea. But if you don't give an old man some peace, I'll never tell you that story about the Italian."

Joe's little attempt at seduction took a while to work; Sam's concerned expression wasn't easily dismissed. But then that wonderful smile did return and Sam gave in. "He was a Sicilian, wasn't he?"

"What difference does it make?" Joe asked.

"'Cause that's what I am," Sam laughed.

IV

Joe nearly jumped out of his chair when the buzzer rang. The *CBS Morning News* had just ended. It must be just after nine o'clock. Who the hell could that be? The East Village was awfully close to the Bowery and there were always bums ringing the doorbells trying to get into the building in order to sleep in the warmth of the hallways. Probably it was just one of those.

Or it could be one of those busybodies always trying to save Joe's soul – or else the soul of anyone stupid enough to let them in.

It was too early for the postman. Almost everyone else who ever visited Joe would still be sleeping or at work. The buzzer went off once more. *Hell, I better see who it is.*

Joe went to the panel where there was an intercom button. He pushed it and said hello.

"Mr. Talbot?"

"Yes."

"This is Henry Dewar, from Son Valley? We got a card from you asking for more information."

The retirement home! Joe had nearly forgotten all about it. "Of course. Come right up. Fifth floor." Joe punched another button to unlock the front door and hurriedly went to put on a fresh kettle of water for tea. This was exciting! That pamphlet had sounded so appealing. Especially now, in the middle of winter in New York City. God, it'd been cold out. It seemed that there was less and less of Joe each year, less and less flesh to protect him from the winter winds. All those pictures of the people sitting around a big swimming pool had been tempting.

The knock came at the door and Joe opened it to greet his visitor. "Mr. Talbot, Henry Dewar. Good to meet you." There was a big hand reaching out in the air. Joe took it and shook.

"Come in, come in. I have a pot of tea I'm making just now. It'll only be a minute."

"Don't go to any bother on my account," the man said.

"No bother at all. Just take off your coat while I get some cups out. You can hang it on that hook there on the back of the door if you don't mind."

While Joe went about the business of preparing the tea and waiting for the water to boil, Dewar shed his heavy topcoat and left it where Joe had suggested. He seemed to sense Joe's love of informality and simply took one of the wooden chairs at the kitchen table. He had a valise with him, which he opened.

By the time Joe had brought the brewing pot over to the table, Dewar had already spread out whole stacks of information. Many of the sheets were just enlargements of the illustrations that Joe had already seen in the Son Valley brochure. But there were some new ones. Joe didn't wait for an invitation to look at them, but gathered up a couple and couldn't help but smile at the images before him.

There were photographs of happy looking older men. Some were playing cards and others were groups around a pool table. There were other images of men alone, or in couples, or in smaller groups talking and reading and watching television.

"We think we've created a unique atmosphere for relaxation and enjoyment at Son Valley, Mr. Talbot." The man seemed to be starting a sales pitch. But he stopped himself. The glow in Joe's eyes as he looked at the photos was proof that he wouldn't need a hard sell to be convinced.

"Is this the only kind of place like it?" Joe asked.

"Certainly the only one for gay men," Dewar smiled.

"I don't know," Joe was remembering some of Sam's objections. "Arizona's so far away."

"And so much warmer than New York."

"Mr. Dewar, that's almost dirty fighting to say that on a day like this." The news had said it was 17° outside.

"Mr. Talbot, Son Valley *is* unique. Located in Arizona, it promises you endless recreation and untold opportunities for companionship with your peers – gay men your own age."

"Well, I do admit that sounds fine," Joe said. It certainly did.

"And it's affordable. Why, with your nest egg, we'll be able to guarantee you a life-long stay at Son Valley."

"My nest egg? How'd you know about that?" Joe was suddenly on edge. He didn't like to mention that Certificate of Deposit he had down at the bank. It represented everything he and Harry had ever saved plus the money from Harry's insurance. It might not be a fortune, but it had kept Joe off welfare and it did make the days go easier for him to know he didn't really have to count pennies all that much.

"Mr. Talbot," the man was smiling, obviously trying to reassure a suddenly defensive Joe, "on your application was a form that allowed us to check your credit references. It was a simple matter for us to do that. We only wanted to have the information necessary to counsel you appropriately."

"Well," Joe thought for a moment, he did remember that form. "Yeah, I did sign it."

"Son Valley is a highly reputable institution, Mr. Talbot. As I said, we just investigated your resources enough for us to know what your situation was. Of course, if it had been necessary, we would have tried to find some assistance for you ..."

"I've never taken a penny of welfare and I never will." Joe's voice was adamant.

"Well, you obviously won't need to."

"How can you be so sure my money will last?" Joe wondered. He just might live for a long time more. It wasn't that likely, but it could happen. His great uncle had gone on till well into his nineties.

"Simple as pie, Mr. Talbot," the salesman promised him. "Simple as pie. All we'll need to do is to convert your investments into an annuity. It still will provide you with plenty of spending money – you'll get a monthly check – and it will guarantee that you can stay in Son Valley for the rest of your life."

"Huh," Joe had heard about these things before – annuities. It was a big financial corporation's way to gamble that you wouldn't live long enough to really enjoy the benefits. But if you did, well it could be a good deal. Joe knew that some other old people had taken them out just to be assured of a steady and predictable income. It could make sense, he supposed.

"Mr. Talbot, let me tell you more about Son Valley and the services we have to offer you. Why, they're endless. You'll see that this is just the place for you to spend your golden years. With your own, all your needs taken care of, financially secure and at peace with nature in the middle of one of the country's great resort areas."

Joe sighed. "I do have to admit it sounds good."

"Then let's talk seriously!" There was an almost unnoticeable change in the smile on Dewar's face. If Joe had been a sportsman, and if Joe had seen it, he would have recognized it. It was the look of a hunter when he's finally gotten his prey in his sight.

• • •

Sam had a fit.

"Joe, you can't just go off to some place like that without seeing it. You can't. Look, why don't you wait a while. Let me get some money together. I've always loved the West. I used to camp in Colorado; I'd have a really good time going back out that way. We'll go together and check the place."

"Sam, you barely have enough money for your rent."

"I have some put away."

"For your next play. Now, stop it. I'm a grown man, not a helpless infant that has to be taken care of. This is just the thing for me. It's what I always hoped I'd find."

"But there are all those stories about what rip-offs these outfits can be." The young man was desperately trying one more time to convince Joe to hesitate before he made such a big move.

"Sam," Joe protested, "it's for gays. Doesn't that make a difference?"

"No, it does not. I still don't know who owns it. I don't know who runs it. I don't know what kind of staff they have."

"You don't need to know. *I* do. And it sounds just fine to me. Now help me close the lid on this suitcase."

Sam begrudgingly went over to the corner where Joe was struggling with a piece of luggage that wouldn't allow itself to be shut. He used his own strength to force the latch.

"There." But Sam had no pride in his accomplishment.

Joe put a hand on the younger man's shoulder and led him over to the kitchen table. He sat Sam down and then took a seat next to him. "I do appreciate how much you care and how concerned you are. But you have to understand that I'm just too old to keep up this pace in the city. I'm lonely, Sam. I want something different from what I got here. I need something more. I've been here for so very long that I've watched all my friends die off or have to move away.

"You kids are great to me. But you aren't going to be here forever. You shouldn't have to be. You're going to take that pretty body of yours and go off and meet some hot man and next thing I know you'll be moving to Hoboken or ..."

"I'll never move to Jersey!" Sam said sharply, then laughed at his own over-reaction.

"Well, wherever. But you kids are all going to move on. And I don't want to end up senile in a charity ward here in the city with ... It's too gruesome to even think about. This Son Valley place is just what I need and what I want."

Sam was still despondent, but he could see that his arguments weren't going to take him anywhere. "Do you promise to write? To call me? To keep in touch?"

"I promise. I swear it."

"On Harry's grave?"

Joe was startled by that. He sat straight up in his chair. For a quick moment he thought the youngster had purposely tried to hurt him by mentioning Harry in this conversation. Then, with a rush of warmth, he realized it was really only a measure of how much Sam really did care that he'd make Joe swear an oath to the one thing that was most important to him in this life: Harry's memory. "I swear, Sam, I swear."

Then, for the first time in all the years they'd known one another, Sam leaned over and kissed Joe right on the lips. "I'm going to hold you to it."

"Damn you!" Joe got up from the seat and moved quickly to give the impression of being busy. "Now, go on, you don't have to watch all this. Let me pack in peace. They're coming tomorrow."

"I know, I know. Don't *you* forget that we're all taking you out to dinner tonight."

"Bunch of sentimental whippersnappers," Joe scoffed, hoping the tone of his voice would hide the tears until Sam left the apartment.

V

Alex Kane was pissed.

I never have a moment's peace, *he told himself. He was swimming laps in the Olympic-sized pool that was the centerpiece for Joseph Farmdale's mansion in Carmel, California.* Not me. I have to fight those bastards all the time. And then? Then I have to watch my "partner" to find out just what the hell he's been doing to my personal life.

The same thoughts – or minor variations – went through his mind over and over again as he kept on swimming. He was slamming his hands and arms into the water, trying to take out his anger and frustration on the pool. *Lousy form,* he told himself. *Who gives a fuck,* he answered.

Joseph Farmdale sat on a chair nearby and watched the body in the water as it trailed a constant wake in the pool. He was utterly unconcerned by whatever was driving Alex this morning. He was used to these bursts of unexplained and strange physical displays. It seemed that Alex Kane was capable of unendurable amounts of exercise. Whenever Farmdale turned around the man had begun his sit-ups or his push-ups or was using the free weights. Just the thought of it all tired Farmdale.

He, himself, never had indulged in such activities. There had been a time in his youth when it seemed appropriate for him to climb on the back of a polo pony, but those instances had thankfully disappeared and Joseph Farmdale had gone back to his own true passions – the stock market, his thoroughbreds, managing his properties, and watching the development of computer science with the greatest interest.

There was no use in trying to catch Alex's attention while he was in one of these masochistic moods. Farmdale knew that. He rang a small bell on the poolside table and in a quick moment one of his many servants appeared. Farmdale asked for a gin and tonic and continued his vigil, waiting for Kane to come out of the water.

When Alex finally realized that he wouldn't be able to exhaust himself sufficiently to drive the annoyance from his mind, he did climb up the metal stairs and onto the concrete patio. He was naked; there had been no need for a swimsuit here. He reached over for a towel and began to dry himself off, overtly avoiding any notice of the older man who so patiently awaited him.

Farmdale's drink had arrived a while ago. He still sipped it as he watched Alex rub the terry cloth over his body. As usual he was vaguely aware that he should have some response to seeing Kane naked. It certainly did seem that everyone else did. But Farmdale couldn't really react. He had never found the male nude erotic – and hardly could remember having thought the female nude was that either. Though he must have, at least at some time. He had fathered four children, after all.

But as Alex Kane bent over and brusquely toweled his thighs and calves, Farmdale could only view him in one way, the same way that he judged his horses, those prize-winners in the stable. Kane was the same perfectly torsoed specimen. There could be no denying those lines, the perfection of the balance and the stunning quality of the skin and hair coloring. This was a prize-winner, no doubt about it.

As he often did, Farmdale congratulated his son on his choice of a lover. He had long ago resigned himself to James's death, and he knew he had done so better than Alex Kane had. But there were still moments of paternal pride in all this. Yes,

yes, as the Farmdales usually did, James had chosen well. He hadn't been restricted by silly social standards when he went after his lover; this offspring of Greek fishermen from New Hampshire was more than adequate. There was that beauty that the Farmdale father could acknowledge, that similarity to the great Hellenes was obviously there. Luckily there was hardly any body hair to obscure it, only the little tufts under Alex's arms and crowning his genitals – so like the ancient statues.

Alex had finished his task and had walked over to Farmdale's chair with a purposeful stride. The towel was dragging behind him. Kane took a seat across from the one Farmdale occupied.

The younger man reached into his bathrobe which had been draped over the chair and pulled out a handwritten letter. There was that look of dark anger on Alex's face. It was focused straight at Farmdale. "Dear Alex," Kane began to read with what Farmdale considered to be an unnecessarily loud and theatrical voice. "I want to thank you very much for my graduation present. I really don't know what to say, it was so generous. Of course I love it! But I really don't know if you should have done this."

Alex slammed the letter down onto the glass tabletop. "What the hell did I buy Danny Fortelli for his graduation!?" Alex's fist was poised in midair to slam down for utterly unneeded emphasis. Farmdale made a motion to restrain the threatened destruction of his furniture. Alex relaxed slightly and rested his elbows firmly on the table.

Then Farmdale sighed with his own bit of dramatic flair. "You have been acting in a totally irresponsible fashion in this entire affair. I'm quite annoyed with you and your misuse of this young boy. Now, if my son had married a woman, she would have re-married at least twice in the more than ten years since his death. But you? Not you! You are trying to act as though your very body is some kind of eternal flame flickering for his memorial.

"Danny is perfect for you. He is someone who cares

deeply for you and for whom you have your own emotional attachment. Yet you will neither admit that nor deny it. You say you're never going to see him, but then you show up, unannounced and carry him off to that dreadful chain motel near campus. You could at least drive forty-five minutes into Boston and use a suite at the Ritz or the Plaza. The idea! Continuing assignations at a suburban Holiday Inn!"

"Where I see him isn't the issue," Kane insisted.

"No, it's not. It's that you do want to see him, selfishly and egocentrically when you want to. He has no way to reach you, he has no promise that you'll ever again show up, in fact you constantly threaten him that you won't. Then you forget his graduation *and* his birthday. The boy's hopelessly infatuated with you and you don't do the right thing for him, not at all."

"You know there are reasons and ..."

Farmdale stopped Alex Kane's interruption. "There are no reasons good enough for this behavior. All I'm trying to do is to make the young man aware that all is not lost. You have no touch for niceties, the little gestures. They mean so much in a courtship."

"I am not having a courtship!" Kane declared. "I don't want a courtship. Danny Fortelli was in trouble. I got him out of it."

"And then you bedded him," Farmdale's eyebrow went up. "That alone was strange behavior. You've always told me you only use your sexuality for recreation or as a tool to barter for information. But then, there you are, all of a sudden, in bed, in a bed in Provincetown, with a very handsome athlete. It seems that the Great Wall of Alex Kane was breached, and you are uncomfortable with those flaws."

"I am not here to talk to you about my psychology. I asked you a direct question and I want an answer. *What did I give Danny Fortelli for his graduation present!?*"

Farmdale let out a disgusted snort. "Simply a small automobile."

"A car? I bought Danny a car?" This was obviously worse than Kane had even feared.

"Well, he'll be stuck out in the woods at that little state college. He's nearly an hour's drive from his parents' house, there's no decent public transportation, an automobile seemed to be quite an appropriate gift. Actually, I never have understood why he is going to go to Mansford State."

Alex Kane was getting uncomfortable. He shifted in his seat and his body seemed to move a bit much. "When he was in trouble his grades suffered. He couldn't get his full scholarship. So, since he didn't want to have his parents go into debt, he chose a state school."

"You mean it was just a question of money? That Danny still could have gone to an Ivy League school, or some other private institution? Why didn't we pay his tuition?"

"I ... I offered. He wouldn't take it."

"Why in the the name of the good Lord not?"

"He wanted to do it on his own. He thought he had fouled things up himself and, well, he could go to Mansford on the money they offered him. He didn't want to be a drain on anyone."

"A drain! Doesn't he know how much money you have?"

Alex glowered into his hands. "No, of course not. No one does."

"I do! James left you a fortune. You could have bought him his own college."

Alex stood up and turned his back on Joseph Farmdale. "I don't like to think of James in terms of his money."

"Well, you had better learn to do so. I'm not going to be around forever and some day you're going to have to learn to look after your own affairs." But that issue didn't interest Farmdale enough to divert him from the real topic at hand. "He wouldn't take that tuition money from you. No wonder you two are so perfectly matched for one another. You're equally as stubborn."

Alex Kane had his own priority to return to. He swiveled on his heels and stared at Farmdale again. "What *kind* of car have I bought Danny?"

Farmdale tried to appear nonchalant. "I told you, it's

small."

"What kind of *small* car?"

"Oh, something from Europe, I believe. Just a two seater."

"What country in Europe?"

"You know I don't pay attention to those details. I simply saw an appropriate automobile in a showroom while I was in Boston ..."

"When were you in Boston?" Alex Kane realized the plot was getting even thicker.

"While you were doing such an admirable job in Alabama, I simply thought I would attend to some of the amenities. After all, your parents have been dead for years. I am the only family you have. It seemed only correct for me to meet the Fortellis. Charming couple. We dined at Locke-Ober's – I hadn't had a chance to go there since I was at Harvard..."

"You took the Fortellis out to dinner? You flew all the way across the country just to take the Fortellis out to dinner?"

"Well, given the way your relationship with Danny should be progressing, they had a right to know more about you and to meet the people who are part of your life now. Yes, I did go to Boston to meet the Fortellis. That's where I found the car."

"You went to Danny's graduation, didn't you?" It was getting clearer now.

"Well, yes, I did. It just so happened that I was there ..."

"And you brought the car to the ceremony?"

"It seemed a nice gesture."

"And you took Danny and his parents and how many friends to Locke-Ober's?"

"Oh, just a few ..."

"The banquet room?"

"Well, they don't actually have a banquet room ..."

"You rented the whole fucking place, didn't you?"

"It's not *that* large."

"You rented the most expensive restaurant in Boston for the night and you took Danny's entire high school graduation class there for dinner. And then you gave him a car. A little European automobile. From what country was it?"

Farmdale was beginning to understand how very disconcerting it must be for some of the men that Alex Kane cornered during his work. "Germany, I believe."

"What kind of car was it? There was a note of command in Alex Kane's voice now, one that wasn't going to be denied, not even by Joseph Farmdale.

"A Mercedes. A small Mercedes coupe."

"Oh my god!" Kane collapsed back into his chair. "I bought Danny Fortelli a Mercedes that cost more than his father makes in three years. And I bet I paid for the dinner at Locke-Ober's, too, didn't I? I took his whole school to dinner."

"I just thought it would be a decent gesture on your part."

"Oh, shit."

• • •

Alex Kane was sprawled on his bed later that day. He wore only a pair of gym shorts; his arms were above his head. Wide awake, he was staring at the ceiling. There was a knock on the door. "Come in."

It was Farmdale. He was dressed in a dark suit now.

"Manuel said you weren't coming to dinner. Aren't you well?"

"I'm fine." There was no emotion in Alex's voice.

Farmdale hesitated for a moment, then walked into the room. At first he went and stood looking out the large picture window. It offered a magnificent view of the Pacific coastline. Then he turned and walked over to Alex. He was stiffly formal as he sat down next to the nearly nude figure. It was an awkward movement when he put a hand on Alex's exposed underarm. The little gesture of intimacy was as much as Farmdale had ever given Alex – or his own sons.

"This strange life you lead has left you without the means to have your own private existence. I feel badly about it. I don't know how to change it. But I wish I could."

"What do you mean?" Alex's voice was softer, the argument between the two men was over. Whatever else Farmdale was and whatever he might have done, this was the only person in Kane's life with whom he had had continuing contact over the last ten years.

"After James was killed in Vietnam – and you had avenged that death – we made our pact: That you were to continue your role as a guardian of your people in your own battle. It created a situation of great contrasts – sharp divisions. For the past ten years you have witnessed – and then done battle with – the most vile elements of society. You have used your body and your skill to fight that horrible reality – the manifestation of utter evil in human life.

"To do it, you have had to do that thing which every warrior must. You have lived in a world of black and white. You have striven to be the best possible man, your own personification of good, in order to justify your struggle against evil. You have – by the way – done a magnificent job of it. I doubt I've ever seen a person who has tried so hard to do the right thing and who has suffered so much when his only alternative was to perform the ultimate judgment on another man."

They were quiet for a moment. Alex Kane didn't like to think of the killing he'd done. He always looked for the option. He had been glad that the threat of The Family had been enough to change Frank Matson. But there had been others. Like the man who had blackmailed Danny Fortelli, the man who had forced the kid into a life that he should never have had to experience, even if only for a few weeks.

"But that dichotomy has left you defenseless in your own time of need. Don't argue with me, Alex. I know perfectly well that you do care for Danny, that you care very much. But you've not the means to deal with the subtleties, the grey areas that relationships demand. You haven't compromised with anyone in so long that you don't know how to do it now, not even in this most personal arena."

"You can do it for me. You seem to like doing things for me." Only the slightest hint of sharpness crept into Alex's voice now.

"Don't begin all that now. Yes, I bought the boy a car. You

should have been the one to do it. But you wouldn't. You're going to have to resolve yourself and your dilemma, Alex. It's not fair to Danny; it's not fair to yourself."

Farmdale's hand still rested on Kane's arm. Alex took it in his own free grip. "Yeah. I know. This in-between stuff isn't doing anyone any good."

"Think about it, long and hard. Perhaps you should wait on this next assignment?"

"I can't. Not with what we know. I have to take care of it."

"Dinner then?" Farmdale stood and looked down at Alex.

"No. I need to think. Tell Manuel to just bring me a sandwich or something light later on. I'll be fine."

Farmdale nodded, then turned and left the room.

All black and white. *Alex thought to himself,* it sure used to be.

His mind was a constant battlefield these days – between his memory of James Farmdale and his yearning for Danny Fortelli. Whenever he'd conjure up the image of himself and James in that bed in their bungalow in Saigon there'd be a sudden intrusion, the recollection of the sweet smell of Danny's body beside his own.

And his work? It had been his dedication to James. When he had seen his lover killed by a fag-hating American sergeant in the jungles of Vietnam, Alex had known what evil was and how it had to be answered. He had avenged James's death right then and right there. The long arm of Farmdale's influence had taken care of the aftermath.

Alex had heard the stories about it all. How Farmdale had received one of those hateful, euphemistic telegrams from the Pentagon informing him of the unfortunate death of his son as a result of "friendly fire." That was hardly an excuse a Farmdale was likely to accept.

Joseph had pulled so many strings in Washington that a Marine Corps general had been forced to fly to Carmel to explain the particulars. "Don't play games with me," Farmdale had said. "I know my son was a homosexual. But how did he die?"

After he had told the true story – all of it – the general had explained that Alex Kane would be tried, and certainly executed, for his part in the affair.

Farmdale had replied: *"The hell you say!"*

No one had ever seen the kind of assault that Washington suffered after that. There was a war in Indochina, there was a crisis in Korea, the Russians were moving in Africa, the economy was in a shambles. None of it compared to the disruption that Farmdale wrought on the capital.

No one had fully understood just how many Congressmen owed him their seats – or felt their seats threatened by the information stored in those computers of his. No one had had any idea of the range of his connections, the import of his power, the ferocity of his obsession.

It had finally risen to the White House itself. A bewildered and angry and very tired President had finally screamed at his staff: "I don't care what the hell y'all have to do. Just get that son of a bitch off my back!"

So Alex Kane had been sent home. But there was no home. There was only the memory of James, the man taken from him by a bigot who couldn't tolerate the sight of two men loving one another. Alex had fought another battle then, one that he had hoped would drown that memory in booze and self-hatred.

But the older Farmdale's connections didn't just work in Washington. They had found Kane and brought him back here to Carmel. That's where the pact had been signed. They would together fight the ignorant forces of society that would rob gay men of their dignity and their dreams. He committed himself to the most complete training that any human being had ever known. And while that was being done, Farmdale had turned his enormous and sophisticated computers and restructured them to see what the law enforcement agencies of the country refused to look at – the patterns of human destruction and degradation that entrapped homosexuals. When those patterns were discovered, Kane went into the field and removed the source – with whatever means he needed to use.

But now?

What could he offer someone like Danny Fortelli? Alex's own death never seemed to be far away. Sure, he was good, he was the best there was ... that he knew of ... so far. But there was always the one who'd be lucky and get a shot off, or there could always be the time when there were just too many of them for Alex to handle. And then? Then, Danny Fortelli would be left the way Alex had been. Alone with memories.

A nineteen-year-old had a right to more than that. And Alex had his duty. He had his obligation. He wasn't the kind of man who could retire; he didn't have the kind of job that someone else could easily fill.

He glanced over at the top of his dresser. There was the book. They were always the same. They came in Spanish red leather bindings, one of Farmdale's little touches. Never in a plain folder. Never in a manila envelope. All the evidence and all the computer printouts were there, carefully and tastefully bound together.

This one was going to be hard. Hard and painful. Alex Kane had read through the data with growing anger and intensifying fury. He had no right to indulge himself in a personal happiness with anyone like Danny Fortelli, not while that kind of thing was happening to others in this world. He had a mission to perform.

Selfish? That's what Farmdale had called him. But the real selfishness would be to abandon this life's work and retreat into a relationship. He couldn't do that. Not while there were always going to be those notebooks, those detailings of unnecessary suffering.

He'd go to Arizona. Tomorrow. He'd go and he'd do what he had to do. He had no right not to. Not while the memory of James still fought for its rightful place in his mind. Not while it still demanded vengeance.

VI

If Joe Talbot had been able to, he would have told Alex Kane to stay just where he was. No one should visit Arizona. Ever.

Joe's trip out had been deceptively pleasant. Henry Dewar had done it up right. That's for sure. The slick man, all nicely dressed in his three-piece suit and smelling of his expensive cologne, had come by nearly every day while Joe was making his decision, and still came by afterwards to make sure the old man didn't waver. There were nice speeches – pep talks, really.

Even after Joe had signed over his savings account to the man, he kept coming by. On the day he was to leave, Dewar even arranged for one of those rented limousines to take Joe and his bags and his memory trunk to the airport. "No need for you to fight with cab drivers and porters," Dewar had smiled.

The flight to Phoenix had been a joy. There had been a cute young steward who seemed to have Joe's number right from the start. God, how times had changed. It used to be that it was the stewardesses who teased an old man and made coy remarks about his still being someone who had to be watched out for. Now it was their male counterparts who did the joking.

His name had been Randy and he had taken obviously special care of Joe. "Now you're sure you're comfortable?"

he'd asked.

"Of course I am. You think I haven't flown before?" Joe had retorted.

"I'm sure you've flown. I can tell how many landings you've made in your day just by the way you're checking out my buns."

"Oh! … Now! … You!" Joe had been flustered. But he joined the young steward's laughter and did even goad along the humor with one quick little pat.

"I knew you were one of those," Randy had said with a big smile on his face. "Like fine wine, just matured into a better vintage, not flat at all."

Well! That would have made Joe's flight right there. He hadn't given a little feel to a man in years, not that way. Randy kept up the banter for the whole flight and made sure that Joe had all the tea he wanted – and an extra free cocktail as well.

After a while, when the other passengers had been taken care of, Randy had come and sat by Joe, asking where he was going, what he was going to do in Arizona. Joe had explained his move to Son Valley.

"That's *great!* Hey, do you have the address? I get to Phoenix a lot – it's my regular route – maybe I could drop by and see you sometime."

"Oh, you have better things to do with your free time," Joe had protested.

Randy had retorted: "You obviously haven't been to a gay bar in Phoenix if you think that. Come on, give me the address."

Joe, just delighted by the attention, had reached into his pocket and brought out the pamphlet. "Here it is, why don't you just take this brochure. The address is on it."

Randy had studied it. "I've never heard of this town." He looked concerned. "All they say is 'in beautiful northern Arizona.' That covers a lot of territory."

An announcement warning of turbulent weather took Randy's attention away. "I'll have to go now. I'll be back when I can."

But the rest of the flight was a busy time for the young man, and there wasn't any time for chatting. When Joe was getting off the plane Randy was standing at the head of the compartment, saying those plastic good-byes to the passengers as they disembarked. He pulled Joe aside.

"I've arranged for our service people to collect your bags for you. Just give me your stubs."

"Oh, you don't have to ..."

"I know I don't. But I want to. Just let me have the stubs." Joe obediently handed them over. Randy handed them to another uniformed airline employee. "Look, they'll be at the door, right where our luggage department is. And you watch out. I'd like to hear more about this place you're going to. Take my card." The young man handed Joe a calling card. "You write me as soon as you get there and let me know just where it is."

"All right, all right, I'll do that. And thank you for such a nice trip."

"Thanks for the goose," Randy smiled, his tanned face crinkling just a bit and those blue eyes of his sparkling brightly. Wow, if Joe had just been a little younger ...

"Now, off you go. They'll handle everything for you downstairs. Just remember to write."

Hell, if he was going to get this kind of treatment from young lookers like Sam Manetti and now this Randy fellow, Joe should just spend the rest of his life traveling, coming and going and getting all this attention. He laughed to himself as he carefully followed the signs to the airline baggage claim. What a life it's turned out to be.

•   •   •

What a life!

It had become a nightmare as soon as Joe had arrived in Son Valley. The long ride through the barren, if beautiful, Arizona countryside had left Joe fatigued. The driver hadn't been very friendly, but Joe just thought he'd been spoiled by

Randy's considerate personality.

But when they'd arrived at Son Valley Joe was really upset. Instead of a nicely designed compound there was just a single concrete block building. There was no landscaped garden. The swimming pool looked tiny. He couldn't see a recreation building. There were supposed to be cottages for the men to live in. That's what he'd been promised.

"Now, now, Mr. Talbot. Don't you worry about a thing." A stranger had walked up to the car while Joe was complaining to the unanswering driver. "Son Valley's just in the beginning stages."

"But I saw the brochure, I saw what I was promised."

"You saw our sketches, Mr. Talbot. Everything's in various stages of construction and planning. You'll see. In a short, short time Son Valley will be just the way we envisioned it. It takes time."

Joe was furious. "I don't want to sit and watch a construction site. Hell, I could have done that in New York."

The stranger stood still for a moment. His expression grew slightly threatening. The white nurse's uniform he wore didn't lessen that impression. A smile was forced across his mouth. He stuck out his hand. "I'm Norman Statton, Mr. Talbot. I'm the Head Nurse here. I see to all the details of your comfort."

Joe begrudgingly took the offered handshake. "But this is such a surprise. Such a disappointment." Damn, he should have listened to Sam Manetti.

"But I've told you, Mr. Talbot, everything in its own time. Come on inside now. You've had a long trip and you're probably tired. It's upset you to travel so far, you're not used to it. A light meal and some sleep, something to help your body adjust to the time zone change, and you'll see just how wonderful Son Valley can be."

Joe sighed. Well, he was tired. And he didn't travel well. A bed sounded just fine, he had to admit it. And he was hungry. "All right, all right. But I want to talk to the administrator first thing in the morning!"

"Of course." Statton's smile was fixed on his face. But it was quickly erased as soon as Joe had turned and begun to walk into the building. "Hurry up with that shit," he told the driver.

• • •

How long ago had that been? Joe couldn't remember exactly. It must have been the trip. That male nurse must have been right: Joe just never seemed to recover from it. He *was* old. He certainly must be old if he felt this badly.

He had taken a pill from Statton after the horrible meal of institutional foods. Joe remembered scowling at it. "I can open cans myself to get this stuff for dinner." But the real edge of his displeasure was lost that night.

He had woken up the next morning and his body seemed drained of all its energy. He had lain on the bed and had had the worst time getting himself up out of it. He had been dressed in a hospital johnny, and his ass was cold from the breeze that came up his rear end. But he was worried that he was so very tired.

He wanted to see that nurse. He had forced himself to his feet and walked out of his room. He had to keep one hand on the wall to maintain his balance as he struggled down the corridor. He was relieved to quickly come to a large room with at least a dozen other older men. All of them were sitting silently and watching some inane game show on the television.

Joe was too weak to make any noise. He had collapsed into an empty chair and just sat there. He tried to find the energy to call for Statton, but he couldn't. Before he knew it, he was asleep.

Statton woke him up – it seemed like much later. "How are you feeling, Mr. Talbot?"

"Fine, fine," Joe muttered. *Wait,* he told himself, *that's not right.* "Where's the administrator? I want to see the man in charge here." Joe's words hadn't come out with any of the force he wanted them to have.

"Oh, Mr. Etson's busy right now. Don't you worry, he makes a point out of visiting with every new resident. Now, how would you like a cup of good coffee?" Statton was holding a cup and saucer in his hand.

"Couldn't I have tea, please?" Joe asked with a whisper.

"Mr. Talbot, we can't cater to every whim in an institution like Son Valley. Coffee will do you fine. Milk? Sugar?"

"Both please," Joe capitulated easily. He took the beverage from the nurse and sipped at it. Strange flavor, he thought. But Joe hadn't drunk much coffee for years. He'd always been one for tea, himself. But the sensation of the warm liquid was pleasant enough. He finished it off quickly.

He must have spent the whole day in that chair. That and all the days that followed. How many? How many? There were tasteless meals served on trays by other men dressed in the same white uniforms that Statton wore. They didn't even put on a façade of friendliness, though. "Come on, hurry up with that plate," the one called Max had yelled at Joe one night. When he couldn't finish it soon enough, Max had taken the partially eaten food away from him.

Max scared Joe. Even in the tired frame of mind he was in, that fear got to him. He'd seen Max smack one of the other men across the face a couple times when the oldster hadn't been able to get to the john fast enough. "Clean up your own mess!" Max had screamed, forcing the man down on his hands and knees and forcing a rag and a bucket of water on him. "I'm not wiping up your piss and shit."

Max was a big bruiser, like Harry had been. He had those same thick biceps with tattoos all over them, and that heavy stomach. But he had none of the tenderness that Harry used to.

Statton kept telling Joe that he was still suffering from the effects of his journey. "It happens, you know, Mr. Talbot. When you get on in years, there's always that chance that a dislocation in your geography can produce a dislocation in your psyche as well. Here, have a pill, this should help you."

Joe had tried to get to know some of the other men who

lived in Son Valley. There was one nice looking man who must have been Joe's own age. One afternoon they had both struggled to converse.

He was Butch Senten. Said he used to be a bit-player in Hollywood. He wished he could remember a movie he'd been in by name, maybe Joe had seen it. But before his memory could work he had nodded off, back to sleep, Joe had been appalled by the look of Senten's eyes. They had been so vacant, so void of emotion or feeling. But that night Joe was even more upset. He had looked in the mirror in the communal john and saw that he, himself, had that same vacant image stamped on his own face.

How long was it until Sam called? A day, a week, more?

Statton had come to Joe in the sitting area and pulled him to his feet. "You have a friend on the phone, Mr. Talbot. Our man in New York mentioned him to us, Sam Manetti? Well, he's concerned about your well-being. I've told him before that you were having a little trouble adjusting to Arizona, the time change and all that, but he insists on talking to you anyway. Come on, why don't you come to the phone and reassure him."

While Statton pulled him over to the office on the other side of the hallway, Joe tried to remember all the things he had wanted to say to Sam. The disappointment, the fatigue, the fear of that man Max and the way he had beaten up the old guy. He needed to remember to say those things.

But both Max and Statton were standing beside him when he was handed the phone. He heard the familiar voice. "Joe, Joe, thank God you're there. They wouldn't let me talk to you. What's going on?"

Joe felt Max's strong grip on his own skinny arm. He was so tired, just standing here made him so tired. "Oh, Sam," he began, what was it he wanted to say? "Sam, I'm just so old. That trip, I tell you, that trip did me in. I just haven't felt the same since." There was something else he was going to tell Sam. What was it? His mind was hazy. Now he was glad that Max was holding him so tightly, he didn't want to fall.

"What's wrong, Joe? Tell me?" Joe couldn't really hear the honest concern behind Sam's voice.

"Nothing, nothing, I'm just old, Sam, I'm just getting old."

"I'll come out there. I'll take the next next plane out there and visit you."

"No, don't bother. I'm okay. I just have to rest for a while, kiddo. I just need to rest. I'm very tired Sam. I'm very tired."

Statton had taken the phone from Joe's hands then and said something to Sam; Joe didn't hear it. Max was pulling Joe back to his seat. "Here, Talbot," the big man said in a short while. "Here's a cup of coffee to perk you up."

Joe took the coffee and actually smiled at Max. Maybe he wasn't such a bad guy after all. Getting him a cup of coffee at a time like this.

• • •

There was another morning when Joe tried to talk to Butch Senten. This time Butch couldn't even get the words out to make a complete sentence. His mouthings were nonsensical. His eyes didn't seem to be able to focus on Joe at all.

Joe remembered his own face in that mirror, the way he had looked when he had seen his reflection. His mind struggled mightily to make all these things coherent. He still couldn't remember how long he'd been at Son Valley. But it had been too long to explain the exhaustion and the other things that seemed to be happening to him.

He did know – somehow his mind did grasp this – that Son Valley was wrong. There was something about this place that was frightening, that was affecting him. The way he went in and out of sleep, the way the staff treated him and the others, as though they were unthinking, unfeeling bodies that just had to receive a minimum of sustenance. None of the hopes he'd had for Son Valley was coming through. He hadn't seen one of the residents do a damn thing but sit and watch television.

Somehow he forced himself back to his room early one

night and took one more look at the reflection of his face in the mirror. Dimly he began to hear Bill Kurtis and Diane Sawyer talking. It was some old episode of the *CBS Morning News.* He was in the brightly lit bathroom and he could swear they were speaking to him. Something about children. Or was it old people like himself? Something. Something about homes. Something about "controlling" residents. Something about drugs.

Something about drugs.

Hell, *Joe thought to himself.* They've been doping me. I'm not sick. I'm not tired.

As woozy as he was, Joe tried to hold tightly onto the thought as he made his way over to his bed. He got in under the thin covers and desperately tried to think. All those pills they were giving him. Every time there was something off in any way Statton gave him a pill. The way he and the others kept having such a hard time with their bowels. That must be drugs too. That one old guy that Max had slapped around wasn't the only one who'd had to rush to the john.

There was a sudden alertness to Joe's mind now. He was certain he had the answer. He just couldn't let it go. Beginning tomorrow, he'd watch out for those damn pills. Maybe then he could make some sense of all this.

VII

Alex Kane didn't have a hard time making sense of Cactus City. It was like any other small county seat in the Southwest. One big main street, a few shops, a courthouse, a couple of middling hotels. It was the center of life for the surrounding area, but not one that was made for a hot time.

Alex had flown into Yuma Airport that morning and rented a car. He'd driven the three hours to Cactus City, admiring the stunning vistas that lined the highway at the same time that he was astonished by the lack of inhabitants. This was one of the most sparsely settled parts of the United States. There had been dozens and dozens of miles that Alex could travel before he saw so much as a shack on the side of the road. All of Arizona's population seemed to be clustered on the banks of a few rivers, none of which came close to this town.

He had spent some time reading local newspapers and wandering through the small stores on the street. He hadn't found a clue about anything to do with his goal in coming here. Normally Alex was able to get information quickly and easily. He'd just go to a gay bar, allow himself to be picked up and he'd have a source, almost always a good and trustworthy one. But Cactus City wasn't going to have a gay bar. Not by a long shot.

When Alex had wandered into the one decent looking

restaurant in town he wasn't expecting anything but a beer and a meal. It was immediately obvious that the other people in the dining room's bar had greater expectations.

It was Friday night and the working people of Cactus City were celebrating loud and heavy. Alex smiled at some of their antics and made his way to the bar. He ordered his usual Budweiser and overtipped the bartender. He turned to face the crowd and study it some more, resting his elbows on the mahogany surface behind him.

As he scanned the people that were gathered he noticed a single male standing in the corner across the way. Alex Kane had no time to waste on seducing straight men; he couldn't be bothered with all the games that came with them. But he did decide that this man certainly looked interesting.

The people here were dressed in the expected western clothes for the most part. Some, probably lawyers, bankers and salesmen, were wearing an embarrassment of pastel polyester – they must have thought that was the "in" thing this year. The women looked as though they shopped out of a J.C. Penney catalog, and they probably did. All in all the group was happy, easily singing along when a favorite country and western tune came over the loudspeaker, laughing loudly to their jokes and just pleased that the weekend had arrived.

It was easy enough for Alex to get moody in these situations. It was always so appealing to look at what appeared to be simple lives and to want to have that kind of existence for himself. If he was just another guy living in Cactus City then most of his problems would be solved. But that was an impossible speculation. He wasn't just another guy, and he never would be again – if he ever had been before.

Alex drove those little touches of self-pity from his mind and scanned the room again. That same man was still standing in his corner, still slouched against the wall. Alex looked at him for perhaps a beat too long. Then he took his eyes away. If this had been a gay bar Alex would have sworn the man was cruising him.

Could he be?

Alex looked back. The stranger had a bigger smile on his face now that he had caught Alex's attention. He nodded his head in a slight but overtly friendly manner. Alex certainly would have been interested if this had been a gay bar. The guy was at least Alex's own six feet. He had a shock of curly blond hair and a thick blond moustache. His teeth gleamed when he did smile. The eyes were a light blue, noticeably light even from this distance.

The jeans and cowboy shirt he wore showed a lot of wear. But they were also made for the man's body. The denim pants hugged his solid thighs and bulged at his crotch. The shirt was only buttoned halfway up. The hair on his chest – so unexpected on a blond – was thick and just as curly as that on his head. The skin was darkly tanned.

The man winked.

What the hell! Alex thought, more surprised than he was used to being. The guy must have sensed that. His smile broke out even more. He stood straight and walked over to where Alex was standing. His hand was outstretched. "Luke McDavid," he introduced himself.

Alex took that handshake and made his own introduction.

"I know you're not from here," Luke said, "I know everyone in this town."

"California," Alex explained. He always used Farmdale's address when he had to have one. The reality was that Kane lived most of his life in a succession of hotel rooms. But that was too difficult to explain to most people.

"Here on business?"

"Yeah. I'm looking into some property near here for someone."

"Ranching?"

"Maybe."

"Well, I have a great idea. If you want to talk ranch land, you *have* to talk to Luke McDavid. I just happen to know everything there is to know about such things in this whole county. And I will insist on sharing all that knowledge with you ... over dinner."

The smile and the invitation were both authentic and added up to an honest to god come-on. Alex smiled, "I'd be happy to have dinner with you. But if you're giving the information, I guess I better pick up the tab."

"Don't be silly. No one picks up the tab in Cactus City when he's with Luke McDavid. You just come on over to the dining room of this establishment and we'll get down to some serious talking ... about business."

Alex followed the big man to the other side of the partition where the tables were set for the evening meal. Luke didn't wait for a hostess, he just picked out a place in the far comer and led Alex over to it.

They sat down and Luke began to ask Alex some more questions about what type of real estate he was looking for. Kane had done his homework for the assignment; he had learned all the right terms and key words about a transaction like this from Farmdale.

A waitress came up and handed each of them a menu. "Rebecca, how's my sweetheart?"

"Oh, Luke McDavid, don't you go playing those games with me. You've broken more than enough hearts in this town, leading poor girls on to think they could get ahold of what they can never have. Bad enough it's you; you don't have to go importing more good-looking men we can't hope for." The waitress looked right at Alex Kane and sighed. "Why are all your *friends* so damn good-looking?" Rebecca shook her head and walked away, leaving the menus in their hands.

"What the hell's your story?" Alex Kane asked, not angrily, with a touch of humor in his voice. "I just don't understand how you can act this way in a small town. You came on to me as though we were in a bar on Folsom Street or Christopher, not in Cactus City. Then the waitress in the local steak house treats it like it's just matter-of-fact that we're gay. You haven't even said anything to me yet. How could you have been so sure?"

Luke obviously enjoyed all this. His eyes sparkled more

181

brightly. "Oh, well, so far as you're concerned, I was sure only because you were looking back. Now, all that sixth sense we're supposed to have about one another is foolishness. But there is a certain way that men look at one another and let each other know that something's going on. You had it. You looked back. I didn't do all that by myself, you know.

"Besides, there are things you notice. You aren't a cowboy, I would've known if you were. But you got the right kind of jeans on and boots and all. And you aren't wearing a gold chain – that's a straight man's dead giveaway, they all wear gold chains around here. No cologne, either, though I didn't know that till I got close-up, of course. You're also too good-looking. Straight men have bellies by the time they're your age – about thirty or a little more?"

Alex shook his head in agreement. "Thirty-two."

"See, and you got a body like a high school athlete. Put all that together and it spells gay.

"Rebecca? Well, after a while, in a small place like this, the word gets around. Small towns aren't as bad as most people think, not really. Now, you can't go and seduce their children and they might have trouble if you wanted to have a gay liberation parade down the center of town or something. And I know you would have trouble if you were a newcomer. But I was born and raised in Cactus City and they all know me and they've known me forever. I just let them joke and I joke back and we all keep it at a friendly enough level.

"They're used to my having a *friend* come and visit every once in a while, though it's been a long while this time around, I must admit. So, they just take a few liberties."

"How do you manage – just with friends visiting?"

"Oh, the old animal urges get to me and I make some mad dashes to Los Angeles or Las Vegas when that happens. I have a little plane of mine out in the county airport for just those events. I used to have some visitors – you know, married men in the dead of night, the kind that are scared to shit that someone will see their car in my driveway, so they'd walk two miles instead. But that got to be more trouble than it was worth, so I cut it out.

"Thing is, I'm happiest here. I've tried to live other places, but I just can't hack the city and its ways. So I don't get laid as often as I'd like, but I get things I care about more. Not that I don't like it when I do get my chance to climb in the sack." Luke lifted up his bottle of beer and playfully toasted Alex.

"Pretty presumptuous, aren't you?"

"Hell, Mr. Kane, it isn't presumption to say I'm the best fuck in Cactus City. I'm probably the only one!" Luke took a deep drink of his beer and slammed it down on the table. "What you see in front of you is all you're going to get here. And something tells me, you've done a hell of a lot worse in your time."

Alex really did like Luke's puckish manner. And if he really was a native, he fit the usual category of Kane's sexual partners: men who had information they'd give in exchange for a night with him. Looking at the way the man's shirt had spread open when he had leaned across the table just now, revealing a larger look at that hairy chest with those well-developed pectorals, Alex was perfectly willing to concede that this was going to be a pleasure.

Rebecca was suddenly back beside them. "Now, what you going to have?" she asked. "Least, what you going to have that's on the menu and that's legal?"

Luke smiled at Alex. "If you follow my lead and have a sirloin steak, rare, a salad with house dressing, a baked potato and we split a side of onion rings, you'll have a damned good meal. You choose anything else, I am not responsible for your doctor bills."

"You win. That sounds fine."

"Two Luke specials," Rebecca said as she gathered up the menus. "You wouldn't have done too bad with the fried chicken. It's not bad tonight."

"All that means," Luke insisted, "is that it's not deadly poison tonight."

"McDavid, you are a pain in the butt. Or at least I wish you would be. Just once, I surely do wish you would be." With an exaggerated sigh, she left.

Luke and Alex talked easily for a while longer. Then Rebecca was back. She put a bottle of French wine on the table. Alex was impressed. He recognized it as a particularly good St. Emilion, one that Farmdale enjoyed. Luke had taken a corkscrew that Rebecca had placed beside the bottle and was opening it. He saw the question in Alex's face.

"Well, you see, when it was time for me to go off to college, my daddy and me finally compromised. I'd study animal husbandry, the way he wanted, if he'd let me go to Cornell, the way I wanted. I picked up a few things out East. Let's just say that a taste for good wine was one of the less exotic."

Rebecca returned with two glasses for them. Luke poured each of them full. "I had them stock a couple of cases of this for me. Private stock, you could say. I eat here a lot. Gets a bit lonely eating by myself all the time. Even if all I get is some background noise from these fools it helps a lot. I got some business in town often enough, anyway, bankers, insurance men and the like. So I try to do it here.

"Back home I get a little more fancy in the kitchen than just steak and potatoes, anyhow. Another of the exotic things I picked up at Cornell."

"A gourmet cowboy?"

"Well, hell, those gay genes got to come out some way besides my cock and asshole!" Luke loved that joke and nearly spilt his wine as he laughed.

The dinner was as good as Luke had promised. The steak wasn't the chemically tenderized stuff of a big city restaurant. It had a firm texture and full taste to it that burst in Alex's mouth. The wine went with it perfectly. The potato was baked to perfection – not microwaved, he knew that. The salad dressing had been made with buttermilk and some tart spices. By the time they were done Alex thought he had gained at least another ten pounds. He was sitting back in his chair, contented and happy with the food and the company.

"I do hope you're expecting this little evening to continue," Luke said. His voice wasn't as challenging or joking now.

It had a touch of seduction in it, soft and alluring in a way, though nothing that came from the big man's mouth could ever be less than masculine.

"Oh yes," Alex replied. "I most definitely am."

"Good. The coffee here's for shit. Why don't we just get along. Don't worry about the check; I insist on paying it. You're a guest in our fair city, I have a tab here, and Rebecca will just take care of it all for us."

"You're on," Alex said.

•   •   •

They drove over the backroads after leaving the state highway. Luke's place was at least twenty miles from Cactus City, but that kind of distance didn't mean much in this part of the country. Alex Kane knew that.

The ride wasn't all that comfortable. Luke drove a monster of a four-wheel-drive truck. It bounced and jerked with every bump. It didn't buffer its occupants from the realities of the highway like Kane's rental car did with its super-suspension and power steering and power brakes and god knows what else.

They stopped at one point. Luke had been giving Alex a guided tour through this part of Arizona, and now he pointed out a large and imposing Victorian mansion. It was slightly out of place in the middle of the near-desert. "That's where I grew up." There was a wistful tone to Luke's voice.

"Do your parents still live there?"

"Nah, they're long dead. It's been at least ten years since." He put the vehicle back in drive and started them on their way again. "My father built it for my mother when they got married. He was trying to make it easier for her to move here. Didn't do much good, the woman always wanted to be back East – she was from Baltimore. She hid it as well as she could, but we always knew.

"She'd keep on trying to civilize everyone around here. She'd have poetry readings and musical evenings and all that.

Dad was the biggest rancher around, so all the wives of all the others would feel obligated to come. But they didn't really have any passion to match her interest in art. She tried to get it going in me. But I was drawn out to the range with my father.

"She was a good woman. Like I say, she tried to hide things, but there used to be this look on her face when Dad and me would go out in the morning, most often on horseback in those days. We'd try to contain ourselves in the house and be proper gentlemen for her, but our hearts were always outside. If she hadn't loved the two of us so very much, I guess she would've left this place long ago. But she stayed till her last days.

"I loved them both. And I loved that house. But it was a woman's house. Dad and me always let it be that. When they'd gone, I just couldn't see a bachelor living there with all the flowery wallpaper and the fine antiques she'd collected. It's off to a corner of the property, so it was easy enough to divide that acre it sits on and let it go on the market. I built myself my own kind of house further in. More my own style."

Alex soon got to see what Luke's "own style" was. The house was a single story building, sleekly lined and showing the sharpest attention to architectural design. It was constructed of obviously local materials – rough stone and hand-hewn wood combined in a way that allowed the structure to almost melt into the natural surroundings. It was understated, at least in the sense that Alex wasn't really aware of how large or luxurious it was at first glance.

After Luke had parked the car he led the way into the house. At first it appeared to be one gigantic room. A state-of-the-art kitchen was separated only by a waist-high divider. Food processors, pasta machines, microwave ovens – all the latest gadgets were evident. The floors of the room were stone, but not cool to Alex's feet when he had followed Luke's example and left his own boots by the door. Obviously there were heating elements in the material.

The inside walls were of the same rock and wood as the

exterior. There was an enormous fireplace at the opposite end of the room from the kitchen. Only a few large pieces of furniture formed an arc facing the hearth. Between them and the cooking area was a huge and obviously handmade dining ensemble. It was almost baronial in size and appearance.

Farmdale would have been comfortable in a place like this, Alex realized. Luke, whatever else, was rich.

The cowboy had sauntered down the other end of the room and was striking a large wooden match to light the already assembled wood in the fireplace. When the flames had begun to flicker he turned to Alex. "It'll take a while for this to really get going. Want to warm up in the hot tub first?"

"Hot tub?"

Luke gestured to the side wall of the room. Alex hadn't noticed the large sliding glass doors. Outside was a wooden platform, the centerpiece of which was a wooden tub. Alex smiled, "This is the life of a cowboy?"

"Yep – 1980s version," Luke answered. He began to unbutton his shirt as he went to the doors. "Come on, let me show you how the latest model works – hot tub, that is."

"I don't need to know how a hot tub works," Alex said as he watched Luke pull his shirt off.

"Well, then, I guess you'll just have to be satisfied with the basic cowboy model's way of doing things." Stripped to the waist Luke walked over to where Alex stood and wrapped his arms around the dark haired man. They kissed. Luke stood back suddenly. "Jesus!" He said the word in two long syllables. "What the hell was that all about?"

Alex Kane smiled. People often reacted to him that way. He had trained his body to be the most efficient tool possible. The countless hours of work and exercise and physical awareness had had a bonus effect. Those same things that had made him a fearsome fighter had created a depth of sexual ability that always seemed to take people by surprise. A simple kiss, a light embrace, a tender caress, any of them became greatly magnified when Alex performed them.

"It's just something you learn." Alex gave Luke his stock

answer.

"Well, teacher, I want some more lessons. Right now." He grabbed Alex's arms and pulled him to the patio.

Luke was naked in a matter of minutes. He was gingerly lowering his body into the steaming, swirling water of the hot tub. The slow entry gave Alex a chance to appreciate just how well-built Luke was. That blond hair seemed to cover all his body with a thick coating, but not one so thick that Luke's muscles weren't obvious.

Finally Luke's torso was submerged. "What's the matter, you shy or something?"

Alex just smiled. He finished unbuttoning his own shirt and pulled it off. He peeled off his socks, then unbuckled his belt and let the jeans fall to the ground. His undershirt came next. Its removal was enough to evoke a low whistle from Luke. "Just like a fucking statue."

Alex Kane's body didn't have the bulk that Luke's did, but those torturous exercises had produced a definition and a sharpness of each individual muscle that left him looking as though he had been the model for most of the great art work of ancient Greece. But when he slipped down his cotton briefs and stood totally naked in front of Luke, the cowboy had other thoughts in mind. "Hell, no wonder they put a fig leaf over that! They'd have half the men and half the women fainting dead away."

Alex smiled again and walked over to the tub. When he put his first foot into the water he understood why Luke had taken so long to immerse himself. It was hot! The cowboy reached over and took one of Alex's calves in his hand. "Smooth like silk," he seemed to say to himself. Then he raised his voice, "Just slide in slow and easy. You'll get used to it."

Alex followed the advice and soon had almost all his body in the water. The unseen jets made the tub into a mechanical massage device. The pounding flow of water relaxed his muscles and the warmth was seductive all by itself – and in addition, Luke was giving it plenty of help. The man had gently taken Alex's cock and balls in his palm and seemed to hold them carefully and almost lovingly.

"Not often I get to have this, a hot man in my hot tub, my hands on his crotch. Feels good." Luke's voice was low and sensual.

"It's a big place for a single guy, Luke."

"Yeah," Luke was still fondling Alex intimately. "I always hoped maybe I'd find someone to move in with me. That's why I wanted a man's house, not something like my mother's, but I guess I always hoped I'd have another man to share it."

Luke probably felt Alex stiffen. "Oh, don't worry," he reassured him. "I know the signals well enough. You're not one to want to move out to Arizona and live in the desert for the rest of your life. I'm not going to make any moves like that on you."

"Sorry, Luke."

"Sorry? Hell, I knew who you were and I had an idea what you were as soon as I saw you. You don't have the hunter's look about you. That kind of hunter I mean anyway. You're an honest, open guy, okay by me. You're a big boy and so am I. This is for tonight, maybe one or two other times while you're in town. That doesn't bother me. But you asked me a question and I gave you an answer."

Luke moved slightly away from Alex. His mind was drifting. "You know, I thought I had that once, that guy. When you asked me back at the restaurant if I did much and I said not recently, it was because of him. Liked him a lot, really did. He was from L.A., that's where I met him. Lust at first sight. So, we thought everything would be perfect. I had the house, he could just get some kind of job in the town to make himself feel independent – it's hard when you got a place like I do and the money to go with it, people are always worried about taking too much from you.

"But, it was like my mother all over again. He was a fish out of water. He wanted theater and movies and god only knows what else." Luke was far, far away now. "It was hard to watch it happen. He did all those things that my mother didn't. He started to blame me, find unnecessary fault in me.

"You could just see it, like it was a movie script. At first he was willing to try anything so long as it meant we could do things together. I taught him to ride and we'd go all over hell on horseback. I was even teaching him how to fly that plane of mine, thinking he could go over to Phoenix or up to Las Vegas when he wanted to to get his culture-fix.

"But then it soured. You could watch his reactions as they changed. Everything was wrong. There was nothing good about the place, the desert, the state, the truck, the plane, nothing had a single redeeming value. Then, one day, he understood that what he was saying was something different. He was saying that *I* didn't have any redeeming value. And that was that. Two years and good-bye!"

They sat in the water silently for a spell. "Do you want me to leave, Luke?" Alex felt he had to ask the question, the cowboy had left him so far behind.

"Oh, hell, no!" It was as though Luke had been awakened from a trance. "Hell, no! After all this time I got a number like you in my paws, you think I'm going to let him go? You're crazy." He pulled Alex to him. Kane let the big hairy man drag him over and embrace him. Luke's hands found Alex's cock again. "I'm perfectly happy with a perfectly honest night with a good man. I'm downright appreciative!

"I shouldn't go on about things in the past. I learned my lesson. I won't try to take any more fish out of water. But that sure as hell doesn't mean I can't try to find myself an amphibian!"

They got out of the tub soon after that. Naked, dripping with water that Luke told Alex to ignore, they went inside. The fire was roaring, its bright flames sending wild and energetic shadows over all the walls. There was a large bear skin spread in front of the fireplace. Luke collapsed on top of it, face up, looking right at Alex.

"Like what you see as much as I like what I see?" Luke asked. He had spread his legs. His cock was slowly but surely filling with lust – it had begun to arc up, away from the nest of blond pubic hair. His balls were pulled so tightly beneath it that they were nearly invisible. But Alex had seen how very large they were.

Kane dropped to his knees beside Luke. His own cock was becoming erect. He reached over and laid a palm on Luke's warm belly, where the beads of water from the tub had plastered the body hair to his skin. Alex ran his hand up and down, each movement taking his palm closer first to Luke's nipples, then to Luke's now fully hard cock. Alex kept up the motion, coaxing Luke on and on to a higher peak of passion.

Eventually his hands found those hardened pieces of flesh on Luke's chest. After a bit of pressure Luke moaned as the nipples were manipulated. Alex kept up the luring actions until Luke surrendered to his peaking passion and lifted his hips off the floor.

"Please, Alex, oh, man ... please."

VIII

Alex sipped the coffee slowly. It was hot, fresh from the pot Luke had just made. He imagined that Luke needed his own cup as much as Alex needed this one. It had been a very, very long night.

"Is that what happens when you leave a man up in the mountains all alone for too long?" Alex finally asked.

"That's right." Luke had a big smile on his face. He was obviously pleased with everything that had occurred. "I told you I had developed some pretty exotic tastes those years I was back East. Haven't had much time to practice on them for a while."

Alex felt the remnants of Luke's practice in his now tender nipples and his well-used body – front and back. "You know, I'm used to being the one who tires other people out. Not the one who nearly has to cry 'Uncle.'"

"Didn't do that, though, did you?" Luke continued. "Are you sure you aren't an amphibian?"

"Sorry, Luke," Alex knew the cowboy was basically joking; he didn't think he had to be defensive any more. "If I'm going to settle down, I'm afraid I already know who it'll be with."

"'If?'"

"If." Alex heard a harshness in his own voice. "It's not at all a sure thing."

"Seems a shame that someone like you is roaming around

unbranded. Seems you should have found something by now – someone."

"Some men just aren't cut out for it. Their work, their obligations ..." Alex let his voice trail off.

Luke stirred his coffee a bit. "Well, I won't argue with you about it. That's a man's own business. But since you are the one who brought up work, why don't you tell me what you really do? Why are you really in Cactus City?"

"I told you."

"Nah, you told a good story, and one that would've fooled a whole lot of people. But not me. I know land and land sales like the back of my hand. You had the lingo down well enough, but you really aren't any kind of investor. It didn't fit. When we were at dinner it didn't bother me much. I just figured you had something you didn't want to tell a total stranger. But I don't think I'm a total stranger any more and I'd like to know just what it is you're up to."

Alex hesitated. But it only lasted a moment. He instinctively trusted Luke. This was a man he could rely on. Whenever he had followed that kind of instinct before it had proven a wise move.

"It's a long story, Luke. A pretty bad one. One that's going to make you really mad and really angry. One that you might just as soon never hear."

Luke looked seriously at Alex Kane. "I'm here to listen to whatever it is you got to tell me. So long as I'm not going to be getting mad at you, you don't have to worry."

Luke stood up and motioned for Alex to follow him over to the big, comfortable chairs that faced the fireplace. The two men sat close to each other and Alex started to tell his story.

He didn't give Luke all the details of his own history – just enough to make the tale whole. He didn't tell Luke that there was a man named Joseph Farmdale who owned the most sophisticated computer set-up in the civilian world, one that did double duty; it didn't just oversee Farmdale's far-flung holdings, it also tracked crime and corruption all across the country. It looked for patterns that law enforcement agencies wanted to avoid seeing, it observed the progress of a people that the rest of the world would just as soon have disappear.

Those computer banks had information that saw the vicious progress of gay oppression all across America and even in other parts of the industrialized world. When all the particles of data came together and formed a message that only they could read, then Alex Kane was brought in. That is, Alex Kane was brought in if Farmdale's army of lawyers and political connections couldn't right the situation through normal legal channels.

They had discovered something right here in Cactus County. And as soon as he began to tell Luke about the discovery, once he didn't have to worry about telling the cowboy too much about his own personal history and his connection with Farmdale, Alex became utterly specific.

"We're able to keep track of obituaries of gay men. Obviously there aren't many that say, 'This man was a homosexual.' But sometimes there are ways to know that that's what's going on. There are the euphemisms: 'He left behind a life-long companion,' or 'His personal secretary of the last three decades will administer his estate.' That kind of thing. The estate aspect gave us more data to fill in. By keeping track of probate courts we could also know what single men had made what other single men their heirs.

"Now, that might not be foolproof, but it's more than a little good. It's as close as anyone's going to get to identifying elderly gays. What we did was keep the survivors' names and addresses in the computers. There were all kinds of possibilities involved, maybe some research at some point, who knows." Alex was hedging a bit now. He wasn't quite honest with Luke. The whole truth was that Farmdale and Kane had decided that if *they* could identify a group of gay men, someone else could find a similar way to do it. Their real purpose was to make sure there was no sudden and otherwise inexplicable motif of harm that came to any of the groups.

"So, we knew about a group of elderly gay men – obviously most of the survivors were getting along in years. Then, without any obvious cause, they started to die, and they started to die quickly. The numbers weren't large enough to bring them to anyone else's attention, but they were too large for us to ignore, especially because of one peculiar connection."

"What's that?" Luke was fascinated by Kane's story.

"Most of them were dying in Cactus County, Arizona."

Luke's jaw fell open. "Here?" Alex nodded his head. "In Cactus County? How the hell ... Alex, I already told you I know everyone in Cactus County. I certainly would know if anyone was really gay. There are a couple closet cases I see in a bar in Yuma or Las Vegas once in a while, but there's no one –"

"None of them is from here, Luke. They just die here. That's the problem. There's no logical connection. But their bodies are discovered in this county. This is where their death certificates are filed.

"It's not that there have been enormous numbers. Not yet anyway. It's the outrageous coincidence that brought it to our attention. Otherwise, well, on a one-by-one basis, there's nothing that would have made anyone else find it strange. One man was dressed as a bum and his body found by the side of a highway. It probably never made the papers. Another man had been registered in a local motel. When the maid found his corpse, the management probably did everything they could to keep it quiet. Dead men aren't good advertising."

"I know about that," Luke said. "Rebecca's cousin was the maid. And you're right, they did hush it up."

"They hushed it up four times in four different motels. The sheriff probably should have made some connections, or the coroner."

Luke shook his head. "They're both half-assed. We don't have much need for that kind of stuff here. We just let some guys who'd have a hard time finding work fill out the forms and such. The few times there's really the need for police work, we call in the state troopers. If we really needed a forensic investigation done, the state would handle that, too. So there have been five deaths here?"

"More. But all the bodies found in such a way that publicity would be avoided or else it would appear to have been an understandable accident. The only thing: they were all old, and rich, gay men."

"Rich? Money's involved as well?"

"It usually is in murder. Not great amounts, not millionaires, but all the men had had some kind of retirement account, savings of at least $100,000. When they left their homes, their accounts were closed. That money's never shown up in any other bank."

"You can be sure of that?"

How could Alex explain to Luke that the one thing that they could always be sure of was Joseph Farmdale's knowledge of banks in the United States? "Trust me, I'm sure."

Luke stood up and paced over to the fireplace. He leaned against it, a hand on the mantelpiece. He was lost in his own thoughts. He didn't speak for a few minutes. "You always think these things – things that happen to us – are in the city. Somehow you get lulled into thinking that it just happens in San Francisco or New York – the political stuff, the things they call 'oppression.' Here in Cactus City I've always been able to prove to myself that it was just a question of fucking and sucking, a private matter that my neighbors wouldn't complain about so long as I didn't make it a big issue. But now you're telling me that old gay men are dying here – and just because they're gay."

Luke turned and looked at Alex. "I guess I'm just going to have to own up to the fact that I can't ignore the shit. I can't make believe it doesn't happen here, that it just happens in some other places, to some other people, by others that are never going to come after me."

Alex was suddenly thrown back in time, back to a jungle in Vietnam. He was holding on to the lifeless body of his lover, James, and looking up at the sneering face of the Marine sergeant who had just murdered him. "No, Luke, you can't think it's going to happen just where you want it to. You never can count on it being in just one place."

They were quiet for a minute longer. "I got the best fore-man in Arizona. I have a full complement of hands on the ranch. There's nothing I have to do that can't wait. I'm working with you on this one, Alex. Honest to god, I'm working with you."

IX

Joe's mind worked for him. Just enough. The morning after he'd realized that the staff was giving him some kind of strong psychotic drug, he started to work against them. It was long, slow and painful. He wasn't able to fool them all the time, but he fooled them enough that his senses started to come back to him – just enough.

He would take the pills they'd hand him and put them in his mouth. But as soon as the attendant's back was turned he spit out the tablet and slipped it into his pocket. The first day he realized he had only taken two of the four doses. The next morning he could already feel the effect: he was much more alert. There was still that feeling of overwhelming lethargy, but it wasn't so deadening.

He was able to keep himself to a maximum of two of their pills a day; often he'd get by with only having to take one. It was a tremendous relief to feel the difference. He had been convinced back there that he had slipped into total senility, but now his mind was sharpening.

But not enough. What was the problem? It couldn't be just the pills. He kept on trying to figure out the source of the waves of near incoherency he'd sense come over him, the confusion that would take away his prized periods of lucidity. He was sipping a cup of coffee one morning, watching that mean one – Max – as he handed out the others. Then it came to him. It was the coffee! That explained so much: why he'd wake up feeling great and then lose that as soon as he had come into the sitting room and take his place with the other residents. Of course, that's why they were always filling up the cups and why they kept on saying that a little coffee would perk up the spirits. Hell, it was drugged too.

He knew he had to be careful. He couldn't let them know that he was liberating himself from the chemical controls they thought they had on him. He kept on sitting quietly in his chair and blankly watching television as though nothing had changed. But he kept on spitting out the pills and only making believe he was downing the coffee, most of which he poured into the big potted plant that stood beside what had come to be known as his chair.

With his clarity he was able to study the place more carefully. And he was forced to see it more fully. Now he realized that Son Valley was even worse than he had expected, even worse than he had realized when he had arrived.

It was the kind of dreary building with colorless construction that was used in so many institutions. The cinderblock walls were all painted in a sickening pale green, the tile floors were a monotonous beige. The furniture was all metal framed with plastic upholstery. There was precious little of it.

As time went on, it seemed that Joe was actually seeing everything for the first time. Things like his room: he had never realized how minimally it was furnished. It had a standard hospital bed with plastic coverings for the mattress underneath the cheap sheets. A bedstand, a metal dresser to match and a single chair was the rest of it. There wasn't even a rug on the cold linoleum floor or a shower mat in the bathroom.

Joe had seen plenty of the new buildings elsewhere that were designed for easy access for the elderly and the handicapped; this place had none of those helpful aids that were supposed to be there – the handles to let you get on and off the pot or the grips to make it easy for you to climb in and out of the bathtub.

Most of the other men were at least as old as Joe. It was

hard to tell because of the medications they must have been on – the same ones the staff had given Joe – but they also seemed to be in much worse shape than he was. The lack of staff was apparent. There was the stench of shit in the air from those men unable to wipe themselves well, and from the stale urine that was trapped in their johnnies. The gowns were changed infrequently.

And there were bruises.

It was bad enough that Joe thought they happened when the guys fell. But he quickly realized that the beating he had seen Max give hadn't been an isolated incident. The staff thought nothing of slapping around one or two of the residents if there was a hint of inconvenience or trouble.

Joe's lucidity was bringing a lot of fear with it. This place wasn't just bad – it was dangerous.

Then Joe finally did meet the administrator – Mr. Etson. He and Statton had stood right by Joe as though he hadn't been there. They obviously didn't feel a need to be careful in what they said in front of him. Joe tried hard to control his anger and not let them know just how aware of them he was.

"That kid call again?" Etson asked. He was a fat man; his western style suit could barely contain the gross gut on him. "Last thing we need is some New York busybody calling in the authorities."

"Don't worry about it." Statton dismissed the question. "We've had Dewar go back and show the kid some photographs we faked. Yeah, he calls, but there's always been a good reason to keep him at arm's length. We even faked some medical records for Dewar to bring him to convince him that nothing's strange. They show the guy's just slipping into senility for perfectly understandable medical reasons."

"The whole point of this scam was that there weren't going to be any families worrying about shit. Now we got that kid and another."

"Another?"

"Yeah, old movie star over there has some other guy all hot and bothered about him. Guess they were in movies together when the other guy was a child actor. Now he wants to move him to some fancy place with the money the friend's got coming in from residuals all of a sudden."

"Well, let him. He won't remember anything. We can put together good enough looking records for him."

"And give up all the cash he signed over? You're out of your mind."

"You're getting too greedy, Etson. Don't hold onto everything too tight or you'll end up sorry."

"Don't give me lectures on how to run this business. You just attend to your duties. Which reminds me, the bills for the kitchen are getting way out of hand. Can't you cut back?"

"More! For God's sake, Etson, they're not even close to the dietary plans they should have."

"Listen to you! Christ, it makes me sick to hear you playing like a real nurse."

"I *am* a real nurse." Etson had hit some painful button in Statton's insides.

"A real nurse, but only by the skin of your teeth. They nearly got you on that rap back in Iowa. You're lucky they didn't throw you in jail."

"Shove it, Etson. We fixed that. I did get a license back."

"Well, I tell you what. You just remember who it was that got that paperwork done – you think about it while you figure out how you're going to cut back some more on those food bills. This ain't no charity."

•　•　•

Joe knew he had to move as fast as he could. He went into Butch Senten's room that night and shook the man awake. "Huh?" Butch had responded sleepily after Joe had jostled him.

"Listen to me, Butch, and listen good. Don't drink the coffee. Don't drink the coffee." Joe whispered as loud as he dared.

The man's eyes looked blankly at Joe. "Please, Butch, you have to stop drinking the coffee in the morning." There wasn't any recognition. Joe decided his best hope was to plant the idea in Butch's mind as best he could. He repeated the message over and over again, shaking the man whenever he seemed to be falling back to sleep. Only when Joe heard voices in the hallway did he stop and then carefully make his way back to his own room.

• • •

The next morning Joe watched Butch carefully. He saw the puzzled expression on Butch's face when the actor studied his cup as though he were remembering something about it. The something Joe had told him. Butch looked up and his vacant eyes searched the room, finally landing on Joe's face. Joe silently shook his head, no.

Joe thought he'd yell for joy when he saw Butch pour the muddy liquid into the paper-filled wastebasket beside him. Butch must have found that same tiny reservoir of resistance that Joe had discovered in himself.

They'd be in this together.

• • •

Joe carefully monitored Butch's caffeine intake for three days before he dared to make his night-time visit again. When he snuck into the room this time Butch was awake.

"How do you feel?"

"Still woozy, still real weak," Butch answered.

"It's going to be okay. Just keep on finding ways not to drink the coffee and don't take any of their pills if you can help it. I just put mine under my tongue and hold it there till they turn around. Sometimes I make believe I've swallowed it if I think they're getting suspicious."

Butch nodded in agreement. "What's this all about? This isn't what I thought was going to happen."

"Me neither," Joe whispered. "I don't know what the whole story is yet, but I know it's not good. Now, you go back to sleep and don't worry. If you can get down to one or two pills a day the way I did, we'll figure something out."

"Okay, partner, but I got to tell you I'm scared."

"You? I'm not just shivering from the cold. I have to get back before they miss me."

Joe had been good when he had acted as though he were still taking his pills. Butch was so good – he was trained at it, after all – that he fooled Joe sometimes. But the two of them became increasingly coherent with every day.

Statton and the rest of the employees obviously were confident that their drugs were doing the jobs for them. They grew increasingly lax in the way they oversaw the residents. They'd come by only at readily predictable times with coffee, meals or pills. Butch and Joe were able to move their chairs even closer together and to talk in soft tones without anyone growing suspicious.

"I heard them say someone's trying to get you out of here," Joe told Butch.

"Who?"

"I didn't hear a name, but some young guy you used to act with when he was a kid."

"Oh," Butch was annoyed, "that was Rick Adams. We were in some western television things together. We'd play these roles, that I was his grandfather, and he never got over that. Keeps thinking I *am* his grandfather, especially once he found out we were both queer. Damn nuisance, that kid. Always coming by and bothering me ..."

"Well, the thing is, he's concerned and he might spring you. He was putting so much pressure on these guys they were talking about letting you be transferred. Look, if you do, you have to get a hold of someone for me, Sam Manetti. He lives on East Third Street in Manhattan. Tell him to get me out of here."

"Hell," Butch whispered back, "I'm not waiting for Rick or Sam or anybody. I'm going to leave myself."

"We have to watch out, Butch. These guys are mean. We don't even have our clothes. Didn't you notice your dresser and your closet are empty? Mine are, too. We have no transportation. Nothing ..."

"We have our rights."

"Keep your voice down! We have no rights here. You've seen what these men are like. They have our money and they don't want to give it up. They're not going to care about rights. They've already broken enough laws to keep them in jail for a lifetime."

"The phone," Butch wondered out loud.

"Yeah, that's the hope. We have to figure out who works the front desk, and when if there's a way to divert him, maybe when there's only one guy on the night shift, maybe the other one of us can call and get help."

"It makes sense to me." Butch's voice was hopeful more than anything else.

"It has to make sense," Joe insisted. "I can't see any other way out of here."

X

Luke and Alex both fell into their chairs at the restaurant. It had been a long day – and it hadn't produced any results. "I just can't think of another place to look, Alex," the rancher confessed. "Just like you thought, they've covered their tracks well. That old horse's ass of a coroner just accepted everything at face value. So did the sheriff. Just cut and dried deaths by natural causes."

Alex was brooding. They had gone back over all the records in Cactus County. None of the officials had noticed anything really out of the ordinary until the questions he and Luke had posed made things seem connected. But there should have been more in a sparsely populated area like this one. For anything this large to be going on, there should have been something that people had noticed – a new building, strangers moving into town, sudden wealth, something.

"I don't think it's happening here in Cactus, Luke," Alex finally said. "They're bringing the dead men here, but the acts aren't being committed here."

"Hell, this county borders on so many others that we're talking about half the state of Arizona – and probably parts of Nevada and California. Besides, they were deaths by natural causes. The county coroner's a fool, but he's not that stupid that he'd overlook an obvious murder."

"Oh, the murders weren't obvious, I agree to that. But

they were murders. I looked at those records very closely, Luke. Sometimes your mind just wants to see certain things, that or it expects them and so it doesn't find anything strange about their being there."

"What are you talking about?" Luke asked.

"There were five deaths that the coroner had records on. He hadn't even done autopsies; he didn't think it necessary. I didn't mention it, but there are at least six more involved in the past twelve months. I just let him talk about the time since the beginning of the calendar year.

"I saw something in those reports. All five men were suffering from one form of malnutrition or another. Now, you see a body of a dead man in his sixties or seventies and you see skin and bones, it doesn't seem all that strange. But it sure does seem strange to me that men who could afford expensive motel rooms and who could afford the automobiles left in the parking lots would have enough money to eat a decent meal every once in a while.

"Maybe one, even two of them would have lousy diets. Lots of Americans do. But none of them should have had such terrible diets that their health suffered so severely."

Luke let these words hang for a while. Then he growled through his clenched teeth, "Damn. What the hell's going on that people can treat men this way? There should be some kind of regulatory agency looking out for these things. What about their families? What about ..."

"They're gay, Luke. They're old and gay. They all probably broke off with their families years ago. You have to remember what it must have been like for them to come out and live their lives so much earlier than we have. We have enough troubles; think what they had to have gone through. And they're so old, well, most of their families would have died by now anyway.

"Since they're gay they probably not only had no one looking out for them, there were probably lots of people happy to see them move on, disappear. They'd only be embarrassments to most others." Alex's face had all the anger in it that Luke's was showing. "They're the most expendable of all.

"Agencies? Retirement colonies and nursing homes are one of the biggest scams in the country. There are barely enough inspectors to keep track of all the shit they pull. They have lawyers to cover their asses when something does come up. Whoever these people are, they probably didn't even bother with a license. Someone would have to find them almost by accident and then it'd take years of legal productions to get them.

"This country doesn't do well by its old people anyhow, Luke, and when those folks are fags, it'd just as soon they did walk away into the desert rather than stick around and bother them."

"Well, I don't know about you, Alex, but I'm not going to give up. I'm going to scour this whole fucking state and the whole fucking West if I have to, but I'm getting to the bottom of all this – fast. I'm not resting till I get my paws on whoever's pulling this shit and that guy's going to be awfully sorry when I do."

"I thought you didn't believe in parades down Main Street? You might be getting yourself in too deep, Luke. You may not like the fallout."

"Hell, I might as well own this county. If I can't raise some ruckus, who the hell can?"

"Me. I'm in it for the long haul. You can leave it to me. I can call and get some reinforcements, I have the resources. Don't go and blow your life apart ..."

"You trying to tell Luke McDavid to go and put his head in the sand? You're full of shit. The traditions of frontier justice are the rules I grew up with. All that riding the range I did with my dad wasn't just macho posturing, Alex. He was handing me a tradition and a respect for law and human life.

"Let me tell you something, Dad used to say this all the time. He'd tell me, there's one thing that civilization's all about, there's one reason we put up with government and law and social restraint: to protect human life. That's the essence, that's the foundation. If human life isn't protected, then society has no right to exist.

"There can't be any limitation on that. None. It's why capital punishment is such an issue, why people get so riled up about babies that aren't perfect being killed, why war is so horrible to us – because it involves a society condoning death."

Alex Kane's face seemed suddenly sad, suddenly terribly sad. "There are such things as evil, Luke. There comes a time when a member of society has to remove it."

"Yes," agreed Luke. "And when the law's been so severely broken that other human lives have been taken, then a man's given up his right to the protection of society. I have some idea of some of the stuff you're doing Alex. I'm worried about it – won't deny that. And I know you're working with a system of values that might not make my Dad understand you, but I think, in the end, he'd approve."

Alex's sadness didn't leave. "That evil can take human form, Luke. It can be part of someone's very being.

"And when you see it and when society can't function, when it can't function to perform its own justice, you do."

"I do." There was no pride in that statement.

"This is the West, Alex. We know about those things. There were decades when the idea of the law was a foreign kind of abstraction, when good men had to take its enforcement in their own hands. We still have some of those responsibilities.

"We have the responsibility of people and the law to protect human life at its greatest vulnerability. That these men are preying on the old, the infirm, people who have contributed all they had to society, that's an abomination. That they would do it to people who were all that *and* gay, that's sin, that's evil, that's totally unforgivable. All we are, Alex, all we want to be, has to depend on our recognition of the rights of the weak to live and to be protected. Without that, we're nothing."

The look on Alex Kane's face went through a transformation, and from a sadness that was almost unbearable to look at came a new force, a strengthening, a rekindling flame of emotion and focus. "Those people will be avenged, and the ones that have survived will never again fear for their safety. I swear it."

Luke McDavid sat back, stunned by the sight in front of him, the tightening of Alex's muscles a manifestation of his grim resolve. Waves of emotion broke over Luke's mind: first awe at the importance of what he saw, then an undirected fear at its intensity, and then, finally, a sense of redeeming anger, a core of burning dedication. *Those people will be avenged.* For a brief moment that Luke knew he'd always cherish, he was one with Alex Kane, he was allied with this strangely handsome man in a manner that transcended their previous sexual attraction. They were to stand together and defend what they – together – held sacred.

They sat and drank their beers together in silence. Rebecca seemed to realize it wasn't the moment to intrude. She wordlessly gave them their menus and left the two men to their contemplations. The voice that finally did intrude on them was from a stranger. "Excuse me, can we ask you guys some questions?"

Alex and Luke looked up at the young man who was talking to them. He was shorter than they, probably no more than 5'8". He had dark hair, closely cropped, and a moustache as neatly trimmed. At first Alex thought he was a local – the guy wore the same tight Levis and the same cowboy shirt as the rest of the men in the bar. But then he smiled to himself, amused at his own gullibility. His cowboy had never ridden a range, at least not one outside city limits. The clothes were too perfect, too perfectly kept and pressed, the colors too nicely coordinated. The guy in front of them was a perfect clone.

If there had been any doubt, his companion resolved it. He was somewhat taller, blond and clean shaven with bright blue eyes. He, too, wore the clone outfit, this one complete with a hooded sweatshirt.

"Sure," Alex said, "have a seat."

The pair took the two free chairs at the table. They were obviously nervous about something. "We're just trying to get some information about some place that should be around here. But no one seemed to know ..."

"Well," the blond broke in, "we don't mean to give you any offense, but when we saw you we figured that you were ... uh ... we thought you might ..."

"We're gay," Luke said, not only amused at their discomfort, but also at the quick way he himself made his declaration.

The two newcomers blushed slightly. "Yeah, well," the dark-haired one was searching for words, "sometimes you sort of know one another."

Luke called over to Rebecca. "Honey, these beers here are as warm as you know what. How about a couple cold ones for us and whatever these fellas are having besides."

Rebecca was back in a moment with four bottles of Budweiser on her tray. "Importing half of San Francisco, aren't you, Luke? Just to make us suffer, ain't that the truth?" Her mock injury left a lightness in the air after she'd deposited the brews.

"New York, actually," the first boy said.

"I'm from Chicago," the blond added.

"Oh, but she had the right idea," Luke said. "Now what kind of information are you looking for?"

"We're trying to find someplace called Son Valley."

"Why, that's up in Idaho," Luke complained.

"No," the New Yorker interjected, "S-o-n Valley. It's here somewhere in Arizona."

"Well, guy, I'm sorry, but I grew up around here and I've never heard of any such place."

The new pair looked despondent. The blond man turned to his friend, "Look, maybe we should just tell them. Maybe they know something ..."

The dark-haired youth took a deep breath. "There's supposed to be a retirement home with that name, for gay men."

Alex and Luke nearly overturned the table as they leaned

across to hang on the newcomer's words.

"This friend of mine, from New York, he moved out there. Well, something's fishy about it all, something I just don't like. I keep calling and they're trying to tell me that Joe's getting too senile to talk on the phone, or to write. I send letters and he never answers them. He was in great shape until he left New York for this place. He was alive and just full of stuff. I won't believe that he's gone batty until I see it myself."

"I was working when I met this guy, the old one. I'm a steward for the airlines. Sam's right. Joe was in great shape, we had a ball together, you know, just teasing and shit. I gave him my address and he left me his. I wrote, no answer. Well, sometimes that happens, you can imagine how many people I meet who are friendly and everything on a plane, but forget you on the ground. I thought it was peculiar, I had Joe pegged for more than that, but, well ... I was willing to forget it, but then Sam was on the same flight a couple months later and when I found out why he was coming to Arizona I knew something funny was going on.

"I had liked Joe more than enough to take some time off and help Sam look for him.

"The more we've looked, the stranger it seems. I mean, there's no Son Valley home registered with the state. There's no such post office name, either. But I know they got my mail. None of it was returned."

Alex worked to keep himself calmed. "What more do you know about this place, this Son Valley?"

The airline steward reached in and pulled out a much folded brochure. "I just happened to have kept this, Joe gave it to me so I'd have the address." He handed the wrinkled paper to Alex.

Luke leaned over to read the pamphlet along with Alex. "What a set-up, every trick in the book. Line drawings instead of photographs, fake pictures – see, there are palm trees and a beach behind these guys, this was probably taken in Florida."

Alex studied the text carefully. "They got mail. What

about this phone number?"

"It works, I called it a couple times. But they now just hang up on me, telling me to mind my own business and leave Joe in peace."

"Luke, the mail must get through because the zip code's right. The post office just goes by that, lots of companies are taking advantage of it. And we have to be able to get a fix on the location from the telephone prefix as well."

"That's the easiest thing in the world! Both. I'll call Jack, he's the postmaster here in Cactus City. Hell, and I can get the telephone's location from information. You just stay right here."

The cowboy grabbed the brochure and went over to the pay phone in the corner. Alex turned to the other two and introduced himself. "I'm Sam Manetti," the first one said, shaking Alex's hand. "I'm Randy Miles," the airline steward offered his own greeting.

Alex began to explain things to the two of them. "We've been looking for this place ourselves, but we didn't have this lead. Look, I promise you, your friend's going to be okay. We'll get him out tonight. You just go back to your hotel room ..."

"I will not!" Sam said. "I flew all the way from New York City to check on Joe. I'm not going to wait in any Ramada Inn for word. I'm concerned, I want to know what's going on ..."

An excited Luke broke up the conversation. "It's in New Charleston. A little town about seventy miles north of here. I got a ... friend who works for the telephone company in Phoenix. He was working a late shift and I had him look up the records on the phone. Place used to be a boarding school for the federal government back when they tried to get all the Indian kids off the reservations to 'civilize' them by removing them from their parents and their own people. When that policy finally got dumped, so did the school. I think I know just where it is, least I know close enough where it is. Come on! We got a job to do."

"We all have a job to do," Randy insisted. "We're going with you."

"This could be dangerous. You don't understand how dangerous these people might be."

"I don't give a fuck, we're going with you." Sam was obviously intent.

"Come in our truck then. There's a back seat where you can ride."

"Alex ..." Luke started to complain.

"It'll be all right, Luke. I promise."

XI

Joe had gotten through the whole day with a single pill and not one drop of coffee. He'd watched Butch and he knew the actor had done just as well. They were in the best shape they were ever going to be.

The time was right. It was after eleven. The late shift had come on. There was just one guard who walked the perimeter of the property and a single nurse's aide at the desk. The desk with the phone.

Joe had memorized Sam's phone number long ago. And Butch had given him Rick Adams's in West Hollywood. Joe had worked hard to get that number down, he had even gone so far as to test it while that one pill had its deepest effect on him. He had scratched the digits out on a piece of paper and handed it to Butch when no one was looking. He'd passed the test.

He waited patiently, it should start right at midnight. That was the agreement.

On cue, like the perfect trooper he was, Butch let out a loud and very credible cry of pain. "Nurse! Nurse!" There was commotion as two men – it must be the guard and the nurse – both ran down the hallway and into Butch's room.

As quickly as he dared, Joe got out of the bed. He opened the door to make sure no one was there. Butch's fake shouts of agony filled the building. "I'm dying! I'm dying!"

"Shut up, you old fool," a voice answered. There was as much naked fear in it as anger.

Joe knew that Butch would be giving the performance of his lifetime. He moved down the hall and sat behind the nurse's desk. He lifted the receiver and punched out the number on the touch tone phone. He listened impatiently as the mechanical device clicked. He could almost imagine what each sound meant, connecting this phone to a central computer in Phoenix, then running a minute electronic pulse to Chicago, it should be getting close to New York just about now. And Joe heard the beautiful sound of the ringing at the other end of the line.

"Come on, Sam, please answer the phone." The ringing went on and on, droning with seemingly endless repetition. Sam wasn't there! "Damn," there were tears of frustration in Joe's eyes. He hung up and waited for the briefest moment. Again he lifted the phone and punched another long distance call. This one to area 213 – Southern California.

The clicks sounded once more. The ringing. *Please, God, please!* "Hello." Joe thought it was the most wonderful sound in the world. But he didn't have time to enjoy it. The drone of a busy signal filled the earpiece. There was a finger on the telephone console.

"What the hell do you think you're doing?

•   •   •

Both Statton and Etson had arrived within a half hour. Joe and Butch were both up and sitting in the common room – but hardly in comfort. They each had a straitjacket on. The arms were attached behind the chairs, underneath that point where the metal arms were welded to the rest of the frame.

"Jesus Christ, can't you do anything right?" Etson was yelling at Statton.

"I found them, didn't I? Senten's an actor, a very good actor, he had all the symptoms of a major coronary. What did you want me to do, let him die of a heart attack right here?"

"Why the hell not?" Etson complained. "Who could argue with that? We could have had it reported right here in this county. We wouldn't have had to play any games with the certificates. You should have let him go."

"I'm a nurse!"

"Hell, you're a quack. You're in this up to your asshole and you know it. Don't try and get all holier than thou with me. You own part of this operation. You knew what it was. Playing your silly ethical tricks nearly blew the whole cover. How'd these two get by without their medications? How'd you let that happen?"

Statton looked at Joe and Butch. "They must have figured it out. They must have ..."

"That's right, they must have figured it *all* out. Do you think they were just calling home for a chat at twelve o'clock at night? They were going to blow the whistle on the entire operation. You'd have ended up in jail – again – and you wouldn't have gotten your license back this time."

"Well what are we going to do with them?"

"Not a damn thing!" Butch Senten piped up. "You just let us out of these things and you let us go on our way. We paid you good money for services you haven't rendered and you have no right to keep us here."

Etson nodded to a sleepy-eyed Max who was obviously not pleased with having his sleep disturbed. The big muscular man walked over to where Senten was tied up and slapped him hard across the face. Blood flowed from the actor's face.

"That's our right to keep you here," Etson sneered. He turned to Statton. "I want them eliminated. Tonight. I want them out of here – for good. You take care of it."

Etson started to walk to the door. "Come on, Max. Let's go."

"Yeah, Max, come on."

Everyone in the room snapped towards the sound of the unfamiliar voice. There was a single man standing in the doorway of the home. He was big, but not nearly as big as Max. He had green eyes that seemed to glare in the evening light.

"Come on, Max, try that on someone who might know how to take it. Someone who might know how to give it back to you."

Max grinned. This was more like it! He'd been the heavy-weight champion of the Seventh Fleet before he got canned from the Navy. He always liked a good fight. Bouncing around these old geezers had been a pain in the ass. He'd been looking for more.

Max didn't even know who the man was or why he had appeared. The voices of the others – Etson, Statton and the three other employees in the room – were barely distinguishable sounds. He didn't care what they were saying. The man had offered him a fight; he'd been challenged. In the primal way that men like Max operated, this was going to be a joy.

The two males had their muscles ready, tensed for each other. They approached. Each was careful: the way to lose a fight is to underestimate your opponent. Neither of them was going to make that mistake.

"Stop them!" someone said.

"Leave them alone," another voice answered.

The pair approached. Their arms extended carefully. Max was vaguely aware of the sharp lines of the challenger's face. The intensity of the eyes didn't obscure the features. Max liked this kind of pretty-boy fighter. He liked this kind of bout. He'd claim his prize when it was over.

Max always got hard when he fought. His prick was stiffening in his pants now. Partially it was the excitement of it all. Max liked to fight. He loved watching noses break and hearing arms shatter. He adored the sound of a skull bouncing on a floor or off a wall. And Max loved to win. He always did. If the guy he beat was good-looking – like this one – then Max kept up the battle, but with his cock, not with his fists. He'd pound the guy's ass till it bled. Max liked that, the sight and smell of fucking a guy.

He moved closer to the man. He wanted the contact of battle, the feel of the bones crushing, the tearing of flesh.

They had told him in the Navy it made him queer. That's why they kicked him out. Max wasn't queer! A surge of fury went through his body. He just wanted to fuck men's asses when they were so weak they couldn't fight him any more. Fuck them and show them what scum they were. That anger went through Max and he couldn't wait any longer. He had to feel the thrill of victory.

But when Max dove at his opponent, he missed. How did he do that? How could that happen? Max found himself sprawled on the floor. He began to turn to face his enemy once more. But as soon as he did a foot caught his chin and lifted him bodily into the air.

Then something was gripping hold of his hair and he couldn't move. He couldn't escape the rain of blows that came.

"How does that feel, Max!" Some vengeful force was slapping Max's face, the left cheek, the right, the left ... *"How does it feel, Max!"* Pain. The pain was unbearable. Max felt something wet flying through air, flying out of his own face, his blood, splattering on the walls, the floor, the red drops scattering in the air. And then Max felt nothing. He wouldn't. Not for a long, long time.

Etson was terrified by the sight in front of him. He had never seen anyone seriously challenge Max – that's why the enormous bruiser had been hired. But now the bulk of the fighter's body was a hump of flesh, barely breathing, barely containing life. The urge to flee had overcome the administrator. He started to run for the door. Two other employees were in front of him. He pushed them aside.

But a hand gripped the collar of his shirt and jerked him hard, stopping the forward motion of his movement so completely that Etson nearly passed out from the force of it.

"Who the hell are you? What are you doing here?" It was the man who only moments ago had beaten Max. Etson, the perfect coward that he was, the kind of loathsome man who always hid behind his paid enforcers, stared into those green eyes and once more the urge to black out nearly encompassed him.

That had to be insanity that he saw. Absolute and utter madness. There was something in that face that Etson had never seen in a man before. Something awesome. Something he wanted to get away from. But he couldn't escape that grip on his neck.

"Let him go. Let him go or I'll kill them."

It was Statton's voice. The nurse was standing by the two old men with a revolver in his hand. "I'll shoot them if you don't do just what I say."

Butch was staring at the black metal of the gun. He looked as though he was hypnotized by it. He didn't watch as Alex Kane released his grip on Etson's clothing and let the fat administrator take a deep breath, one he hoped would let him regain his composure.

The old man was waiting, sure that this was his swan song. This wasn't one of the movies that Butch had played in. That fight wasn't a stunt man's exercise. In all the years he'd been in film he'd never seen such violence. Never. Whoever the stranger was, he was capable of doing things that Butch had only pantomimed.

But those ideas weren't very clear in Butch's mind – not with the gun so close to his head, so close to his head while he was so entirely entrapped in the cloth of the straitjacket. He closed his eyes and waited.

There was a loud *CRACK!* It must have been Joe. Oh, God, the man killed Joe. Or the stranger. They were all going to die. The horrible sound of human pain and surprise filled the room and Butch didn't dare open his eyes. That scream! That horrible scream!

There were more sounds – shuffling feet and other motions. Butch still didn't dare open his eyes. He didn't want to watch real death. He didn't want to know when his own was coming on him.

But then hands were undoing the straitjacket. "Take it easy, old-timer. Everything's all right now, you just relax." A soft voice was speaking to him now. One that had the tones of the West in it, those tones that Butch and his fellow actors were always trying to capture on the screen. Amazed, Butch had to look.

"What the hell?"

The attendants were face down on the floor. That strange man who had beaten up Max was moving quickly to tie their hands behind their backs. Statton was standing nearby, clutching his right hand. It had been the one holding the gun, but now it was empty – empty and bleeding copiously onto the linoleum tiles.

"What happened?" Butch asked as the man with the frontier accent went about releasing Joe. "How ..."

"I won a whole lot of sharpshooting contests in my day, old man. A whole lot. Shooting a gun out of a dude's hand was a piece of cake."

"You've ruined my hand. You've fractured the bones. I'll never ..."

"Don't worry about a thing. You're not going to have much use for that hand for the next few years – maybe not for the rest of your life." The real cowboy spoke as he finished untying Joe. "Arizona prisons are a great place to recuperate anyhow."

Alex Kane had finished binding the rest of the staff. He walked over to the phone and called the operator. He gave her instructions; the local sheriff and the state police would be on their way soon.

• • •

It was dawn by the time the authorities were done. They had walked through the corridors of Son Valley and discovered over forty living bodies, bodies that could barely sustain life they were so full of drugs and so lacking in basic nutrients.

"I ain't never seen the like," the state trooper in charge had finally said. "I ain't never."

Alex Kane and Luke McDavid stood and watched the activity, their faces masked with a silent resolve. In the sitting room Sam and Randy were sitting and talking to Joe and

Butch.

"I wanted to help. But those two tricked us," Sam complained. "Somehow they knocked us out."

"But it's strange," Randy said. "How did it happen? I don't have any bruises. I know they didn't give us drugs."

Alex had walked over and had heard the two younger men speaking. "It's just something I picked up," he smiled. "Luke and I knew that this could have been dangerous. We couldn't take the chance that you'd get in the way – or get hurt."

"Well, you could have said something to us instead of doing that," Sam complained.

"No way, you two were determined to play cavalry and rescue these guys. You don't have the skills. We had to do it alone."

Sam wasn't appeased. But Joe knew enough to divert his attention. "Sammy, can you get me another cup of tea? I could really use it."

While the Manetti youngster went on his errand Joe spoke to Alex and to Luke who had just walked over to join them. "What happens now?"

"They go to prison. There are enough broken laws inside these walls that they'll get long sentences, and there's a good chance we can convict them for murder."

"Murder?" Joe's worst fears were confirmed.

"Murder," Alex said. "They certainly wouldn't have let the two of you live after your attempt at reaching the kids. They also have a lot of dead bodies to answer for. They'll get everything that's coming to them."

Butch broke in, "But what happens to us? They have all our money."

Alex reassured him, "We'll find a way to keep you comfortable until you can reclaim your savings." He knew Farmdale would pick up the tab with a minimum of complaints. "The sheriff says there are a couple of legitimate retirement homes in the area that have enough vacancies for all of you. There'll be special people brought in to monitor your progress and make sure you're okay."

"Joe's not going to another nursing home." Sam Manetti had brought back the requested cup of tea. "Not ever again."

"Sam, you can't afford ..." Joe tried to complain.

"I don't care what we have to do, Joe. I'm not sending you back to one of these places."

"But the other homes will be legit," Randy suggested.

"Joe's not going to one of those straight places where a bunch of old biddies are going to hound him." Sam rejected the idea again. "I'll get a job out here, anything, waiter, dishwasher. We can get a small place until you get your strength back and your money comes through. Then we'll head back East."

"Sam, the money's not a problem ..." Alex began to explain.

"Hell, no," Luke interjected. "And there's no need for you to go renting any place. I have a huge house, extra bedrooms and all. You two and Butch can just come on over there and spend time on my ranch. We'll get some good range cooking into you and get you on your feet in no time."

Alex started to talk again, thinking he'd explain to Luke that there were the Farmdale millions to draw on. But then he saw the way Luke was looking at Sam Manetti. Alex just smiled and kept his peace.

• • •

"Oh, good god, this is the life!" Joe Talbot was luxuriating in the big hot tub on Luke's patio. The warm water swirled around him, loosening his muscles and gently kneading away the tension.

"Never had this kind of layout in my movies," Butch agreed. He, too, was naked and immersed in the warm water. "This is what I thought Son Valley was going to be like. Stars in the skies, no pollution to hide them, empty desert as far as you can see."

"Oh, you old buzzard, you wanted some of those pretty

young attendants to look at too, the ones they had in the pictures that looked like they worked in a bath house. You probably thought you could pinch their behinds every hour on the hour and make believe you could still get it up."

"What do you mean, *still* get it up. 'Course I can still get it up."

"Couldn't prove it by me," Joe grinned. "I ain't never seen it."

"You move that collection of ancient bones any closer and you will."

"Yeah?" Joe's eyes were teasing now.

"Yeah. Just 'cause you're older than god doesn't mean that someone wouldn't find you ..." Butch stopped his talk and realized what he was saying. "Wait a minute. It's one thing for us to get it going over some young thing, but we're old men!"

"Yep, real old," Joe agreed.

"Well, we shouldn't be talking this way to one another."

"You're right," Joe agreed as he moved over to Butch. "We should be doing it."

• • •

Alex had stayed around for a few days until all the legal technicalities had been taken care of. He wasn't going to let any of Etson and Statton's shyster lawyers spring them. A few calls to Farmdale had insured that some of the best legal minds in the country would be flown in to oversee the court proceedings. Others were hard at work retrieving the money Son Valley's residents had handed over to the crooks.

It seemed that everything was being handled well enough. Alex had spent hours on the phone. Now he was looking at it and wondering if he should make one more call – to Massachusetts. He picked up the receiver and began to punch the area code into the console. Then hung up. *Leave Danny alone,* he told himself. If Luke hadn't been there with his rifle, if he hadn't been a good enough marksman to shoot the revolver out of Statton's hand, if it had been one of their men with the gun hiding behind the door ...

"Alex, come on over and have a beer with us," Luke called. The rancher was sitting on one of his couches facing the fireplace where the flames were billowing. Sam Manetti was there too. His head was resting on Luke's lap, his legs sprawled over the length of the furniture.

Alex didn't take up the offer for the beer, but he did join the two of them. "How's everything going? The old men doing okay?"

Luke laughed. "Well, unless I've lost my mind, the sounds coming from that hot tub tell me they're doing just fine."

"And you?"

"And me," the rancher beamed. "I found me an amphibian. An honest-to-god amphibian."

Sam Manetti seemed embarrassed. He rolled over and hid his face against Luke's stomach. Luke reached down and ran his hand through Sam's hair. A look of placid excitement beamed from Luke's face. "The guy loves the West. Cooks like a dream. Has the body of ..."

"Stop it!" Sam's voice complained playfully, muffled by Luke's body.

"Body of life and cock to match," Luke wasn't going to give up his monologue. "Did you know he's a writer? An honest-to-god writer? Had a play on Broadway ..."

Sam sat up now, "Luke, it was in a tiny off-off-Broadway theater. It got one review. One fucking review in a gay newspaper and they didn't like it. Maybe five hundred people saw it – tops! It ..."

"It must have been a smash hit. Least it will be when it's produced right, with enough money for publicity and promotion and decent sets." Luke had his own reality and it wasn't going to be denied. Sam just collapsed down against the rancher's body again.

"I figure, Alex, I'll do it right this time. I got the best crew any rancher has right here on the farm. So, I thought, this time I'll do the traveling too, maybe that's the way to handle things, me being a little bit of an amphibian myself."

Sam wrapped his arms around Luke's chest and used the big man's body to pull himself up and deliver a kiss. "Only if you teach me how to ride."

"Done!" Luke kissed him back. "That, and we'll figure out a way to take care of Joe for you, too. Though, way things are going, looks like that means Joe and Butch. No problem, we'll get us a houseboy and we'll work something out."

"You don't need a houseboy. I'll do the work that Joe needs done and I'll keep the house, I'll earn my keep ..."

"Boy, you are going to be much too busy to do any of that. And I don't mean learning how to ride a horse."

Alex Kane smiled and stood up. "Excuse me. I have to make a phone call."

"Who now?" Luke asked. "I thought everything was settled."

"It is. I just have to call Boston and let someone else know it."

XII

"So how's college?"

Danny Fortelli looked up from his dinner and answered, "You call me in the middle of the night and say you're going to catch the next plane from Arizona to Boston. You tell me to meet you at the Ritz for dinner. And the only things you've said since we met are, 'How are you?' followed a half hour later by, 'How are your parents?' and now, another half hour later, 'So how's college?'

"I'm flattered, Alex, really I am. But it does seem a little weird to have three sentences of nothing after all the build-up."

Alex dropped his fork on his plate and sat back in his chair. "I'm sorry, Danny. You ... I don't know all the ways I'm supposed to act around you. It's hard for me. All this ..."

"All what?" The look on Danny's face didn't show questioning as much as it did patience. It made Alex think that Danny was much more on the ball in this one than he was.

"You, me." Alex took a sip of his wine. He had found the same St. Emilion on the Ritz wine list that had been served in Cactus City. He had ordered it as much for the coincidence as for any love of the vintage, though he did like it.

"'You, me' doesn't seem to be much of a regular item these days. I'm sorry, Alex, but you just have me too confused. I don't know if you're coming or going, if you want me to come or leave. I try not to be a pest and then I get these phone calls. I make believe nothing's going on and then there's a car in the driveway and the keys are in a birthday card."

The two of them sat silently. The quiet, elegant crowd around them seemed to be speaking in nothing but whispers. Waiters and busboys flowed through the tables as though they were liquid; the best training made them act that way.

Danny finally began speaking again. "I don't know everything about what you do, Alex, but after all that stuff here, when we met, when I was in trouble, I guess a lot about it. I assume that's what you were doing in Arizona, something like that. Well, this has been going on for so long, this stuff between us, that I think you owe me an explanation."

Alex motioned to the nearest waiter to take away their plates. He ordered coffee for both of them, and a cognac as well. "This is going to take some time, Danny, we might as well make it worthwhile."

Only when the beverages had been served did Alex begin. He started in Vietnam. He told of a young man from New Hampshire who'd gone to that part of the world to fight for something that might be decent, and then was able to only find one other man who could keep that in mind – the idea of decency in the midst of an utterly barbaric conflict.

He told Danny about James. He talked about what that year with the young son of Joseph Farmdale had been like, what it had meant for him, for Alex. Then he told about James's murder – and his revenge.

Then the rest had begun. The commitment to fight his own war here in the United States using his talents and strengths and Joseph Farmdale's seemingly unlimited resources. There had been many battles, too many battles with too many casualties on both sides and some of them had been caused by Alex Kane's hands.

He had dreamed once that the war would end, that the victory would be as easy as he had thought the victory in 'Nam was going to be when he, himself, was an eighteen-year-old Marine. But now he saw this war he was fighting as a never-ending one – one where the opposition was so enormous, the scales were so unbalanced, the odds so bad, that Alex Kane knew he was in it for his whole life.

"I didn't know the details, Alex, but I had figured out most of it anyway." Danny was sipping the cognac and looking right at Kane's face. "You haven't spoken about the main subject though, the 'you, me.' Tell me about that."

"What can I say? There's no way I can have a lover in the middle of this. I can't expose you to the dangers. If some of the people I have to go up against ever knew you existed that way, that you were waiting back home, unprotected, they'd find you. They'd use you as a pawn to neutralize me. They'd …"

"Fuck you, Alex." Danny said the words with an angry hiss. "Just go fuck yourself."

"What do you mean, Danny? What did I say? I'm just trying to protect you."

"You are so maddeningly self-centered sometimes. You think you're so goddamned important to the world that you can't see that maybe someone else has a contribution to make. You …" Danny broke off speaking. He sipped the cognac again.

"You are only thirty-two. You're not an old man. You don't have to spend the rest of your life alone. There can be someone else. It could be me. But you have to wake up to see that it might not happen in the way you expect it to. You have to ask me what *I* want, what *I* would like to do."

"You want to be my lover." Alex thought that's what they had been talking about.

"No, Alex, you want me to be *your* lover. That's why you're carrying on this way. You're talking yourself out of it with this stuff about a defenseless me stuck at home acting like a sitting duck that some bad guy's going to come and knock off.

"Now, why don't we start all over again, Alex. Why don't we start by asking some different questions. Like, why *do* you want me to be your lover?"

Alex flushed. Damn. Danny – and only Danny – could

make him lose this control of himself. With anyone else he was in charge all the time. Any other gay man and Alex set the rules and everyone followed them. Just because ... Alex knew the answer to Danny's question. "Because I love you."

"Good, so far you're doing just fine." Danny obviously wasn't going to give Alex back his control very easily. "Now, if we were lovers, what would it look like? I mean, what would we do? Where would we live? Come on, Alex, keep on going. Just what do you expect from me?"

"Well ... it's obvious. You're in school, and I guess you'd stay there. We'd get a house and you'd live there. I'd have to keep working. And when you graduated, you'd get a job." What else could Danny expect?

"And what kind of job would I get, Alex?" Danny's voice was beginning to display a certain exasperation.

"I don't know. Whatever you wanted. Something that would let you stay in training, I suppose."

"Now, Alex, I want you to know something. This body that's sitting across the table from you is the one that came in first in more events than any other in the history of the Massachusetts High School gymnastics championships. This body – in its freshman year of college – is the first ranked collegiate gymnast in New England – not just in our division, in the whole region. All by itself it's going to win Mansford State a league championship in its first year.

"This body – in case you've forgotten what it looks like, since this is the first time you've seen it in months and since it does have clothes on right now – this body is something I've trained and nurtured for every conscious moment of my life. Don't you think I might have something on you, Alex? Don't you think that maybe I'm a little ahead of you in development?"

Alex stared at Danny; he didn't understand what the guy was saying.

"Alex, goddamn you, don't you realize that I've already begun the training that took you years of work? Can't you look at me and see something besides a docile housewife

229

who's going to stay home and wait for you while you're on the road? Don't you think that maybe, just maybe, I have as much commitment and concern and conviction as you do? Couldn't you just for one minute look at me and see a potential lover who's also a potential partner?"

"Danny, you can't mean ..."

"But I do mean just that. I mean I want to share your life. I mean I can't even look at any other men because of you. How could anyone compare to you? To what you are and what you do in the world, not just with me. Everything you've told me tonight only confirms what I had felt all along. I want to join you, Alex. I don't want to be some dependent help mate, I want to be with you – in every way."

"I can't let you."

"Why? Because you want all the glory to yourself?"

"No, no, that's not true, there is no glory."

"What is there that I can't share?"

"The danger. The sight of all the things that go on in this world. The knowledge of how cruel it can be, what it can do to other people."

"Alex, I may have just turned nineteen, but I have seen all that – more than my share – more than enough to be able to know that I can take more."

The waiter came by and filled their coffee cups. Neither of them drank. "Alex, do we have a room here?"

"Yeah."

"Good, let's go fuck, I'm tired of all this talk."

•   •   •

"You seem so far away. What are you thinking about?" Danny asked Alex as he shifted his body to lay his leg over Alex's thigh.

"I was thinking that the smell of you is the most wonderful perfume in the world," Alex said, flexing an arm to pull Danny closer.

Danny waited a little before continuing. "Alex, why don't

you try again? I mean, try to imagine what it'd be like if we were together."

"Well, it looks different this time around. It looks even better. I met this man in Arizona, he worked with me on this last thing I did. He had this big ranch house out in the middle of the country. It had a big fireplace, his own furniture, no neighbors nearby to bother him. He hadn't anyone to live there with him – until just now. And the house had seemed too big before, but now it seems just right.

"I'd like to live like that. In my own house. On a lot of property. With someone. I'd like to have someone with me at least sometimes when I travel. I'd like to be with someone I can trust, not just emotionally, but someone like Luke, a guy who'd be able to handle an emergency when it came up, a guy I could rely on to be there when he was needed and who'd know what had to be done."

"This is sounding much better." Danny nuzzled his face against Alex's chest.

"I just wonder about taking your youth away from you. What about a career? What about the Olympics? You wanted to train for them once."

"I won't rule that out, Alex. But that same training is something that I can use to train for our work together. My youth? I lost a lot of that already. Maybe not the way you did in Vietnam, but close enough for me to know what's involved.

"What I want is to be with you. How can you worry about things like 'career' and 'training' and think that they'd be important enough for me to give you up? Or to think that the kind of life you're offering me this time is something with less meaning, less importance? That's not what's going on.

"I know it sounds like a cliché, Alex, but what I want most is a life that has some meaning to it. Your life certainly has that."

• • •

Carl Anwell was astonished. "Are they still at it?" he asked his assistant manager.

"Hardly taken a rest break," Tony LaGadio responded. "It's six o'clock. They've been going for five hours now."

The two pros were looking at the pair of men who were spotting each other with free weights in the middle of the South End gymnasium that Carl and Tony ran. Both the customers were dressed only in gym shorts. There was no shirt to hide the incredible muscles that were pumped up from the long exercise.

Both Tony and Carl were caught in the midst of conflicting emotions. At one level, they were professionals at this business of building muscles and in that way they had nothing but admiration for the two bodies they were observing. The older of the exercising men was almost totally hairless, and no part of his torso was hidden from their view. The lines seemed to have been etched from marble, not something that could have been developed on a human form.

The other, that younger guy, was as well-built. The fine coating of dark hair on his chest and the lush growth that came from under his arms and over his legs only seemed to accentuate his physique. The sweat had matted the body hair to his skin anyhow. Right now he was bench pressing, the strain was bloating his chest and his upper arms into inspiring size.

On another level they were both secretly struck by the sensual beauty of these two men. They had faces that went with the nearly perfect bodies, handsome, sexual. The older man's was dominated by his eyes, sharply piercing green eyes. The younger one had a mouth of great beauty, one whose lips were full and red, almost as though they had been artificially colored. But there was nothing artificial about either of these guys. Tony and Carl knew it.

But the most striking thing about the pair was the way they worked together – if "work" was the right word. They seemed to be in absolute synchronization with one another. Carl and Tony had noticed that earlier. There had been moments when they had been doing stretching routines while they had faced each other and while other men might have frowned or grimaced from the exertion, these two had smiled, just smiled in obvious appreciation of how the other looked.

Even now the older man was coaxing the younger into lifting more, to keep on going, to do the maximum possible. There was a softness in his voice, an encouraging tone that seemed to strengthen his partner. And the kid did keep on going, he did refuse to give in to the pain of the effort.

Carl and Tony couldn't take their eyes off the image in front of them, the vision of two men existing in a state of complete cooperation and coordination. In all the years they had worked here in the gym together they had never seen anything quite like it, the sexuality of body building, the emotion of the male bonding at its most emphatic.

All the time the two pros spent at the gym they had treated the male form as a machine, something that had to be fed fuel and sculpted by strain and admired with an aesthetic distance.

Tony didn't always feel that way. But he had hidden the other appreciations he had from everyone's view, especially his boss's. He had never indicated, in any way, that he might ever have looked at Carl as anything but an asexual athlete. But watching these other two for so long had eroded his iron discipline. Once more his cock was trapped in its hardness inside his jockstrap. His balls were heavy with painful excitement.

Carl had honestly never looked at a man "that way" before. But as he looked at Alex Kane's body bent over Danny Fortelli's prone form, he understood why men were gay. If he ever had a man look at him that way, appreciate all the things about his physique and his mind in that obvious manner, it might not be so bad; it might be something he'd like.

While Carl was letting his mind wander into a fantasy land he had never allowed himself to travel into before, Tony was dealing with a blunt reality – the fact that Carl was standing so close to him. Carl, Carl whose body Tony had worshipped all these years, Carl who had been unknowingly tempting him every time they had stepped into a shower together, who had fed Tony's own lustful dreams every time he had lent the Italian bodybuilder one of his jockstraps.

Their separate worlds suddenly came together. Tony's hand was the means. He had no conscious intent when it happened. He didn't think about it at all. It just happened. All of a sudden his palm was resting on one of Carl's heavy, hard buttocks and his fingers were kneading that flesh that he had looked at so longingly while it had been framed by the elastic bands of Carl's jock, as though its real purpose was to force Tony's attention to center there, on the two mounds, on the deep crack.

The touch of his partner's hand on the part of his body that Carl would have sworn was inviolate up till this very day sent pleasurable spasms up and down Carl's spine. He closed his eyes so he could concentrate on the wonderful sensations. "Yeah," he moaned.

Carl's own arm went around Tony's waist and caused even more messages to run through his nervous system. He had never thought of Tony's waist this way before, the hardness of the Italian's stomach, the contrasting softness, so well shaped, on the sides. It was so warm, the touch of his flesh was so compelling ...

"I think we better go into the office," Carl said.

As they turned to head to the doorway, the doorway that would soon be closed and give them the privacy to finally explore one another, Tony turned to the pair that was only now leaving the weights behind and moving to the shower. Their magic had made this all possible. He only hoped he'd have a chance to thank them some day.

• • •

Alex stood under the pulsing shower. He leaned back and let the water soak his hair. He felt wonderful. Sex in the morning was one of his favorites – and sex with Danny was always his favorite. They had gone at it for hours, taking only short breaks for breakfast and talk. Every inch of his skin was sensitive from their lovemaking. For a nineteen-year-old, Danny had remarkably few inhibitions.

The workout had been fantastic too, as though it were just a continuation of all the sex they had had. Watching Danny test his young body to its limits had been incredibly beautiful. But that didn't mean he could let the kid get away with all the stuff he had pulled. "You were being a hot dog out there."

"What do you mean by that?" Danny asked from the next shower.

"It would have been all right for you to say you had had enough. You were pushing yourself too hard to prove to me you could keep up."

"I was not! Alex, I work out at least two hours every day, you know that. Of course I went to the limit, what's the use if you don't? But don't flatter yourself. I wasn't trying to prove anything to you."

Alex pulled his head out from underneath the water and looked over at the body beside him. Danny took it as an invitation. He moved over and wrapped his arms around Alex, lifting his head to receive Alex's kiss. Their liquids merged, their tastes blended. When the kiss was done Danny looked at Alex, "You're going to have to learn some things. You think you're going to be this great teacher for me, and I'll take the lessons you have to give.

"You have some you need, too. Like believing that we don't have to compete about anything – exercises or love. That I don't need to be protected all the time. I have my own strengths. You just have to learn, Alex."

Alex looked down at Danny and realized something even more important. If Danny had been almost any other man in the world, he would have reacted to Alex's touch, to his kiss. Just as Luke had experienced sex with Alex as something way out of the ordinary, so would other males. But not Danny. With Danny, Alex's powers were useless. With Danny, Alex was the one who melted.

Alex realized that he hadn't been afraid of other people using this man to neutralize him. That wasn't going to be the problem. It was Danny who was nullifying Alex's protective armor.

It was just like James. Just like the first time that James had kissed Alex in that hotel in Saigon and with that one kiss had removed all the pretense and all the sham that had kept Alex from loving men.

"Most people don't get this even once in their lifetime," Alex said suddenly to Danny. "I've gotten it twice. It's a charmed life." Not caring if he had made sense to anyone, even Danny, Alex fell to his knees and took Danny's cock in his mouth. Oblivious to the falling water and the rising moans that came from his lover's mouth, uncaring about any intruders, Alex gave thanks on his knees, made his offer of thanksgiving to the swelling flesh.

• • •

There was snow falling on the streets of Boston when Alex and Danny stepped outside. They were both warmly dressed in leather jackets and scarves, both had knit hats on their heads and carried their gym bags in gloved hands.

They made their way through the narrow streets and alleys of the South End, arguing boyishly about where they'd eat dinner. "Room service," Alex insisted. "We're at the Ritz, for god's sake, the least we can do is have room service."

"I want a gay restaurant. At least one with lots of gay waiters."

"What do you think the Ritz is? Who do you think works there?"

Danny's laugh was cut off. He lurched forward, face down into the snow that covered the sidewalk, his bag flying to the side. *"Danny!"*

A clump of a snowball was packed against the back of Danny's hat. Alex was immediately on alert. He turned quickly and ducked just before another white missile would have hit him squarely. There were five men right behind them. The sound of the snowball hitting the brick wall behind Alex told him what had happened: This wasn't a little game. There had been a rock embedded in the snow, a rock thrown with more than enough force to have hurt Danny badly.

"You bastards!" Anger – raw and unbounded – flooded every part of Alex's being. He dropped his own bag and moved toward the threatening group.

He knew what they saw, two gay men straggling through the dark streets of the city. Two easy marks. But this wasn't going to be easy on them. *If Danny …*

The five moved forward. One brought out a link of chain. Another reached into his pocket and soon Alex heard the unmistakable "click" of a switchblade. They had deceptively innocent freckled faces of young Irishmen. They were the street toughs of South Boston, the kinds of punks who preyed on the unsuspecting gay men of this area – them and anyone else they thought they could roll.

Fury ruled Alex. Blind fury that matched – surpassed – anything he had ever felt before, at least since Vietnam. It was Danny that had just been attacked. Danny who might …

Alex sent a foot out, striking the crotch of one assailant with blinding speed, sending him sprawling onto the street with screams of agony. The one with the knife in his hands lunged, sure that Alex's concentration must have been broken. But he made a mistake. It was his hand that was broken, not Alex's nearly insane deliberation. His shouts of pain made a heinous duet with his other fallen companion.

But these weren't the kinds of punks who ran from a fight. These were young versions of Max, men who, no matter how young, found energy in the sounds and sight of violence. The three that still stood moved closer, their carefully coordinated movements making them confident that they could take this one.

Two of them made their moves in a physical harmony that even Alex had to appreciate. But both met with one of his fists before they had a chance to deliver the blows they were so sure they were going to land. Both felt their noses break into splinters. Both sent waves of red blood onto the virgin snow.

Alex turned to take care of the last one, the one who had been menacing him off to one side with that link of chain. His muscles ready to meet the expected attack, Alex stood and then looked in amazement. The man was already out. His arms draped formlessly over the snowbank, the chain harmlessly sitting in the middle of the road.

Danny stood nearby rubbing the sore back of his head. "What a cheap shot. A rock in a snowball. You'd think they could have come up with something better than that!" His voice was full of disgust when he said that. But it lightened when he looked at Alex. "See. I passed my first real test. With flying colors and ..." he rubbed his head some more, "hard knocks."

· · ·

Danny won the choice of restaurants. "So all I have to do is deliver a single knock-out punch and win all the arguments?" he teased.

They were in a dining room not too far from the Ritz, but across the expressway that separated downtown Boston from the predominantly gay South End. The place was surprisingly comfortable and attractive. Surprising because not one piece of the old wooden furniture matched, nor did any of the old flatware they were eating with. It seemed a potpourri of silver and stainless steel that had been purposely chosen so that no two forks or spoons or knives could ever become part of the same set.

The colors were stylishly light and warm. The food was the best of the latest nouvelle cuisine fashion. The portions were small, but every single element had been created with the greatest care. The promise of rich desserts and the lingering satisfaction over the flavor of the impeccable cuisine eliminated any desire Alex might have had to complain. All that – and the sight of the handsome and obviously gay waiters.

"If you keep on coming up with places like this, I might have to resign the position of restaurant chooser altogether." But there wasn't a lot of joy in Alex's voice. Even the great meal hadn't taken away the evening's earlier events. "Danny, I ... I don't know what I would have done if ..."

"But 'if' didn't happen. It was a rock. They were lucky it hit me. They were a bunch of assholes. It would have happened if you had been there or not. Things happen. They happen to people and no one notices. They just put it down to the stuff that goes on in the city. It's what you were telling me before. You have to look to see the patterns.

"We know they did it because we were gay. But if we had been someone else who had complained to the police, they just would have said it was only a coincidence – that they were simple muggers out after anyone they could get.

"But there was hatred mixed in with their greed. The hatred of who we are and what we mean. Isn't that the whole point, Alex? Isn't that why we have to do what we're going to? Because we're the only ones who'll always see that hatred and we're the only ones who'll be willing to fight it?"

"But if it means you getting hurt ..."

"It will always mean that I might get hurt. But at least if I get hurt, I'll be in the middle of doing something about it. If you really believe in all you've told me about the way things are going, do you really think I'd ever be totally protected anyway? Don't be stupid, Alex. What could you do? Put me on a mountaintop where no one could ever find me? Try to hide me? I'm gay. I'm always going to be and there will always be people who know that, who can see it.

"You're not putting me at risk by having me by your side. I'll always be at risk, I'll always have to be careful. And I'll always have to fight."

"But you shouldn't. Not at your age. You should just be going to school. You should just be being happy."

"You bozo. Sometimes I think you watch too much television. You worry that I see too much and you don't realize the rest of it – that because of all this I see so much! So there's some danger that comes with the property. So there's some risk. But it's all part of the package that brings you to me and that makes my mind want to grow and my perceptions want to stretch. Get over it, Alex. I'm not just all right about things. I'm happy and I wouldn't change a second of it."

Alex took a sip of wine. "Would you change your hazelnut torte for a quick fuck back at the Ritz?"

Danny thought for a minute. "You know what? You just defined the limits of love and lust. No. I don't want to do that."

Just then the waiter brought the desserts to them. As he poured the coffee Alex pressed the issue. "Do you mean to tell me that a hazelnut torte is more important than I am?"

Danny was lifting his fork. He paused and stared at the pastry it was carrying. "At this moment in time: Yes."

XIII

It was six months later that they received the invitation. "Will you go with me?" Alex asked Danny.

"Of course."

They flew down to New York on Friday afternoon. They had a room at a hotel in midtown. Alex fumed at the tuxedo he had to wear. "Goddamn cities."

"You look great," Danny encouraged him as he knotted his own tie. "I never thought I'd see it, but you look great."

"All this hullabaloo."

"Alex, it's opening night! What do you expect?" But Danny had learned enough lately to let Alex just keep on complaining when he was in one of these moods.

They walked to the theater. Just as they arrived a stretched limousine pulled up to the entrance, so long it seemed like an engineering impossibility. The crowd gathered automatically as the chauffeur opened the door. Then they seemed to disperse in disappointment when they couldn't recognize the face of the man who stepped out.

"What the hell are you doing here?" Alex demanded of Joseph Farmdale.

Farmdale dismissed the driver with an imperious flick of his wrist. "I – if you must know – happen to have bankrolled half of this production."

"Can't you keep your busybody self out of other people's

241

business just once in a while?" Alex shouted.

Farmdale ignored him. "Danny, so good to see you again," he clapped the other man on the shoulder. "You're looking very smart. Black tie looks so natural on you. Unlike some people who seem to wear it as an ill-fitting masquerade."

"You old ..."

"Come on, you two. Enough of all that. We'll miss the curtain."

When they were seated next to one another Alex whispered, "Why did you do this?"

Farmdale didn't turn his head, he kept his eyes on the stage. "I'm not quite sure yet. It is either a brilliant investment or a horribly expensive charity. Why don't you shut up and we'll see which."

. . .

Over a late night supper at the Algonquin, they discovered that Farmdale had once again backed a winner. Sam Manetti was ecstatic over the first edition reviews. "A stunning introduction of a promising young playwright."

"Hell," Luke muttered, "they don't say you're brilliant. I haven't seen the word 'masterpiece' yet!"

Sam and Danny had only just met, but they had an automatic understanding of one another and their mates. They smiled over the the thankless task of educating the preceding generation.

Alex ordered the most expensive champagne on the wine list – six bottles for the whole table. "He'll pay for it," he told the waiter as he pointed to a scowling Farmdale.

Then he turned to Luke. "How's it going?"

"Well, I guess it couldn't be better. But it's a whole lot of complication. Nothing bad, mind you, just a whole lot of it."

There were at least fifteen people at their table – the actors, director and others from Sam's play production and Farmdale and Danny as well as Joe and Butch. The conversation was loud and celebratory. There was a small bar off to the side of the lobby. Its quiet seemed appealing to Alex. "Come on, let's talk over there," he said to Luke.

The two men wandered away from the table, oblivious to the appreciative eyes – male and female – that followed their progress. No tuxedo could hide Alex's form. No amount of city living could shield Luke's masculinity.

Alex had a club soda; Luke had a beer. "So, what is it?" Alex coaxed.

"I always thought I'd get me someone out at the ranch and it'd be quiet and peaceful like it's supposed to be. You know? Just me and my guy.

"Well, my guy is the most sex-starved thing on two legs you ever saw and he runs me *ragged*. He's been telling me that it's the tension about the play and all. I don't know. I mean, I'm not really complaining, I like it, but I just forgot how much *work* it can be. That, and all the construction going on ..."

"Construction?"

"You don't know? I thought Mr. Farmdale would have told you. Well, Sam wouldn't let Joe go back to New York – you knew that and that was just fine with me. Then him and Butch got it going and they haven't stopped yet. So Butch stayed. Then we started getting all these visitors. Seems that Randy guy, the steward, well he keeps coming up to see the two old-timers and that's fine.

"But his lover comes along with him. And his lover turns out to be a social worker. They're all talking about things and they're all talking about Son Valley and what they had hoped it would be – about the needs of gay old folks and everything. So I'm sitting there one night and there's Joe and Butch and Randy and his friend and I have my arm around my guy who's going to have his big play produced in New York City and I'm feeling pretty good and I got half the land in northwestern Arizona and I said, 'Well, go and do it. I'll give you the property.'

"Next thing I know they're all on the phone to Farmdale talking about the money they got coming back and tax-free status and incorporation and then they call that friend of Butch – the one that was the big child actor and now's a bigger man actor who seems to be minting money with his macho movies. So," Luke took a deep breath, "they're building Son Valley. In Cactus City. On my land."

"It gets awfully contagious, Luke. But tell me more about Sam and you. Did he make you do this? Is this some problem?"

"Oh, hell, no. Not at all. I mean, you didn't take those complaints about all the sex seriously, did you? No way. Luke McDavid is as pleased as punch by it all. I never, ever thought a guy could be that good to me. And his play and all is just infectious, the excitement and everything. It'll all calm down, but he's made me feel alive and involved.

"Sure, the project and the play and all the people create a lot of motion and action, but we're real good about finding time alone. We're real good at it. I just think I must have been a fool to have wasted so much energy on the idiots that came before him.

"Hard? Bad? No. None of that. I'll tell you what, though. I had to learn some lessons. One of them just really knocked me out."

"What?" Alex asked.

"I had to learn that I was the one who had to become an amphibian. Sam's just right at home on the ranch, rides like a natural and his favorite way to get away from the others is for the two of us to ride out with our gear and cook a meal over a campfire and then sleep in a bag made for two. He's not a fish out of water, he's a fish that can swim in two seas. Me? I'm the one's got to learn all the lessons."

"I know just what you mean," Alex Kane said as he looked over to the table where Sam and Danny were talking to one another easily and with soft animation. "We both have a whole lot to learn."

JOHN PRESTON

Born in Portland, Maine, John Preston was an influential author of fiction and nonfiction, dealing mostly with issues in gay life. He was a pioneer in the early gay rights movement in Minneapolis. He helped found one of the earliest gay community centers in the United States, edited two newsletters devoted to sexual health, and served as editor of The Advocate in 1975.

He was the author or editor of nearly fifty books, including such erotic landmarks as Mr. Benson *and* I Once Had a Master and Other Tales of Erotic Love. *Other works include* Franny, the Queen of Provincetown, The Big Gay Book: A Man's Survival Guide for the Nineties, Personal Dispatches: Writers Confront AIDS, *and* Hometowns: Gay Men Write About Where They Belong.

Preston's writing was part of a movement in the 1970s and 1980s toward higher literary quality in gay erotic fiction. He was an outspoken advocate of the artistic and social worth of erotic writings, delivering a lecture at Harvard

University entitled "My Life as a Pornographer". His writings caused controversy when he was one of several gay and lesbian authors to have their books confiscated at the border by Canada Customs. Testimony regarding the literary merit of his novel *I Once Had a Master* helped a Vancouver LGBT bookstore, Little Sister's Book and Art Emporium, to partially win a case against Canada Customs in the Canadian Supreme Court in 2000.

Preston served as a journalist and essayist throughout his life. He penned a column for Lambda Book Report called "Preston on Publishing." His nonfiction anthologies, which collected essays by himself and others on everyday aspects of gay and lesbian life, won him the Lambda Literary Award and the American Library Association's Stonewall Book Award. He also wrote the "Alex Kane" adventure novels about gay characters. These books, which included *Sweet Dreams*, *Golden Years*, and *Deadly Lies*, combined action-story plots with an exploration of issues such as the problems facing gay youth.

Preston was among the first writers to popularize the genre of safe sex stories, editing a safe sex anthology entitled Hot Living in 1985. He helped to found the AIDS Project of Southern Maine. In the late 1980s, he discovered that he himself was HIV positive. He died of AIDS complications on April 28, 1994, aged 48, at his home in Portland.

About ReQueered Tales

In the heady days of the late 1960s, when young people in many western countries were in the streets protesting for a new, more inclusive world, some of us were in libraries, coffee shops, communes, retreats, bedrooms and dens plotting something even more startling: literature – highbrow and pulp – for an explicitly gay audience. Specifically, we were craving to see our gay lives – in the closet, in the open, in bars, in dire straits and in love – reflected in mystery stories, sci-fi and mainstream fiction. Hercule Poirot, that engaging effete Belgian creation of Agatha Christie might have been gay ... Sherlock Holmes, to all intents and purposes, was one woman shy of gay ... but where were the genuine gay sleuths, where the reader need not read between the lines?

Beginning with Victor J Banis's "Man from C.A.M.P." pulps in the mid-60s – riotous romps spoofing the craze for James Bond spies – readers were suddenly being offered George Baxt's Pharoah Love, a black gay New York City detective, and a real turning point in Joseph Hansen's gay California insurance investigator, Dave Brandstetter, whose world weary Raymond Chandleresque adventures sold strongly and have never been out of print.

Over the next three decades, gay storytelling grew strongly in niche and mainstream publishing ventures. Even with the huge public crisis – as AIDS descended on the gay community beginning in the early 1980s – gay fiction flourished. Stonewall Inn, Alyson Publications, and others nurtured authors and readers ... until mainstream success seemed to come to a halt. While Lambda Literary Foundation had started to recognize work in annual awards about 1990, mainstream publishers began to have cold feet. And then, with the rise of e-books in the new millennium which enabled a new self-publishing industry ... there was both an avalanche of new talent coming to market and burying of print authors who did not cross the divide.

The result?

Perhaps forty years of gay fiction – and notably gay and lesbian mystery, detective and suspense fiction – has been teetering on the brink of obscurity. Orphaned works, orphaned authors, many living and some having passed away – with no one to make the case for their creations to be returned to print (and e-print!). General fiction and non-fiction works embracing gay lives, widely celebrated upon original release, also languished as mainstream publishers shifted their focus.

Until now. That is the mission of ReQueered Tales: to keep in circulation this treasure trove of fantastic fiction. In an era of ebooks, everything of value ought to be accessible. For a new generation of readers, these mystery tales, and works of general fiction, are full of insights into the gay world of the 1960s, '70s, '80s and '90s. For those of us who lived through the period, they are a delightful reminder of our youth and reflect some of our own struggles in growing up gay in those heady times.

We are honored, here at ReQueered Tales, to be custodians shepherding back into circulation some of the best gay and lesbian fiction writing and hope to bring many volumes to the public, in modestly priced, accessible editions, world-wide, over the coming years.

So please join us on this adventure of discovery and rediscovery of the rich talents of writers of recent years as the PIs, cops and amateur sleuths battle forces of evil with fierceness, humor and sometimes a pinch of love.

The ReQueered Tales Team

Justene Adamec • Alexander Inglis • Matt Lubbers-Moore

Mysteries from ReQueered Tales

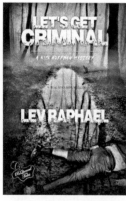

Let's Get Criminal
Lev Raphael

A Nick Hoffman / Academic Mystery, Book 1 – Nick Hoffman has everything he has ever wanted: a good teaching job, a nice house, and a solid relationship with his lover, Stefan Borowski, a brilliant novelist at the State University of Michigan. But when Perry Cross shows up, Nick's peace of mind is shattered. Not only does he have to share his office with the nefarious Perry, who managed to weasel his way into a tenured position without the right qualifications, he also discovers that Perry played a destructive role in Stefan's past. When Perry turns up dead, Nick wonders if Stefan might be involved, while the campus police force is wondering the same about Nick.

"*Let's Get Criminal* is a delightful romp in the wonderfully petty and backbiting world of academia. Well-drawn characters make up a delicious list of suspects and victims." — Faye Kellerman

"Reading *Let's Get Criminal* is like sitting down for a good gossip with an old friend. Its instant intimacy and warmth provides clever and sheer fun." — Marissa Piesman

Originally published in 1996, the first book in the Nick Hoffman Academic Mystery series is now back in print. This edition contains a new foreword by the author.

The Edith Wharton Murders
Lev Raphael

A Nick Hoffman / Academic Mystery, Book 2 – Nick Hoffman, desperate to get tenure, has been saddled with a thankless task: coordinating a conference on Edith Wharton that will demonstrate how his department and his university supports women's issues. There's been widespread criticism that SUM is really the State University of Men. Problem is, he's forced to invite two warring Wharton societies, and the conflict between rival scholars escalates from mudslinging to murder. Nick's job and whole career are on the line unless he can help solve the case and salvage the conference.

> "Is vulgar literary taste sufficient motive for murder? Actually, killing is too kind for the vindictive scholars in Lev Raphael's maliciously funny campus mystery *The Edith Wharton Murders*."
> — Marilyn Stasio, *The New York Times Book Review*

> "A savagely funny satire of academic pretensions and posturings. Definitely on my list of the year's best!" — Dean James

> "Among the pleasures of this mystery is its detailing of the day-to-day domesticity between Nick and Stefan – and of that essential mystery that lies at the core of even our closest relationships."
> — Katherine V. Forrest

Originally published in 1998, this edition contains a foreword by Gregory Ashe (*Hazard and Somerset* series) as well as a new introduction by the author.

In the Game
Nikki Baker

A Virginia Kelly Mystery, Book 1 – When businesswoman Virginia Kelly meets her old college chum Bev Johnson for drinks late one night, Bev confides that her lover, Kelsey, is seeing another woman. Ginny had picked up that gossip months ago, but she is shocked when the next morning's papers report that Kelsey was found murdered behind the very bar where Ginny and Bev had met. Worried that her friend could be implicated, Ginny decides to track down Kelsey's killer and contacts a lawyer, Susan Coogan. Susan takes an immediate, intense liking to Ginny, complicating Ginny's relationship with her live-in lover. Meanwhile Ginny's inquiries heat up when she learns the Feds suspected Kelsey of embezzling from her employer.

> "The auspicious debut of a black writer who brings us a sharp, funny and on-the-mark murder mystery."
> — *Northwest Gay & Lesbian Reader*

> "An entertaining assortment of female characters makes Baker's debut promising" — *Publisher's Weekly*

> "It has adventure, romance, and some of the best internal dialogue anywhere." — Meagan Casey

Nikki Baker is the first African-American author in the lesbian mystery genre and her protagonist, Virginia Kelly is the first African-American lesbian detective in the genre. Interwoven into the narrative are observations on the intersectionality of being a woman, an African-American, and a lesbian in a "man's" world of finance and life in general.

First published to acclaim in 1991, this new edition features a foreword by the author.

The Lavender House Murder
Nikki Baker

A Virginia Kelly Mystery, Book 2 – By night – the bars, the music, the sexual energy. By day – the beaches, the bay ... basking in the sun and the scent of suntan lotion. And everywhere the women of Provincetown.

Among these women in the sun is Virginia Kelly, a woman of color, on vacation from the mostly white world of finance. Ginny has come to P-town with friend Naomi, and without lover Emily. They stay at Lavender House, a hotel for lesbians run by Sam, a woman with whom Naomi has had some dramatic history. Other inhabitants include Anya, who works for the inn; Joan, a writer and sometime guest; loud Barb and her quiet partner. And in P-town, Ginny is drawn to another woman. Then ... murder shatters the vacation bliss. For among the people brushing up against Ginny and Naomi for these few sensual days is a ruthless killer. And a victim whose death will change the lives of Ginny and Naomi.

> "Nikki Baker's second novel is one of the best mysteries Naiad has published ... Baker has produced a winning character in Ginny Kelly ... Read it by the fire one cold autumn night, then smugly recommend Nikki Baker to your friends." — *Deneuve*

> "Titillating whodunit!" — *Publisher's Weekly*

Nikki Baker, author of *In the Game*, is the first Black voice in lesbian mystery fiction.

First published to acclaim in 1992, and nominated for Lambda Literary Award for Best Lesbian Mystery, this new edition features a foreword by Ann Aptaker (*Cantor Gold* series).

A Body to Dye For
Grant Michaels

A Stan Kraychik Mystery, Book 1 – Stan "Vannos" Kraychik isn't your everyday Boston hairdresser. Manager of Snips Salon, which is owned by best bud (and occasional nemesis) Nicole, Stan thought this day was an ordinary one. A delivery van backed into the salon's rear driveway and accidentally spilled gallons of conditioner, leaving Stan and hunky Roger) embracing in a gooey mess trying to staunch the flow, with little success as they slid and slipped with Nicole watching on with rolling eyes. Later Roger is found murdered.

Stan's client, Calvin Redding, who owns the apartment where Roger's body was found, can't explain why the body is dressed in little more than bowties. Enter Lieutenant Branco, dark, muscular, Italian, (straight) of Boston PD Homicide who immediately suspects everyone, especially Stan. In an attempt to clear his name, Stan travels to California, takes up mountain climbing, eavesdropping, spying, schmoozing, and a little bit of schtupping, all in an attempt to find the truth.

Grant Michaels' zany series of adventures starring Stan Kraychik garnered multiple Lambda Literary Awards including a 1991 nomination for Best Gay Men's Mystery. For this new edition, Carl Mesrobian reminisces about his brother Grant in an exclusive foreword, and Neil S. Plakcy provides an introduction of appreciation.

And don't miss ...

Love You to Death: Stan visits a chocolate factory after a patron drops dead at a chi-chi cocktail party

Dead on Your Feet: Stan's new boyfriend, choreographer Rafik, is accused of murder

Mask for a Diva: Stan nabs a gig as wig master to a summer opera festival but the final curtain for one star comes down early

Time to Check Out: Stan takes a holiday to Key West but a dead bodies turns up anyway

Dead as a Doornail: In the midst of renovating his new Boston brownstone, Stan becomes the (unintended?) murder target

Sunday's Child
Edward O. Phillips

A Geoffry Chadwick Misadventure, Book 1 – Lawyer Geoffry Chadwick is 50, Canadian, single, gay and, after a brief struggle with a hustler who tries to shake him down, a murderer. Herein lies the device for this macabre, funny, first novel. Although Geoffry must dispose of the body – which he does by dropping off sections of it around town at night – the trauma of the murder affords him the opportunity to reminisce and ruminate: on the recent termination of his affair with a history teacher; on the not-so-recent deaths of his wife and daughter; on the alcoholism of his mother; on growing old; on being gay. The visit of a nephew and the New Year's festivities only serve to intensify his thoughts. Although Chadwick is abrasively disdainful early on, he is fascinating when he loosens up. Phillips keeps the reader hopping with throwaway quotations from Donne and scatological references and puns.

First published in 1981, and a Books in Canada First Novel nominee, this new edition contains a foreword by Alexander Inglis.

And don't miss ...

Buried on Sunday: "One of the problems with weekends in the country" says Geoffry Chadwick's genial host in *Buried on Sunday*, "is that people feel free to drop in unannounced." And sometimes that includes criminals on the lam: forget the hors d'oeuvres, everyone is now hostage. Winner of the coveted Arthur Ellis Best Novel Award from the Crime Writers of Canada.

Sunday Best: Geoffry gets roped into planning a wedding for his niece Jennifer, but the groom has closet issues and a sexy latino chauffeur has a mixed agenda. Then there is widowed Montreal socialite Lois, mother to the groom, who casts her net for Geoffry ...

Working on Sunday: Geoffry Chadwick has a stalker. But between avoiding Christmas parties, gift shopping, moving his mother into a senior living facility, handling his recently widowed sister, and dealing with the loss of his long-term boyfriend Patrick, Geoffry Chadwick does not have time for a stalker.

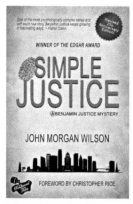

Simple Justice
John Morgan Wilson

A Benjamin Justice Mystery, Book 1 – It's 1994, an election year when violent crime is rampant, voters want action, and politicians smell blood. When a Latino teenager confesses to the murder of a pretty-boy cokehead outside a gay bar in L.A., the cops consider the case closed. But Benjamin Justice, a disgraced former reporter for the Los Angeles Times, sees something in the jailed boy others don't. His former editor, Harry Brofsky, now toiling at the rival Los Angeles Sun, surprises Justice from his alcoholic seclusion to help neophyte reporter Alexandra Templeton dig deeper into the story. But why would a seemingly decent kid confess to a brutal gang initiation killing if he wasn't guilty? And how can Benjamin Justice possibly be trusted, given his central role in the Pulitzer scandal that destroyed his career?

Snaking his way through shadowy neighborhoods and dubious suspects, he's increasingly haunted by memories of his lover Jacques, whose death from AIDS six years earlier precipitated his fall from grace. As he unravels emotionally, Templeton attempts to solve the riddle of his dark past and ward off another meltdown as they race against a critical deadline to uncover and publish the truth.

> "Wilson keeps the emotional as well as forensic suspense up through the very last sentence. The final scene is not only a satisfying explanation of the crime, but a riveting study of the erotic cruelty of justice." — *The Harvard Gay and Lesbian Review*

Awarded an Edgar by Mystery Writers of America for Best First Novel on initial release, this 25th Anniversary edition has been revised by the author. A foreword for the 2020 edition by Christopher Rice (*Bone Music*) is included.

The Always Anonymous Beast
Lauren Wright Douglas

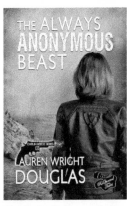

A Caitlin Reece Mystery, Book 1 – Val Frazier, Victoria's star TV anchorwoman, is Caitlin's newest client. She is the victim of a viciously homophobic blackmailer who has discovered her relationship with Tonia Konig. Tonia is a lesbian-feminist professor, an outspoken, passionately committed proponent of nonviolence. She is enraged by her own helplessness, she is outraged by Caitlin's challenge to her most fundamental beliefs, and by Caitlin herself, whom she considers "a thug".

As Caitlin stalks the blackmailer and his accomplices through the byways of the city of Victoria, she uncovers ever darker layers of danger surrounding Tonia. And she struggles against a new and altogether unwanted complication: she is increasingly attracted to the woman who despises her.

> "A very accomplished first novel, which is distinguishable by an elegant flair for description and an obvious love of the language." — Karen Axness, *Feminist Bookstore News*

> "Douglas' book is snappily written, peppered with wit and literary allusions, and filled with original characters."
> — Sherri Paris, *The Women's Review of Books*

Douglas's debut novel in 1987 began a six part series for Caitlin Reece. This new edition includes an introduction by the author and a foreword by legendary Katherine V. Forrest.

And don't miss ...

Ninth Life: Caitlin is hired by a woman code-named Shrew, to pick up a package. Caitlin is sickened to the depths of her being by the contents of the package: a blind and maimed cat, and photographs of animal experimentation. And now Shrew is dead. As a member of the militant animal rights organization Ninth Life, she had infiltrated Living World, a cosmetics company. The other members of Ninth Life suspect she was betrayed by someone within their own ranks and murdered because of what she learned.

More from ReQueered Tales

Like People in History
Felice Picano

Solid, cautious Roger Sansarc and flamboyant, mercurial Alistair Dodge are second cousins who become lifelong friends when they first meet as nine-year-old boys in 1954. Their lives constantly intersect at crucial moments in their personal histories as each discovers his own unique – and uniquely gay – identity. Their complex, tumultuous, and madcap relationship endures against 40 years of history and their involvement with the handsome model, poet, and decorated Vietnam vet Matt Loguidice, whom they both love. Picano chronicles and celebrates gay life and subculture over the last half of the twentieth century: from the legendary 1969 gathering at Woodstock to the legendary parties at Fire Island Pines in the 1970s, from Malibu Beach in its palmiest surfer days to San Francisco during its gayest era, from the cities and jungles of South Vietnam during the war to Manhattan's Greenwich Village and Upper East Side during the 1990s AIDS war.

> "It's the heroic and funny saga of the last three decades by someone who saw everything and forgot nothing." — Edmund White

> "Harrowing and sad, and very funny, *Like People in History* manages to bridge the unnerving chasm between the queer present and the gay past." — Andrew Holleran

In a book that could have been written only by one who lived it and survived to tell, Picano weaves a powerful saga of four decades in the lives of two men and their lovers, relatives, friends, and enemies. Tragic, comic, sexy, and romantic, filled with varied and colorful characters, *Like People in History* is both extraordinarily moving and supremely entertaining.

Published to acclaim in 1995, winner of the Ferro-Grumley Award for Best Novel, this 25th Anniversary edition for 2020 features a new foreword by Richard Burnett and an afterword by the author.

Mountain Climbing in Sheridan Square
Stan Leventhal

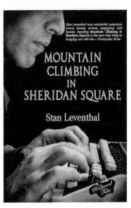

A series of discrete episodes among friends provide snapshots of one gay man's life. There are parties, concerts, dinners with everyday life – and death – interwoven in the rich story-telling. An actress, a painter, a set designer, a writer – all sweating and surviving in Manhattan, all scoring their first successes. Part autobiography and part documentary, artfully written, it details the lives of these creative people. Young and professional, they know there is more to life than money. There is trust and the sort of love that trades in deeds of kindness.

> "Stan was a literary activist who always gave to, built and endorsed literature and writers. I can see still see Stan in his apartment window on Christopher Street, next door to the Stonewall Inn, overlooking Sheridan Square as he typed away." — Michele Karlsberg, LGBTQ publicist and friend

Leventhal's debut novel was welcomed warmly as a Lambda Literary Awards Finalist in 1988. This new edition features a foreword by Christopher Bram (*Gods and Monsters*).

And don't miss ...

The Black Marble Pool – There's a dead body at the bottom of a pool in the backyard of a guest house in Key West. Who is he? And what caused his untimely demise? Maybe it's suicide. Or an accident. But more likely – murder! And who's responsible? One of the guests, the people who run the guest house or one of those mysterious women in town?

> "The pace is brisk: the plot keeps twisting, as no one is at all who they seem." — Keith John Glaeske, *Out In Print*

Second Son
Robert Ferro

Mark Valerian, the second son in the Valerian family, is ill, but determined to live life to the fullest – and live forever if he can. When he discovers Bill Mackey, a young theatrical designer who is also suffering from this disease neither wants to name, he also finds the lover of his dreams.

Together they develop an incredible plan to survive that will take them to Europe, to rustic Maine, and finally to the wonderful seaside summer mansion of the Valerian family, where father and son confront the painful ties of kinship ... and the joyous bonds of love.

"*Second Son* is transcendently beautiful; exquisitely written, exquisitely restrained. Its skillfully drawn characters come alive with an incandescent power as they struggle to preserve the romance, the passion, the tenderness that is vital to body and spirit. The accomplishment of *Second Son* reminds us of what literature has always been about – the deep examination of the soul. Rich, poignant, unforgettable, it leaves one with a rare feeling of having been in touch for a little while with the things that really matter." — Anne Rice

"I admired *The Family of Max Desir*. I love *Second Son*. The surprising story of the love between two men threatened by illness is full of fine authentic details and broader realizations about the human condition. Ferro's new work is entirely original, affecting, and yet strangely upbeat and heartening." — Doris Grumbach

Originally published in 1988, it was Ferro's final novel, completed in the months leading to his death from AIDS as he cared for his lover Michael Grumley. This new edition contains a foreword by Tom Cardamone (*Crashing Cathedrals: Edmund White by the Book*).

Life Drawing
Michael Grumley

Born in Iowa to the sounds of Bob and Bing Crosby and the Dorsey brothers, Mickey grows up to the comforting images of his living room TV and the reassuring ruts of his parents' life. During the restless summer of his senior year in high school, drifting away from the girlfriend he could never quite love, Mickey spends a night with another boy, and his world will never be the same.

On a barge floating down the Mississippi, he falls in love with James, a black card player from New Orleans, and in time the two of them settle, bristling with sexual intensity, in the French Quarter – until a brief affair destroys James's trust and sends Mickey to the drugs and sordid life of Los Angeles.

> "A simple, classic, engaging, and beautifully written tale of a boy who ran away from home, a man who didn't make it in the movies, an artist who found himself earlier than most and did it all west of the Mississippi, in places which, while very American, few Americans have ever been." — Andrew Holleran

> "*Life Drawing* affirms the rich complexity of passion in the story of a small-town boy's difficult journey to manhood. Michael Grumley's crisp, direct language brings to life the demanding wonder of sexuality and the delicate tightrope of love between black men and white men." — Melvin Dixon

Originally published in 1991, it was Grumley's only novel, completed in the month's leading to his death from AIDS as he was cared for his lover Robert Ferro. This new edition contains the original foreword by Edmund White (*A Saint from Texas*) and afterword by George Stambolian (*Gay Men's Anthologies Men on Men*), close friends of the couple.

Murder and Mayhem
Matt Lubbers-Moore

An Annotated Bibliography of Gay and Queer Males in Mystery, 1909-2018.

Librarian and scholar Matt Lubbers-Moore collects and examines every mystery novel to include a gay or queer male in the English language starting with Arthur Conan Doyle's "The Man with the Watches". Authors, titles, dates published, publishers, book series, short blurbs, and a description of how involved the gay or queer male character is with the mystery are included for a full bibliographic background.

Murder and Mayhem will prove invaluable for mystery collectors, researchers, libraries, general readers, aficionados, bookstores, and devotees of LGBTQ studies. The bibliography is laid out in alphabetical order by author including the blurb and author notes, whether a hard boiled private eye, an amateur cozy, a suspenseful romance, or a police procedural. All subgenres within the mystery field are included: fantasy, science fiction, espionage, political intrigue, crime dramas, courtroom thrillers, and more with a definition guide of the subgenres for a better understanding of the genre as a whole.

A ReQueered Tales Original Publication.

The Male Homosexual in Literature: A Bibliography *and* The Male Homosexual in Literature: Supplement (2020)
Ian Young

Ian Young's bibliography has served as a basic guide to English-language works of fiction, drama, poetry and autobiography concerned with male homosexuality or having male homosexual characters. Entries include titles published through 1980. Works are identified by author, title, place of publication, publisher, and date. For easy reference, entries are numbered and a title index is provided. Five highly acclaimed essays on gay literature by Ian Young, Graham Jackson and Dr. Rictor Norton, including essay on gay publishing, round out the listings. A title index of gay anthologies completes the work.

The present *Supplement* includes titles overlooked in the *Bibliography* Second Edition, plus works written before the 1981 cut-off date but published later, including works published for the first time in book form.

Cg

**If you enjoyed this book,
please help spread the word
by posting a short,
constructive review at
your favorite social media site
or book retailer.**

**We thank you, greatly,
for your support.**

And don't be shy! Contact us!

*For more information about current and future releases,
please contact us:*

E-mail: *requeeredtales@gmail.com*
Facebook (Like us!): www.facebook.com/ReQueeredTales
Twitter: @ReQueered
Instagram: www.instagram.com/requeered
Web: www.ReQueeredTales.com
Blog: www.ReQueeredTales.com/blog
Mailing list (Subscribe for latest news): https://bit.ly/RQTJoin